Lace

Book 1 in the Vampire-Fairy Series by

Wendy Rathbone

Description: Lace is a being from another dimension on Earth. He cannot die and humans call his kind "vampire" and declare war on them.

Firi is a human military soldier, a trained guard, who has met Lace twice in his young life and formed a bond with him.

In a world where humans and vampires are arch enemies, where vampires are eradicated in horrible ways, where being a vampire-lover means a death sentence, can Firi and Lace ever find each other again and explore the feelings they have for each other?

Will Lace be able escape his government prison, and the amnesia that keeps him from accessing his true powers?

Can Firi, the boy he met in the woods ten years ago, ever hope to help him?

A male/male romance about secrets that can get you killed, impossible rescues, and old lovers who cannot be trusted.

Dedication

For Della, for everything

and

*Special thanks to Christina E. Pilz
and Kelly Dunn*

$\mathcal{L}$ace

Part One

Lace

Chapter One

Every hour of every day the amber light made the same spherical shadows on the concrete walls. He breathed scents of filtered dust, disinfectant, air flaring with the starched odors of the royal blue uniforms of the guards.

For now, he could not remember his name. Or much past this room, the endless months. Or was it years?

Brief images trolled his dreams: inkwells and quills merging into cell phones and tablets. Gas flame behind glass in tiny lamps. Fluorescent lights in warehouse-sized stores. Rockets from an unnamed star. A brown owl in a dead tree staring at him across a dusk-pink lake.

Images old. Images new. How old was he?

He heard the slick tapping of footsteps on the hallway's terra cotta tile, echoing into his dim room. The sound was familiar along with the sensation of trapped wings fluttering in his chest. A hollow catch of breath, a hopeless, mild sting against the underside of his eyelids.

A voice in his mind said, "Hide. Lie." It was automatic.

But hide what? Lie about whom? About himself?

He only knew he existed, day in and day out, in a haze of timelessness, a daze of gray static, frozen here, waiting for the return of identity, of soul.

His room stretched ten by ten with a narrow bed covered by a maroon blanket. It contained a porcelain sink rusted with brown spots from age, and a toilet he never needed to use. There was nothing else, not even a comb.

He wore paper-thin black trousers, a white shirt with long lace cuffs that brushed the top of his hand. Both garments, ancient and threadbare, clung to his tall form, the cloth furred with nits.

He never thought about asking for different clothes. He didn't want them. And no one ever offered any that he could recall.

He could not know if, when he slept, it was for minutes or hours. Or days. He last dreamed of bygone lilies drooping at a black chasm cut into the heart of the earth, and kept smelling their wilted-sweet scent even after he woke. It seemed he often dreamed of chasms and destruction, too much destruction, and cemeteries all over the Earth, their groves of markers, their eerie wrought-iron entrances. He dreamed of blackbird sunsets and sparks of light, the memory of stars like broken lavender glass on torn black satin. Before them hung three moons, those silver-mad bowl-lamps, and moving like contorted shadows the owl-men who lived within them.

One owl-man was familiar to him, a man coming down from the sky so long ago that time had left this dream-memory in dust. He dreamed the man had said three things:

Pass through.

One world, neither alive nor dead, in the forever falling leaf.

Be blood and bone of mind.

When the owl-man embraced him, he pecked his shoulder hard. It bled. In the dream he caught a fever. Or was it a real memory? On a frightened, winter-gray night he died, his body still as stone in a blue cottage by a bitter stream that ran with blood from some distant, ancient war.

When he woke from death he had changed.

*

Footsteps on terra cotta. Echoes. Wings in his chest. Where were those three moons now? Here in his concrete room it was never night. Or always night.

He grimaced when he heard the heavy door swing open.

Lost boy. Lost man.

They'd come to take him away. Again.

*

Dark uniforms. Men and women. Blue-eyed, green-eyed, brown-eyed, all with the same untrusting gazes. Suspicious. Officious. Conferring. Secretive.

He sat today chained to a chair in gray room much like his cell, except this room held a large table and four chairs. It had no sink. One wall hosted a window-sized mirror. In it he could see his own tattered self, the thread and lace that was left of his ancient clothes, his long hair, cool shades of brown mixed with black, hanging in his eyes. His eyes of gilded frost might be called gray or very pale green. But they scintillated with a silver light. They were the main feature that made him look different from the rest of them. Not human. Other.

Two silent men with stern looks stood on either side of the door. He could smell the fresh oil from their holstered guns. He could also smell—and almost taste—the salts of their skin.

A third man carrying a flat black case entered, the door giving a soft creak as it opened and closed.

Suddenly he remembered other times in this room. Endless questions, the most earnest one being: *Where are you from?*

How to answer? One of the moons? The past? Some fairy mind?

These people who held him and kept him and questioned him—they were always so easily irritated. They knew he was different. Of course they wanted to know why.

But he didn't truly know. And they didn't truly believe him.

Today the man who stood before him in the crisp, shiny uniform had green eyes and a mustache and brown curly hair. He could see the man's curls at the nape of his neck were still damp from a recent shower.

"Good morning, Lace," the man said.

He had not remembered him until he heard that voice. They'd conversed before, two, three, maybe a hundred times.

These people called him Lace. How had he forgotten that? And was it really his name or just a label they had stuck on him?

Lace met his gaze. "Is it morning?"

Without answering, the man said, "Do you remember me?"

"Somewhat. Not your name."

"I'm Evan. We've talked before."

Lace said, "Yes. You ask me questions. But you answer none of mine."

"That's one of the rules," Evan said.

"What rules?"

"Rules of this facility concerning professional and personal engagement with prisoners of war. Now, you have a great many files and a lot of interviews amounting to, well, not a lot. Let's call today a new start, all right?" His forced smile plumped his cheeks; he opened his thin case and took out a keyboard and a computer tablet.

Lace watched him turn it on with one press of a small button. A screen lit up in an aurora of colors.

"May I see?" Metal chains clanked against the arm of his chair as he tried to lift his hand.

"No you may not." Evan touched the screen several times. Colors changed. Black words in tiny type scattered across the surface of the device. His forefinger slid across the smooth glass, changing the pages.

Lace wanted badly to touch it. He could only watch, mesmerized.

Finally, Evan asked, "How are you feeling today?"

"Feeling?"

"Yes. You had some treatments. Then you slept for quite some time. Anything? Dreams?"

"Treatments?" The flutter in his chest began again.

Evan made a notation by tapping a few things on the small keyboard. "Ah, you don't remember."

"No." But it seemed his body did. The muscles tightened. His skin heated just a little, enough so that he noted the flush as a sort of pain. The chains at his ankles and wrists jingled.

Evan looked up. "Something?"

"It seems you and others like you always want to know two things. Who I am. Where I am from. But these are mysteries even to me." And why did a part of his mind suspect these people already knew the answers?

"Very good. At least you remember that much."

"You chain me up and keep me locked away at all other times. I don't know who I am or what I've done. But you seem to have an idea. Why don't you tell me?"

"I can't." Evan offered a cool, half-smile. "The rules."

Lace lowered his head. This was maddening. To clear his head he studied the smooth table-top looking for flaws, concentrating. He saw a half-inch scratch by the edge to his left. It was the barest marring of white against the slate-colored surface. He studied it. It could be a crescent moon. He centered it in his mind. He saw an owl's round gold eyes.

He heard the sound of a creek, ancient voices, a rusty language that seemed part and separate from him.

"What was that?" Evan asked.

Lace blinked the room back into focus? "What?"

"You mumbled something in another language."

"Did I?"

"It sounded… Swedish?"

"I wouldn't know. I speak the same language as you. I think all my thoughts in this language."

"The tape of it will be analyzed."

"And when you have an answer will you tell me?"

Evan did not reply.

From his slim computer case, Evan removed a small notebook and a blue crayon. He slid them across the table, then motioned over his shoulder to one of the door-guards. The man came to Lace's left side and loosened the chain until Lace could lift his hand and put it on the table.

Before the door-guard turned away he briefly met Lace's gaze. He had sad eyebrows that almost met, wide-set deep brown eyes, a pink mouth turned down. Despite the uniform, and the edginess required of his job, he was lovely. The small hairs on Lace's body rippled.

"Write down your thoughts for me, if you will," Evan demanded. "We've done this before so I know you can do it."

Lace stared at the top of his hand on the table. "Obviously. You released my left hand. You must know I am left-handed. So, yes, we've done this before."

Evan kept touching the screen of his tablet, barely nodding.

Lace took up the crayon and placed the tip on the first blank page of the notebook. Why a crayon? Did they think he was a murderer who used quills or pens as weapons? Was he?

He drew a tiny blue star in the corner of the page. Evan glanced up lazily from his screen and gave a slight frown.

Lace stared at the page. His fingers moved the crayon back and forth. *When I was a boy*, he wrote in seraph-swirled cursive, *I made up stories, myths, worlds. Dawn to dusk I played in the kingdoms of my imagination. In one kingdom, I was imprisoned in an alien place by strangers in stiff uniforms. I called you all* **The Wardens of Blue**. *You were famous for your dungeons.*

He put the crayon down and slid the notebook toward Evan's busy tablet.

Evan looked it over, then slid it back calmly, politely. "Try again."

Lace held the crayon tighter. It broke in half. His eyebrow muscles twitched. He stared at the words he'd written and thought them beautiful.

Evan said, low, almost bored, "I have all day."

Lace replied, "So do I."

Producing another crayon, green this time, Evan repeated his instruction. "Try again."

Lace took the new color and added a green star on the corner of the page. Now the blue star would not be lonely.

He wrote: *I was a little boy, hungry and alone, on the cobbled streets of a timeless time. I stole to survive. By age twelve I traded sexual favors for bread and blankets. Most of my clients were kind. But the cruelest ones, the stingiest ones were the ones I called* **The Wardens of Blue**. *They liked it rough. They sought to whip me, chain me up, use me in pairs or groups. When they were done, they paid me by sticking gold coins in my mouth or up my bottom. They never paid what was agreed upon, and they tore my clothes without offering to give me new ones.*

He pushed the notebook across the table and stared past Evan's shoulder to the guard with the grieving face, taking in all the details of this man even though he knew he would later forget them.

The guard had nice hands, smooth and tanned, the nails neatly clipped. On his left wrist he wore a watch that glimmered silver just beneath the stiff cuff of his uniform. The uniform fit him perfectly, tapering at the waist and hips and ending in matt-black boots. The skin of his face was honey-colored, the jaw-line darker from an unclose shave. Lace's fingertips prickled as if he could almost feel the stubble there. The guard's black hair was cropped short but Lace had a sudden image of him with long coils of hair, coarse but soft, a rippling mane of night.

He smelled salt on the young man's skin, but then a whiff of something more. Blood. Fresh. As if somewhere on his body was an unhealed cut.

Evan's stern voice broke his reverie.

"When you are done playing games, do let me know."

Lace leaned forward. "Tell me what you want me to write and I will do it. And sign it with a flourish."

"That's not the point of this."

"Then tell me what is the point. I can't remember anything."

"I know you're not stupid. Surely you realize that you don't eat. You don't defecate. You don't sicken or age. Your blood, well, that is different. Though otherwise, except for your eyes, you look human enough."

Lace perked up. This was information. He so rarely got it. "I know I'm not like you. But not human?"

"No."

"Are there others?"

Evan smiled as if pained. "You tell me."

Lace leaned back. "Are there no good techniques, other than writing with a crayon, to jar my memory?"

"Believe me, we've tried them all. You are a stubborn one."

Was Evan implying he'd given himself amnesia on purpose? Or was lying? If so, there must have been a very good reason. Lace took up the crayon again and stared at the notebook page. He wrote, *The owl-man.* Then stopped.

12

He glanced again at the handsome door-guard who stood, eyes straight ahead, unflinching.

The crayon moved in his hand as he composed. All were thoughts put down as they came to him. Pieces of recurring dreams. *The owl-man came to me when I was still human. He counseled me. Then he killed me. The moons crumbled filling my eyes as I died. I moved into the stars and watched as he and his many 'selves' cut my body open. He drank my blood and ate my heart. He took away all my natural organs. When my body was hollow, he climbed inside me and sewed my skin back together. I woke in a room of concrete walls in the land of the* **Wardens of Blue.** *The end.*

Lace stopped writing. He stared at the paper for several minutes before Evan invaded the silence. "Well?"

"It's nothing."

"Let me see it anyway."

Lace jammed the crayon on the page, making big slicing lines through the green text.

Evan jumped forward and grabbed the notebook. Part of the page ripped. He sat down.

Lace took a strong breath, trying to ease the tension in his jaw.

Evan shook his head. "I should've known. You and your owl-man. You're very sensitive about him. And moons? There is only one moon, you idiot. And we know you didn't come from space. Where do you come from? That's what we need to know."

Lace ignored the insult. "I've talked about the owl-man before?"

"A hundred days… a hundred weeks. All bullshit."

More information. Lace stowed it away in his mind to think about later, if he remembered. Had he really been here two years? Or longer?

He didn't want to help them, but he wanted to help himself. He said, "It's a recurring dream. An image that repeats. So I wrote it down. You asked about my dreams."

"And you continue to give us no real information."

"So you keep me here because I am a mystery. Your mystery."

Evan seemed not to hear him. He typed a note.

A tremor snared Lace's body. "Am I here because I deserve it?"

No answer.

"What did I do? And why do I wear these old, torn clothes?"

Evan said as if in dismissal, "You obviously don't remember that we have offered you different clothing. You refused to put it on."

"Why?"

He let out a short laugh. "Maybe you're fashion conscious and the colors don't suit you."

Lace said, "I'm not."

Still smiling coolly, Evan said, "Would you like to try again and see what happens?"

"What will happen?"

"Oh, you'll freak out, of course, and there'll be a lot of yelling. And shredding. And the clothes will be thrown back at the unfortunate guard who brought them."

"I don't remember any of that."

"Yeah, so you say, you don't remember *anything*. Except maybe your fairytale of some goddamned owl-man."

Two years. He kept thinking of it, that he'd been locked away at least that long. But then what about all the other missing years? He remembered kerosene and candlewicks but they seemed so distant, so long past. There was nothing like that here. The lights in this facility were glass bulbs and tubes that flickered on at the touch of a button. Not to mention the things that were called computers and cell phones.

"How old am I?"

Evan replied, "Please. Answer your own question. I'd like to know. How old are you?"

"I don't know."

Evan asked, "Do you have anything else you'd like to write for me?"

"How was I brought here? How was I caught?"

"You tell me."

Lace looked into emptiness, hollowness, a journey of blind, black steps, everything a blank. The only real things he knew about himself were traits of character he had: manners, inner stillness and a hyper-patience that made his unknown duration of imprisonment thinly bearable. Or maybe it was the amnesia that did that. He simply did not recall if he suffered, when he suffered, or to what degree.

He said to Evan, "Maybe I made a mistake?"

"What?"

"I made a mistake and that is how I was caught."

Evan's body straightened. "Tell me more."

"I don't know more."

He tossed his hand up. "Go with the thought."

"There's nothing there. If I made a mistake I can only assume I didn't hide well enough, or play my life correctly, or trick whomever it was I was trying to deceive well enough. Or I was betrayed. Or I betrayed myself. Turned myself in. If I knew what I had done, maybe I could remember myself more."

"Maybe what you've done is so horrible you can't bear the memory, can't live with it. And you can't die..."

"Is that my truth?" Lace interrupted. "So I am here maybe of my own free will, maybe not. And you are studying me. All of you in your blue uniforms and hard gazes offering me nothing, no reprieve, no forgiveness, no way out, and absolutely nothing for me to build on." His chains scraped the metal of the chair arms. "Is this cruelty my own making? Or yours?"

"Believe me, if there is cruelty by your own making or ours, it is earned."

Lace could not quite grasp what that meant. Did they earn the right to be cruel or did he earn the punishment? Maybe both.

If he'd done something too horrible to comprehend, maybe his only protection, his only path to survival was the amnesia. Or he was completely mad and all this was just another dream on that dark, narrow cot in his concrete, amber-lit room.

He looked down at his hands. They were completely normal-looking, average hands, long-tapered, neat nails that never broke, right middle finger with an indentation as if he might have worn a ring on it for a lifetime or two. Those hands, were they capable of horrible acts, of gestures and deeds that might cause him to turn away from himself, to run, to forget?

Evan leaned back in his chair. "Anything else on your mind you might like to write down for me?"

Lace frowned. "I feel you don't believe me when I say I have nothing, no memories to offer you."

"If that's the case, this day will definitely not be a good one for me. Or for you."

"It isn't a choice that I have nothing more to offer, it's a fact. If we've done this before many times then you already know this."

"I do. But the problem is none of us here believes you."

"I know."

"And if you were completely honest, don't you think that if you did remember anything about yourself you wouldn't say anyway because no matter what, whether you tell us what we want to know, or not, you're never getting out of here?"

Somewhere deep inside, Lace had already decided long ago that this place was not a stopping off point, but a final destination. And yet the wardens of blue who kept him here were human. They changed, they aged. Eventually they would go away. All of them. Even if he had to wait decades, millenniums, they and this place would decay, fall to dust, to ruin.

It might hurt, but he could wait. Some day it would happen. He saw himself walking away from it all, walking into the deep indigos of a future era clad only in string and wind but looking outward, always outward.

Past the smug visage of Evan, Lace stared at the stone expression of the door guard who'd loosened his chain. A tremor of the room's yellow light made his eyes, for an instant, the color of writhen gold. Slowly, the guard lowered his gaze.

A sudden thought flashed through Lace's mind. There could be others like him. Maybe he was not unique. Not alone. The question then was, if there were men and women like him, people who were also not human, who did not eat or age, were they allies or enemies?

He couldn't even begin to speculate. And tomorrow, and the day after that, he would most likely forget all about it as he waited, day in and day out, for the wardens of blue to come into his cell and take him away over and over again.

*

Chapter Two

Evan had not lied.

The day strode by on ever more shaky legs and unpleasant scents. It was definitely not a good one.

The guards unchained Lace from the chair and reconnected the chains from ankles to wrists. *Like being weighted with strings of crescent moons,* he thought. How strange. But not strange. Because this had to be some mad fairytale.

They led him down long tiled halls with closed doors; all was silent behind those locked, metal rectangles.

His pulse began to climb. His body remembered something he did not.

They took him to a well-lit room.

He stopped at the threshold of the door, canting his weight back. The guards pushed him but he did not budge.

Within the room were devices. Medical tools, small computers on wheels, countertops littered with jars, towels, electrical cords, boxes of gloves. From one device beside an upright hospital bed hung clear intravenous fluid bags.

The guards muscled him across the threshold where he allowed his knees to buckle. They caught him as he collapsed and dragged him to the bed. He kicked out with his feet, the chains tripping him up, and lashed with his fists to no avail. Metal held him tight, and there were more guards now, the blue arms and torsos surrounding him, holding him, strapping him down at the shoulders, adding ties to his already manacled hands and feet.

He heard a muffled yell, his own throat closing, opening on gasping air. "Take me back to my cell," he hissed.

They ignored him.

This was a bad room. Nothing good ever happened here. It was no use to struggle but his body didn't seem to

18

care. He lifted his head, pulling at the cuffs, both cloth and metal, body curving left and right, hips rising.

A man entered the room not in uniform but dressed instead in black cotton pants, a black pullover shirt. He had silver at the edges of his sideburns and an ever-concentrating, creased forehead. His gruffness and preoccupation only contributed greater tension to the atmosphere as he set about checking I.V. bags and their descending tubes.

"Let me up!" Lace must have said it at least five times, the last with a twisted grimace, spitting the words. Everyone in the room ignored him.

The man in black spoke softly to two of the guards who came to his side and held him steady at the shoulders and wrists. Lace squirmed as he watched the doctor push back the cuff of his shirt and insert the first I.V. into the top of his left wrist.

It didn't hurt. Yet.

He waited as he suddenly remembered waiting many times before, breath held.

The doctor pushed a button on the I.V. machine.

The first sensation as the liquid hit the artery of his hand was a pressure, then a sting. Quite rapidly a hard pain of searing cold crept into the skin there. Cold like wind grieving over a grave. Like blizzard sleet. Like the edges of space from which no one ever returns.

The agony pushed slowly upward as Lace's teeth ground together. His body twisted. He heard his own groans like animal wails. Echoes of frantic voices fleeted through his mind but he could not understand them. As the liquid traveled through his shoulders to his chest and from there to the rest of his body, he saw blue guards and a white, whirling room. Then he was somewhere gray, held down by an invisible weight, frozen, but still alive.

His mind wavered in and out of the gray.

He dreamed the owl-man came down again from one of three rain-shrouded half-moons.

The bite to his shoulder, at first a seeping bruise, sank slow and steady, red-deep. The pain left his skin in tatters. His soul.

His body felt as if it lifted up, translucent in his shock. He sat with the stars.

They left him standing on a field ribboned with green-dusk light. Chest burning, heavy, the stitches still new from where the owl-man had cut him open and sewn himself inside, he turned under the smoke-woven sky and yelled. Howled. Wordless and alone. Tear-scorched and afraid.

But he wasn't truly alone. The owl-man was in his mind, now, a winged and ancient being flapping back and forth against his skull.

The owl-man was made of night. Frosted stars and hunchbacked moons. Snow and beaten wind. The things of yore and bane and sprite and fae. Winter hearths and fir. Holly, wick and wax. Ash and Jack-be-quick. Ice coated apples and cider ale. All the pent-up beckonings of trees. Sweet cold mist and a mist-imp's breath. Lace became them all. He wore the billowing sleeves of cloud on his shadow, a string of ruby Saturns at his throat.

Lace collar, lace ties, lace cuffs.

Before the stars had finally set leaving him so alone, they'd clad him in all these things, and their own tiny scrims of lace.

They gathered him, bound him, kissed him.

Named him.

Lace.

He screamed.

There were needles in his arms and more loss and death running into his veins.

The owl-man might have killed him, but he had done nothing as terrible as this crush of void leaking into him drop by drop, this living torture. The owl-man had remade Lace into a being like himself as best he could, given him gifts that withstood time and space itself. He was the maker.

20

The ones who did this to him now were the un-makers. The ones who lived in a perpetual, mortal world of decay. The humans.

He screamed again.

The wardens of blue ignored it.

*

When he woke he could not remember his name.

In his dreams, the owl-man came down from some distant moon.

Again, and again.

*

He woke in a narrow cot lying on his side.

He did not feel cold but his body shivered.

A man stepped into his vision and his mind supplied drabbles of information. *A Warden of Blue. A guard.*

The guard said, "I put the blanket over you but you threw it off. If you're cold, then I'm sorry."

Lace's memories, faint but insistent, supplied more details. His own name, for one. And the fact that guards rarely spoke to him.

But this guard seemed familiar. Close-cropped black hair. Did he know him?

"You're not supposed to talk to me," Lace replied, turning onto his back and clasping his folded arms across his chest to still the shaking.

"I happen to know that Ivana always takes a smoke break at ten o'clock sharp every day. She's not watching the camera. We have ten minutes. Lace."

The sound escaping Lace's mouth was a short, sharp laugh. No smile. "Why do you call me that?"

The guard shrugged. "It's your name."

Lace turned to look him up and down. "Are you going to hurt me, too?"

No answer.

"Do you know me?"

Softly, "We have shared the autumn wine."

"What?" Lace asked.

Silence.

Lace added, "I don't know what that is."

"You were once a… a great being."

Lace sat up frowning.

The guard continued. "The best and most beautiful and powerful of your kind. You don't remember. And vampires are now almost gone."

"Fairytales," Lace murmured.

"Yes, fairytales."

"Then who are you?"

"A Halfling. You told me so yourself." He glanced at his watch. "I can't say more."

"But at least your name…"

The guard averted his eyes, an edge of gold reflecting there, and ignored him. He unlocked the heavy door and without turning back left Lace alone again.

*

Time, the enemy, never vanished.

*

Chapter Three

He was a fallen star in chains.

He waved and undulated in the dying dark. Through myths and gods he fell. Through schools of meteors and flocks of rockets. Within the mothwing galaxy, he passed by tiny rooms of stars. Past age and solitude and the eternal glaze of moons. Beyond wicks and runes and cold mouths of space. Through dead forests and blackened seas, he fell. He landed upon the grim earth.

Bloody, hurt, weeping.

Groveling.

He breathed in. The poison of cities and years filled him with dust. He coughed, gagged.

His dreams always ended in destruction.

Lace lay in a concrete room under a maroon blanket that smelled of sweat. The pillow beneath his head pushed roughly into his cheek and jaw. His long bangs spilled over his eyes. He blinked their sting away. A blue guard stood just inside the wide door threshold.

Moving up his dry, cracked throat, words tried to form. "I'm thirsty."

"Did you say you're thirsty?"

Lace tried to sit up. "And hungry."

"I'll go get the boss."

He heard the guard's boots clatter against the hallway tile.

He tried to sit up. Heavy chains against his wrists tangled in the blanket. He pushed it back. The chains tugged at his ankles where they were also fastened. The metal pressed against the leather of his ankle boots. His skin there felt bruised. He tugged his feet over the side of the cot and finally sat, barely balanced.

A chill roamed all over his body. He shut his eyes against the room's sickly light. More footsteps sounded down the hall. Rapid. At least three men.

Three wardens of blue came through the doorway. One came directly to his side. "Do you know me?" the man asked.

Lace looked up into wide green eyes. The mustache over his upper lip, yes, that was familiar. And the disturbingly calm tone of voice. "Evan."

"That's right."

"I talked to you yesterday, I think? Was I in a hospital?"

"Close enough. Can you stand?"

Lace's body ached but he managed, standing on shaky legs.

"My guards tell me you're thirsty? Hungry?"

Lace nodded. "Very."

"What else do you remember?"

"Not much. What happened to me? Is this a… a jail?"

"A lot has happened, yes," Evan confirmed. "But this is a good step. A big step."

"Was I sick? I feel sick." He looked down at his clothes. Strange. Old. Another question for later.

"You were in isolation, in a kind of coma."

"Oh." His gaze moved to the two guards whose expressions conveyed some surprise although they seemed to work at keeping their emotions guarded. One guard frowned a bit more than the other, the liquid in his eyes shimmering in the pale, old glow of the room. He was very familiar. Lace remembered they had talked. Lace decided he looked upset, but he could not get the man to look at him. A strange hollowness seemed to expand within him as he watched the guard. He couldn't understand any of this.

"Let's get you something to eat for now," Evan said. "Guards."

As they escorted him down the hall, Lace's stomach grumbled.

*

They loosened his chains so he could eat.

The table was brown, lacquered wood. They sat in a large room, an empty cafeteria, with pale blue walls and metal light fixtures overhead. The floor had been recently mopped and smelled of bleach and lemon, nearly overpowering the food. Lace didn't care.

He held a fork in his left hand and shoveled heaping portions of mashed potatoes into his mouth. It was as if he hadn't eaten in years. He salivated heavily as he ate, feeling as if he'd never be full. A hamburger patty with gravy edged into his potatoes. Evan told him it was Salisbury steak. He cut it into pieces with his fork and mixed it in with the potatoes. There was also a sliced apple with a pale green peel, and a clear, cool glass of water. All fit for a king in his starved condition.

The guards stayed silent and apart but Evan watched him eat.

Lace looked up from his food for a moment. "Are you hungry, too?"

"I've already eaten, thank you," Evan said.

High windows rimmed the cafeteria's ceiling. A silver light fell around them, adding its gleam to the artificial illumination. It caught and tugged at the pale hairs on the backs of Lace's hands, making them appear glitter-dusted. His fingernails looked polished with a clear translucence.

His shirt and trousers hung on him like thin rags. They did nothing to keep him warm. The material was so worn he could see the flesh of his arms and legs through the cloth.

Why were they so old? Why hadn't anyone given him better, stronger clothing to wear? Then he remembered someone—was it Evan?—telling him he threw new clothes away.

He drained a plastic glass of water and asked for more. One of the guards approached the table with a pitcher. Beads of condensation dotted the surface of the table.

He had so many questions. Why couldn't he remember anything?

I walk the world a wraith. Now where had that thought come from?

He swallowed hard and asked, "Will my memory return?"

Evan shook his head. "I hope so." But there were secrets in his eyes. Hidden flares.

He'd already made up his mind when the man first walked into his cell that he would not trust him. But that guard with the sad eyes—he was another matter. Lace wished he could talk to him, not Evan. But of course there was some sort of hierarchy and door guards did not seem to amount to much.

He wanted to look out the windows of the cafeteria but they were too high. How had he forgotten the whole world? He suddenly knew of cities, roads, cars, mountains, stars, seas. But he couldn't picture the world right at this moment in time. He wanted to see outside, touch wind, stroke the sharp bark of a tree, the leather of a leaf.

He swallowed another bite of food, then said, "I can tell."

"Tell what?" Evan asked.

"It's something bad. Something I've done." A deep breath didn't help the quick pang of anxiety. "Is that why I'm here? What did I do? And why don't I remember it?"

"That I can't say. I'm not at liberty to discuss it with you."

"Then who is?"

Evan leaned back and simply smiled.

The food in Lace's stomach twisted, recoiled, then re-settled. He wanted to turn away but couldn't. He was afraid to ask anything more. But he couldn't contain one last question. "What will happen to me?"

"If others decide it, you may be tried in a court of law. But later. Much later. We have different work here. Either way, justice will happen to you."

"Then I was a… a criminal?"

"Something like that."

"Where are the others?" Lace asked.

"What others?"

"Other prisoners. This is a prison, isn't it?"

"As I said before. You are in isolation."

"You didn't answer my question."

Evan rested his folded hands in front of him. "I'm not allowed to answer most of your questions."

"Please take me to whomever is allowed."

"All in good time."

But Lace knew, somehow, it was a lie.

Evan studied him like he was a trapped insect or an animal in a cage. This was no ordinary incarceration. For one thing, the long halls leading to more empty rooms, and the empty cell he'd awakened in, and the echo-haunted cafeteria itself were too immense, and probably expensive, to house just one man. There had to be other people here.

Lace's chains rattled against the table's edge. "Everything's a mystery."

"I'm sure it is," Evan replied.

So many pieces of things, words, and scents and images, traveled through Lace's mind, but he'd only just awakened. He had not had time for any assimilation. If he could just be quiet and think. If he could just hang onto even one tiny fragment. But it was all like some bad dream. If he tried to focus on any one image, it immediately blurred, fell apart.

He did not trust the men in the blue uniforms. *The Wardens of Blue.*

*

Two guards escorted Lace back to his cell. The one with black hair strode closer to him than the other, and carried a bag over his shoulder.

When they reached the cell, he went in with Lace while the other guard remained outside. The bag revealed green cotton drawstring pants and pullover shirt, socks, underwear, and canvas shoes. It also held a comb, a toothbrush, toilet paper and a razor.

"These are your things," the guard said softly.

"This is all new, not mine," Lace said, looking at everything laid out on his bed.

"You didn't need all this until now," the guard said.

"Why not?"

The guard simply shook his head.

"Will I be able to have a shower?"

"Yes. After your appointment this afternoon."

"What appointment?"

"I can't say."

"You can't or won't?"

No answer.

Lace wanted to ask more questions about the clothing he was wearing, so old, thin, practically rotting off of him. But he kept quiet.

Finally, Lace said, "Am I to remain isolated?"

The guard merely shrugged.

"Forever?" Lace added.

"I'm sorry this is happening. I..." The guard seemed about to confess something. Lace watched as his lips trembled with the barest shudder.

"You're sorry?" He turned away. "I don't even know who I am."

"It's... it's not right, I know," came the soft reply.

Lace turned back to face him, the dark eyes almost too flat, too still, as if secrets raged behind them that were forbidden in the light of day. There were no windows here to reveal the day, but he'd just had lunch in a cafeteria that had seeped white light from high, small casements. The first natural light he'd seen in so long. Here in his cell the ichors of chemical light, jaundiced and never-changing, gave the cell an atmosphere of energy-suckling stasis, definitely anathema to any kind of useful knowledge like weather and seasons, let alone deeper contemplations of heart or memory. Any wisdom that might attempt to reside here, Lace decided, would be immediately stripped of any life-intrinsic meaning. The silence and the chill, not of the air but of emotion, kept these things at bay. Warmer thoughts, the past, anything that led to making up a life, or a lifetime, could not, would not thrive here. No wonder he felt so empty.

So hungry.

For a moment it seemed the guard looked at him very strangely.

"What is your name?" Lace asked.

The guard ignored the question and said, "If there is anything you need, pound on your door. We'll hear you."

As he nodded his understanding, the guard opened the door and left.

Lace heard the clunk of the lock settle in place.

He turned around three times surveying his kingdom. His breath hitched in the back of his throat. A dampness tingled against the skin under his arms and between his shoulder blades as if his body remembered deep pain.

To the air he whispered, "What have I done?"

*

Uncounted time passed and they came for him again. The wardens of blue.

He sat on a hospital bed and a man with gray sideburns in an unbuttoned lab coat put a needle into his arm and pulled back on the plunger.

The blood that came out was bronze-gold, gleaming like tainted mercury reflecting the golden sun. It all looked very wrong.

The doctor shook his head, made a silent motion with his hand to the guards. They came over to Lace and pushed him back and although he was chained, they still secured him with tight bands to the bed.

Lace tried to speak "Wait! What's wrong!"

They ignored him as he lay tense and still, heart pushing at the increasing rapids of his veins.

A pinch. Another needle. His breath came rough as he remembered a past quick image, the white sea of the bed, the tubes, the bags of liquid, and himself screaming until he had no voice.

"Wait! No…," he tried to say.

But it was too late as he felt a cold ache creep into the top if his hand and move up. The pain knifed up his arm, slicing his arteries to ribbons, moving on toward his neck, head, chest and then his whole body. The ice-knives inside him became such agony that the room whirled; his eyes rolled up. He heard himself groan, the sounds escaping him through no will of his own. Then came the screaming. He thought maybe there were words in among the sounds he made, words like "no" and "please" and "stop" as he begged for it to end.

But the horror went on and on.

He tasted ash. His mind soared into a gray-ghosted nihility and he hung there by invisible threads as if at the center of a blind reverie he could neither comprehend nor control. Someone had forgotten to paint the scene so did he even exist? Even in this quiescence, this scrawless trance, there was no reprieve. The pain undulated through him in a formless dance, a frozen, autumnal star-dive where you perpetually burn but never die.

After an eternity, he heard distant words. "The treatment's been done for half an hour. Make him walk."

"He can't."

"Help him."

He was lifted by invisible arms. He still could not see. The smoke-washed void he was lost in stitched him inside-out with acid piercings, as though he were patchwork now, taken apart and put back together, every piece of him sewn askew. His own weight seemed to throw him forward upon the nothing. But strong arms held him up. He thought he might still be screaming but could trust none of his senses at this moment.

Lace's feet trailed behind him as he was dragged, boneless, boots scraping over hard tile.

Slowly he began to orient, a wetness on his face, body still echoing glacial fragmentation and rippling shock.

A voice in his mind whispered, *I may have sewn myself inside you, but I was never so cruel.*

He opened his eyes. Neither of the guards had spoken.

The door to his cell stood open.

The dark-haired guard took on all of his weight, saying to the second guard, "Wait outside. I'll get him settled." He shut the door.

He lifted Lace toward the bed and set him upon it. Lace fell back, head hitting the cement wall.

"Shit. Sorry."

A soft hand cupped the back of his head, pulling him forward, and the guard placed a pillow behind him.

Lace pulled his now loosely-chained hands up to his bent knees. They trembled violently. It was so strange to see that, and feel his gasping breaths as if he still had no control over his lungs.

The guard took his hands in his. "Do you remember the last time I spoke to you?"

Lace could barely remember his lunch today, let alone what this guard was saying. He tried to focus, looked into the dark eyes and remembered how this one had seemed to watch him more. Had he seen gold lights at the edges of his gaze? He had to have been dreaming.

Softly, "Ten o'clock sharp. Ivana takes her smoke break. Chaz is outside. No one is on the camera for this moment." He glanced up to a green light in the corner of the cell.

Lace shook his head to convey he didn't understand, and tried not to gag.

"There, deep breaths. It'll pass. Not quickly enough, though." One hand came up from his trembling wrist to stroke back a fringe of wet hair at his temple. "Breathe with me."

Lace watched the man's lips open slightly, the chest rise. The guard breathed in and out, a shushing sound that was both comforting and odd. Comforting because it seemed normal, ordinary. Odd because it was so familiar, and because he had known no comfort here, not in a very, very long time.

Lace concentrated on those steady, dark pink lips. Breathed. Thought *Ivana. Chaz.* When his throat felt not so tight, he said, "What is your name?"

The lips pressed together lightly as if to form a smile but instead made a frown. "A strange one. Firisian. Firi. I've told you before, but you never remember it."

Lace blinked. His eyes still stung.

"I'm so sorry this is happening," Firi said. "I would do more for you but I can't. But I'm here."

Lace felt him squeeze his hand. Firi's smooth, brown skin twitched at his jawline. His eyes brimmed with extra moisture.

"I'm so tired," Lace said, trying to move his whole body onto the bed now. "I think I'm dying."

"I know."

Lace stretched his feet out straight. "Can you help me?"

Firi took the blanket and placed it over Lace's body. "I'm trying."

"I have so many questions."

"I don't have time to answer them. I'm so sorry." He touched Lace's forehead briefly.

It was a beautiful gesture in a prison that had left him insular and asunder for too long. Just that brush of fingertips sent a wash of warmth through him that banished the remaining vibrations of pain. He wanted to cry out at such rare tenderness. His raw throat protested. Instead, he whispered, "Thank you, Firi."

He closed his eyes and slept.

*

Part Two

Firi

Chapter Four

Fairies.

That was *not* what the news reports called them when mass sightings swept the globe and proof of their existence was obtained. The other word, *vampire*, the word which was a scarier, more alarmist way of describing and labeling these intruders into the world of Mankind, was what fell most often from the lips of everyone, adults and kids alike.

The reports of vampire encounters began as silly stories on the news when Firi was nine. Within only a few months, rumors of vampire attacks quickly turned the world into a fearful, paranoid war-zone. Firi had never known anyone who had ever been attacked, let alone seen a vampire with the exception of himself.

But Firi had noticed fairy-beings all his life, though they hid well. He felt their peach-wind breaths in summer, saw their glass-locked fires in winter gliding through the woods across the deer meadow behind his house. He *knew* them as rare, hidden things. They were in his bones.

They were the fairy people of the wood. To him, as a child, it was normal to believe in them. He told no one. It wasn't until much later that he realized how abnormal his childhood beliefs really were.

Why they had suddenly come out of the woods and into the realm of humans, well, that was another matter. Something had happened to them. Something bad. But he knew inside himself that they had always existed.

Just after the world went a bit crazy, after the hysteria took firm hold and the vampire wars were beginning, Firi finally met one of them down by the old swimming hole. It was sitting by the little beach beneath a jade dusk. Its skin was an almost pale greenish-gold hue, eyes silver and flecked with mica. In an unearthly rain of leaves it sat and watched the water of the creek tremble in a falling breeze.

Firi had just turned ten that very day, still so small, still a child though he didn't feel like one anymore. He'd run away for a few moments from his birthday party in the garden, his swift, ten-year-old legs taking him past the meadow and into the woods. It was as if he'd been drawn to the creek and the little gray sand beach there where he and other boys often played before the war.

Nowadays, he was always warned by fearful parents and teachers to never go far from home alone, that if he ever saw a vampire he was never to approach it, let alone talk to it. The lesson failed to impress him.

As Firi walked toward the creek, the vampire did not turn to look directly at him but spoke to him like an old friend. It said, "Why aren't you afraid?"

Firi shrugged and sat on a flat rock some distance away while the monster continued to stare into the coming night.

"You should run home to your mother," the vampire fairy said in a fragmented, rusty voice.

That was when Firi noticed it was wounded. The grass around which it sat was glistening in golden moisture.

He'd heard his parents and other adults talk. He watched the nightly news. He knew these things had liquid bronze for blood. *Not like us*, the reports would say, as if it were a deliberate rudeness and a horrible crime on their part to be different, to be un-human.

If you ran into one you were instructed to run like hell, go home, lock all the doors. Maybe a silver cross around the neck and garlic over the door and some salt on the windowsills also wouldn't hurt.

People were pretty superstitious, as always.

But somehow Firi knew salt and garlic and silver wouldn't keep them out. If they had wanted in, they would've gotten in. Home invasions, however, were rare. But the news continued to report stories about vampire trespassings in vague terms.

When the un-human race was discovered, what once was myth became dreams made flesh. The shock of such a reality shift created an instant nightmare reaction in most humans. Despite all the mystical stories in all the human bibles people had made no room in their day to day living for the supernatural to *really* exist.

Now they had no choice. In their shock, it was easier to say anything unknown was of The Devil, of the Hell on some un-named plane after death. It was easy to vilify the other and make the decision to rid the Earth of them.

Shock and fear also brought out the more violent and mob tendencies in humans. Their appetites for total annihilation of a magical species seemed unlimited. An unknowable enemy gave extremists, which now consisted of a majority, excuses to conduct their violent urges any way they saw fit. This violence within was not seen as monstrous on their part because it was only perpetrated upon monsters themselves. Myth, rumor and nightmare had come to life.

There was also the universal, racial fear that these vampires were a threat because they were stronger than humans. On TV programs that were less popular, religious fanatics conjectured that these demons who appeared one day as if from the bottom of the Earth, who were gold and silver-eyed, strong as standing stones and never aged, were superior to humans. All jealousy aside—they were immortal; they were beautiful!—of course they could never be allowed to live.

There was also the added fact that, though the night-fairies never needed to eat, they did enjoy elixirs made of blood—each other's, animal and human—and that alone infused an ancient fear.

The word *vampire* came immediately to the foreground, taken up by every news organization, blazoned across every headline, and brought with it the baggage of ten thousand stories, plays and movies from a scant few hundred years.

The fairy vampires never had a chance.

Now the wounded one who sat before Firi and turned the grasses golden, slumped. But Firi wasn't scared. He could see he had been severely weakened. But vampires were very difficult to kill. Firi suspected that unlike a mortally injured human he might simply get up and walk away trailing his coppery garlands of blood, suffering until he fully renewed himself.

But Firi wasn't sure. He didn't know what stories to believe, what was true or made up; he just knew he always questioned everything even as the child he was. He couldn't help himself.

Sitting there by the river bend, this one wore a billowy, gold-flecked white shirt with bundles of intricate lace hanging by his throat. He had a beautiful sash made of sewn leaves and a leaf crown in his brownish, black-streaked hair.

Taking a deep breath, Firi asked in a thin, child-voice, "What happened to you?"

"Ah, stabbed with silver and wood through and through. Soldiers in a distant forest. Even through their nets of silk I got away. I've been running for hundreds of miles. I wasn't tired at all until now. But you're too young to know such things, aren't you?"

"No."

"I see. Maybe I have judged you wrongly."

"Will you die?"

"We don't die. Our bodies can be banished and destroyed, but we never die."

Firi knew from the war reports that most weapons didn't work on the vampires. Humans went to great extremes to dispose of the monsters. They would not die if burned, shot or cut, although wood, silver and silk nets slowed them down. If cut, their fragments would grow new flesh, new limbs.

He had heard stories that if caught, many vampires were bundled together in silk and iron, two strong elements that seemed able to contain them for a while, and dumped into volcanoes. Or they were locked away in metal containers and thrown into the deepest seas.

He shuddered.

The monster turned to face him. Firi was overwhelmed by the handsome features in that face, the even-handed kindness in the relaxed visage, despite the wispy otherness in the eyes. "I smell our kind upon you," it said. "Have you met one like me before?"

Firi shook his head.

"You are Halfling, then."

"What's that mean?"

"It happens. Not often. A drop of fae blood here and there… over time. Lovers' trysts, a faerie prince and a milk-maid sneaking into ever-after, changelings, a youngest daughter sold for protection to the beasts of the wood. It happens. The mixing of the blood, but it's very rare."

"I know those stories are called fairy tales. But they're not just stories, right? I know you've been here forever. I've felt it, smelled it."

"As a Halfling, you would. It's normal. How about your dreams?"

"The night-fairies have always come to me in my dreams."

"You don't use the word *vampire*?"

"Is that what I'm supposed to call you?" Firi asked, suddenly confused.

"No. You are a smart boy, aren't you?"

Firi remained silent.

"It isn't true," the monster began, in his slightly shaky voice, "that we have been here in your world forever. It is all one world, yes, but we lived in another realm to the side of it, west and east, down and out. You might call it another dimension. Where I am from, it used to be that all the air and ground were made of candles, wind and leaves. It's very unstable for humans, which is why you rarely found us. Without a link to one of us, our world would barely hold you aloft. But if you are linked to one of us and wander in, it's stable, much like your Earth right here, right now.

"In my homeland the pink skies are dusted with green clouds. The stars at night shine purple. And there are three moons called Raven, Bleak and Wise."

"Wynken, Blynken and Nod," Firi said, remembering his child's Garden of Verses book on his shelf at home.

The monster, whom he now thought of as just a different kind of man, could have been cast right out of those pages, poem of a myth with stanzas of dark goblins and ambrosia on trees, lines describing immortal neverlands, unending autumns, and frosted faces on playroom windowpanes.

As the monster continued his story, Firi realized he'd slipped from his rock perch, his body creeping closer across the weeds and dirt toward the little sand beach.

"I'll tell you a secret, child. We were once mortals like you and your family and your friends. A long time ago, death existed in our realm. Then strangers came with owl eyes and wings. From one of the moons they flew, or so we thought. And they didn't fly like birds do. They came in starboats with rocket noses. Like you humans, we fought them because they were different and we were afraid. They fought better. We lost. Those few who survived were fed their blood. I was a young man when I drank the blood and was raised from the dead. One of the first. It was so long ago the years blur."

As if in a daze, the vampire kept talking.

"I could describe to you such sights that you wouldn't believe. Our faerie towers are made of red dusk and mist. When the flowering lotus-lights of the royal gardens mature, they rise to the skies and become stars. And there are a dozen emerald seas with uncounted drowned cities 100 thousand years gone, the cities of our mortal forebears."

Firi listened, entranced. He could picture it all in his mind as if he'd been there. The monster's words reflected dreams he'd had since he was barely able to walk. In his blood, in his very skeleton itself, he knew these creatures, sleep-danced with them across caterwauling skies, and had always felt different for it, set aside. It was as if even his friends at school could smell the otherness on him, alienating him. They saw it in his outlander gaze, saw his love, though never spoken aloud, for all things the humans of Earth called monsters.

In his dreams, Firi had walked their rain-swept cairns and secret, December-lit castles. Even now, as his parents and all other adults declared war on non-humans, hunted them, gathered them chained in giant metal containers and dropped them into volcanoes or sank them in the deepest seas, Firi lived in his "Child's Garden" believing in a different point of view.

"I'm sorry this is happening to you. This is your world, too," Firi insisted.

"I am impressed you understand, being so young."

"I just know the grown-ups want to rid the Earth of you all. But that would be like… like taking away all the trees."

"Have you heard the saying: 'What goes around comes around'?"

Firi nodded.

"We were as you are now. But we didn't have all your earthly resources. We had some magic but most of it was useless against the strangers. But I really think we fought so badly because of their terrible beauty. We were enthralled, poisoned by heart-shaped faces, downy wings of snow, midnight hair so thick and long it caped and hooded them. They walked like black shadows with alabaster wings and eyes of ruby that lit the night. They spoke in poems. They killed with their tears."

"How can water-drops kill?"

"Not the tears themselves, child, but pure grief telepathically focused. Despair of such magnitude it would stop our hearts. During our war with them their anguish at our violence bled into us so intently it released toxins into our brains. Our exposure to their darkest emotions caused our bodies to turn on us. Only their blood could heal us."

Firi asked, "After the survivors were changed, where did the strangers go? Are they among you still? Is that why you're here?"

"No. They went elsewhere. Into other dimensions, perhaps, to do it all again."

"Then why have you left your own realm?"

"With age and time our home is shrinking, slowly disintegrating. It will soon be completely gone. The seeding ground of our people will die. The space of our realm is so small now that it was necessary to expand. We thought we could blend in here. We're good at hiding, at secrecy. But mistakes have been made. We are paying for them."

Firi was silent for many seconds as his brain soaked it all in. "So, the ones who changed you, made you strong and so you can't die, their blood healed you?"

"Yes."

"Does it work that way now?" Firi asked. "If I was hurt, could your blood heal me? Or mine, you?"

One tooth gleamed through the bluing shadows as the vampire smiled. It was a princely smile. He radiated an aura of soft, white light.

"It is unfortunate your vampire myths have made it impossible to exist here without engendering such terror. And maybe there are a few among us who have taken advantage of human weakness, making it bad for the rest of us."

Firi drew back even as he felt himself compelled forward. The vampire had not quite answered his question, but he knew the answer anyway. His body, seemingly of its own accord, crawled across the old grass to the vampire's side. He could smell the fresh blood now, tart like cider, sweet like honey. He looked up at him—he'd never been this close to one of them before—and saw merely a man's shape, long hair like shining dark leaves, and silver-green eyes, brighter than human but also wiser, and sad. He wasn't scary. And he wasn't all that different.

Gold blood shimmered on the grass and on the man's beautiful, white shirt. He was hurt in his chest and right shoulder. The shirt at two places was torn and the blood seeped slowly down the greenish-pale skin.

The man said something very softly. It sounded like another language.

Firi sensed the ritual of those words. He shivered as his body intuited the danger. "Will it hurt?" he asked.

"I wouldn't hurt a child," the vampire said. He reached out and touched the top of Firi's hand. "But just one drop of your blood would help me very much."

"Just one drop?" He knew he shouldn't trust. He was told over and over again by his parents and teachers of the dangers of the vampires. Of their threat. Stories of murder, of chaos, of massacres. These stories always happened in some far-off land to people no one knew. But that didn't mean they weren't quite real.

"With your permission, of course." The man gently stroked his hand. "And it might hurt. A little."

Firi took a long breath. He was scared, but not terribly. A unnamed part of him wanted this, craved the contact. "Okay." The word seemed to breathe out of him. His tone was not at all steady.

Voice like a breeze, the vampire said, "We call it the autumn wine."

Speechless, Firi could only nod.

"A link will form between us. But it won't harm you. I'll simply be able to find you wherever you are. And you might feel me as well, but it won't displace you. It won't interfere with your life at all."

"I think that yes, it's okay." Firi allowed the man to lift his hand to his face. He couldn't look. He shut his eyes tightly as he felt the monster's breath on his skin, cool and steady. A pressure. A pinch. And something wet. Then his hand was free.

Firi opened his eyes. The first thing he did was look at his finger. There was no sign of injury, no blood.

He forced his gaze up the man's body to his chest. The blood there had stopped seeping, had already dried.

Inside his heart and mind, a spark of wonder began to fill him, like first snow, like starlight.

"Thank you," the vampire said.

Firi's lips curved up until he was grinning. He was no longer scared.

*

Chapter Five

No one in Firi's family ever suspected he'd had contact with a vampire.

It wasn't until eight years later that he met the vampire again and learned his name.

Indian summer thickened the land with falling leaves and dust. Reddish rain came from the stars. The war had savaged the economy but the humans were winning. So they said.

For all the years after his first encounter with the vampire, not a single day passed for Firi without thoughts of him, without feeling that flicker of another life inside him, heart and brain.

Firi dreamed of his vampire faerie every night. At first the dreams were innocent, like his favorite childhood fables and ballads that filled him with wonder and beauty.

When he hit puberty, much to his shock, and sometimes chagrin, the dreams changed to those of a more adult nature.

The monster he'd met was a part of both sets of dreams.

He went through endless cycles of both fear and loathing, love and longing until he came to accept himself more easily, and decided that even the physically intimate focuses of his dreamings were part of the nature of having shared the *autumn wine*.

The monster had been honest. A link definitely had formed between them. But Firi had given his permission.

He could have concluded, being only ten at the time, that he had been coerced. But he knew that was a lie. He had offered. He had wanted to help heal this creature of the wood who'd called him a Halfling.

Maybe it was simply his Halfling nature, whatever that might be.

He spoke of his infatuation with the nameless creature to no one. Aside from immediate derision and alienation, he would have become the target of bullying from his peers and disgust from his parents. He would have become an enemy of the state.

Vampire/human liaisons had been illegal since the war began. Strict laws existed. The word 'traitor' was used for those who had even rudimentary contact with vampires. Before the war, before vampires were even known to be real, there had been vampire/human love stories. Famous fictions. Movies. Now even the idea of a vampire with a human was met with prejudice of the highest degree.

All those past classics depicting love between vampires and humans were now banned. Burned. Destroyed.

Firi had heard rumors of secret vampire-loving factions. But he was afraid to even research it, too young and unsure to trust himself and his own thoughts, let alone the confidences of others.

He kept to himself most of the time and earned a reputation for being a loner.

He watched the daily televised reports saddened that they never seemed to change over the years, reports of vampires being exposed, captured, taken away to dark oceans or lava pits.

Video never accompanied the reports. It was illegal to show the actual battles, or the captures. Vampires were never filmed and speculation was it was because they did not show up on camera. Like the myth of not being able see their reflections in mirrors, people believed in it.

But Firi knew that was untrue. On the night he'd actually met his vampire, he'd seen the man's reflection in the rippling, black waters of the swimming hole in the creek, white and spectral.

Daily, the news relied solely on official government reports. Since the government owned all legitimate news networks, no professional reporters questioned those reports.

Free-lancers who did question were immediately and publicly disgraced.

Once the country had free-speech. That no longer was the case.

If you were in the military it was a foregone fact that you had seen and interacted with the creatures, but all soldiers signed security clearance contracts never to speak of their roles in the battles, the arrests, the disposals.

Firi had heard rumors of civilians who had seen vampires and even met them. He longed to find such people but if they existed they were silent, hidden, nameless.

Over time, he searched computer archives when he felt bold, brave, knowing there was no privacy, that the government could track such activity at the push of a button. But he figured they wouldn't bother with a teenage boy who was introverted and shy. He wasn't any threat. They probably would not see a point in wasting time even glancing his way.

In his searches he found only anonymous fragments of pre-war, non-contemporary humans encountering vampires, and nothing that was ever concrete. Those fragments were rare, a poem here, a paragraph there. In old forgotten documents in university library archives, his search might pull up a diary entry from one hundred or more years in the past.

...I saw the creature on the knoll, fire-eyes and translucent skin, blue-green pallor as if from plague but comely in its demeanor...

...hair of glossy flame, eyes of diamond light, she beckoned at the winter window, vanishing as I approached to let her in...

...the wine of his gaze, the spectre of his skin...three times in three years I saw him ghost through the fading summer dells outside my home...he was not a wraith, he was not a human...

Some of the people who wrote these old journals admitted in their daily entries that they drank whiskey all day long, or were themselves afflicted with fever, illness, or fantastic dreams. Yet Firi hung onto their words as if they were holy incantations, memorized them, spoke them aloud when he was alone and wanting.

*

In the eighth year since Firi had met the vampire, current news assured viewers that the horrific vampire dangers were minimizing, the war had accomplished its goals and was nearly won. Few vampires remained at large, so said the reports. All their hiding places had been revealed, though the reporters never stated where those hiding places were. The reports were artful in their disclosures with very few specifics.

Finally, people breathed freer. Adults projected less tension toward their children.

The war was fading, like a long ago memory of fear and grief. Soldiers returned to their homes. Final battles were, they said, mere skirmishes now, nothing to worry about.

The vampires had gone extinct.

When he was ten and the vampire round-ups had just begun, Firi had been over-protected by his mother and father.

It was easier, at 18, with the war coming to an end, to escape the house alone now and walk along the deer meadows. His parents didn't watch his every move anymore. Nor was he considered a wild child.

*

Tonight, Firi felt pulled to be outside, to walk in places that had been forbidden to him for eight long years.

Firi moved into the feathered greens and blues of the meadow, looking up through distant trees at the approaching auburn dusk.

An ache permeated his body as if he could feel the burning of the clouds as the orange sun penetrated them. The dust scents of this time of day, the rime, the watery moss, the fading September rusts on the edges of life itself came into him, pungent, smoky, drenched in loamy wind.

In an impulsive gesture, he dropped to his knees, hands in the weeds and soil, needing to feel it against his skin, that drift and delft of brush, rock, dirt. Light-colored moths flew up. On bent and fading long grasses, he lay back and stared at the gold-stained sky.

He watched the brass sun set. He watched the first star come out to rule the ancient night.

Something seemed to ghost in on the wind that night, an essence of frozen sky, a quivering nightfall that brought sounds of old footsteps, images of bedraggled coats and gas lamps from a hundred years ago or more, or maybe from another realm.

The campfire skies of September invaded the pores of the skin and sent the heart a message of such longing, the mind was forced to say, "Time for a journey."

But it was just a feeling, nothing more, he told himself, gazing at a rising moon until it baked his brain in feverish despair and delight. It was just a memory from sleep that kept repeating: emerald storms and black suns and sylvan haunted music infecting the skull, tunes of runes, leaves, green love out in the pastures where the deer drank down the sky.

Whatever it was, Firi fell into a reverie.

In a flush of fantasy, he plummeted deep into a shadow-woven dreamwood where the familiar faerie monster vampire man appeared at his left shoulder, dressed in a white shirt with lace at the collar, and began to whisper in his ear.

But this was different from his usual fantasies, everything containing more depth, scent, feeling. The colors of the dreamwood were brilliant in his mind.

He saw himself standing first in the meadow, then in the wood, the shadow from his past beside him. Had he gotten up? Was this real?

The breeze frazzled him. He most definitely was not asleep. The trees of the waning month, of this strange new wood, were goblin-armed, reaching to snare any passersby.

"Is this real?" he asked breathlessly. Hopefully. For so long he'd wanted to meet this being again.

The vampire at his side said, "We meet again, Firi. It is very real. Let's go down by the hot spring where the moss is velvet and the water warm as autumn wine."

What hot spring? he thought as he willingly moved along with the shadow, matching its pace.

The tips of the vampire's fingers brushed Firi's arm and they walked as if through a dream.

At the touch against his arm his skin flamed. Already today, the things he'd been thinking before he'd gone to lie down in the meadow had him in a restless state, a fever. Overwhelmed, embarrassed, he let his arm fall away, slowing his stride just a little in hopes the vampire wouldn't notice.

But they were linked. Of course he noticed.

And damn, this had to be real. It *felt* so real.

Above them the sky wheeled in jade-tinted blackness. Tiny sparks of stars pulsed and trembled in purplish undulations.

All around them the goblin trees thickened and Firi thought he saw wrinkled old-man faces in the trunks.

Three small moons rose upon the tree-tangled horizon. He remembered: Raven. Bleak. Wise. They hung like crystals in the leafless trees, chiming.

He heard a fall of water, the slaps of a thousand droplets upon the surface of a pool, and smelled the clean mist scent, the bracken-like rain.

A sound of wings from an invisible creature paused by his head, then rushed on.

He wanted to say, *You came back. You're here.* His heart swelled but he remained silent.

As they came closer to the water, everything looked edged in blue light. The vampire was whispering again.

"They say the original seeds of our people come from this very area of land. A lot is disappearing. Remember this."

That was when he truly knew this was no fantasy. Something had happened in his mind in that meadow. Something had come into his dreams and led him away. It was very real.

His excitement increased.

"Where are we?" Firi asked. If they had gone through some portal, he didn't remember it.

"Land of a thousand autumns," the vampire replied.

They came to the pool where a waterfall spilled. The moons made a tri-fold reflection on the dark water. There were skeleton faces in the night clouds. Everything smelled so sweet, honey-dew and pear, wine and ivy.

"Why are we here? Why have you come to me?"

"I told you we were going to the hot spring."

"But why are you here? Or rather, why am I here?"

"For your sake, Firi."

"I never told you my name."

"I've known your name for years, since the day you helped me."

"I have never known yours."

"Lace," was the single answer he received.

Firi felt a little gasp inside his throat. It was such an odd name, but beautiful, too. *Lace*, he repeated to himself over and over in his thoughts. There was some kind of power in knowing that small detail and his body responded to it in its heightened awareness. The name, so sylph-like, was heat and strength, power in delicacy. The name was like a caress. What did he expect? A hard and common name like Ed or Bob? A mysteriously complex name like Darian or Sharife? Or like his own weird name: Firisian?

"You didn't answer my question," Firi said, working hard now to hold his voice steady. "Why are we here? Is this your world? It's sort of familiar, but..."

"We must exchange the autumn wine again. You must drink this time. We must drink together."

"Are you hurt again?"

"I'm fine. For now. But you are rare, one of the Halflings. Now that you are of age, your blood must be quickened so your strength will increase. Have you not felt it?"

"I don't know." Firi had felt a kinship to the vampires, most certainly, and an empathy for them. As well as obsession, both mental and physical. Especially for Lace. But it embarrassed him, all of it, the forbidden nature of his feelings forcing him for years to be secretive and shy, to feel bad at the idea that he was fraternizing with the enemy. And worse, since puberty his swift arousals whenever he thought of the vampire left him with such guilt and longing.

"Are there others like me?"

"Halflings are very rare. Mixing our blood with humans results in carriers within the human race. Carriers can pass their gene down for centuries without producing a Halfling. In all my long life I've only encountered two, not counting you. They are gone now. There are probably more. Finding them would be near to impossible."

"You found me."

Lace turned his head and gazed softly at him. "No. You found me."

The falls were loud, the water sparkling in triple moonlight. In a near-whisper, Firi said, "I want to be like you."

*

Chapter Six

"It is not quite the way you say it," Lace explained. "You're human and you will never lose that self. Our conquerors *turned* us. They made us, as best they could, to be more like them. But we were still different. For one thing, they had wings. In a millennium, we never managed to grow them."

"But I can be changed?" Firi asked, shivering at his own question.

"For Halflings who drink the fae blood, the effects are extended life-spans and added physical speed and strength. Other changes may occur as well, in the mind, but you will still be yourself. Still human. And it strengthens the link between human and their fae donor."

It didn't really answer his question, but Firi nodded; he had so many more questions. He had been thinking on it for eight years and still he understood almost none of it. But he wanted this intently. Had dreamt of it so many times. His body yearned for a kind of completion he couldn't define. Some might have called it love. Was that all it was? Was he in love? It seemed like more, something ripping at his insides wanting to get free, something pulling and pressing. It was insidious. It was exhilarating.

"I know it's not enough information. You can't completely understand. But you will. Over time," Lace added.

"It doesn't matter. I still want it." Why did his voice sound so small out here in these alien woods?

"You're shaking," Lace commented.

"Just nerves." Heat rushed the skin of his face. He'd wanted this since he was ten. It had never been a question.

"Do you see that still pool over there by the triangle rock?"

Firi nodded.

"The water there, it's warm with soothing minerals."
Lace's lips curved up. "It's good for the nerves. Let's go for a
swim first before we commit to anything."

Just that suggestion calmed Firi instantly. They walked
to the big rock which Firi could see, as they got closer,
sparkled as if covered in glitter.

At first Firi was shy.

Lace never hesitated. He sat down and took off his
boots, then his shirt. When he stood, he stripped off his black
pants and set them on the sand. All he wore now was a dark
band about his hips and groin that revealed most of his hips
and buttocks and covered him only in front. Lace's skin was
not as greenly pallid as it had been on their first meeting.
Tonight he was golden in the moons' light with lean muscles
all over.

Firi glanced away and slowly took off his shirt. He
heard the water splash. When he looked back, Lace was
submerged. Steam rose from where his body had entered the
little pool. Gracefully, his head came up and his bright-dark
hair spilled all to one side and stuck like a dozen wet snakes
to his shoulder.

Quicker now, Firi sloughed off his boots and pants
until he was down to white underwear, then he joined the
vampire fairy monster in the warm spring.

The water was a lot hotter than he'd expected and his
body relaxed as his skin tingled in refreshing relief to its
elements.

As he leaned back and floated on the majestic liquid of
the dark pond, he thought, *Am I still in the meadow back home?
Am I dreaming under white specks of stars beneath a single moon?*

When he floated back, the lamps of the three alien
moons had risen further into the trees, drenching them in rose
and silver. Ghost-feathered clouds like tatters of antique
curtains wisped across the blood-dark sky. A small breeze
came over the water, wrestling with the steam. For a moment
he smelled the autumn meadow he'd been reclining in before

Lace had come and taken him away. *I'm still there*, he thought. Then, *No*.

This was real. It had to be real.

Lace came up alongside him, standing on the bottom with his head and shoulders above the liquid surface.

The water licked Firi. His body heated, burned.

Lace said quietly, "This sharing of the autumn wine will not be like when you were ten."

"It will be more blood than just a drop?"

"Yes."

"How much?" His heart pumped strong and quick at the meaning behind that question.

"Maybe enough to make you quite dizzy."

I'm already dizzy, he thought.

"It's a lot to ask from a child."

"I'm not a child," Firi protested. "I'm 18."

"Ah."

Lace nodded, but Firi did not see much agreement there. He then realized how ridiculous his words must have sounded to a millennia-old vampire, but he wanted Lace to also understand that he was not really a boy anymore, and hadn't been for quite some time.

The water swirled, warm and light against his skin. It smelled of summer and fall twined, of old rain, but drifted and dreamy like October dusks.

He bent his head back so his shoulder-length, thick hair swayed behind him and the back of his head was submerged. He was aware Lace was watching him. He shut his eyes tight, floated in free-form a moment, then said, "Who drinks first?"

He had forgotten about everything else except that moment, forgotten his home, his parents, his few friends, the fields he loved, the skies he called home. Nothing else existed. He didn't want to be anywhere but here. Forever.

"You choose," came the answer.

"You first, then." Flailing a bit, Firi opened his eyes and attempted to right himself in the water. His hand broke the surface as if reaching. Lace took it and pulled. He glided into him, his legs bumping Lace's thighs. The moons in the goblin tree branches throbbed.

Lace pulled him to a shallower alcove in the spring and his feet melded with the sandy pool-bottom. There was no beach; it was more of a rocky lagoon surrounded by bending fronds of jade and lavender. A large gold flower, lamp-shaped, bell-like, draped itself in the air above them. Its scent sugared the air.

Lace still had hold of Firi's wrist. Firi watched Lace lean back against one smooth rock and his bare chest gleamed with droplets of water. He had no hair there, and the muscles were fine, the thin ribs delineated under the satin skin texture.

The grasp on Firi's wrist tightened and Lace held his arm up higher. "It won't be your finger this time." He turned Firi's hand so that the underside of his wrist was exposed.

He tensed. "My wrist, then?"

"Yes."

Firi shuddered. "Okay." But his breath trembled.

Lace reached down with his free hand, under the water, and brought up something from his hip. A tiny crystal knife. Firi decided he must've had a hidden pocket in that loincloth of his.

Firi saw the glimmer of it, like glass, and made a small sound in the back of his throat.

Lace pulled him closer, and for a moment Firi thought the man-monster-vampire would embrace him. The silver-green eyes glowed steady as they half-stood, half floated, neither making any move. He said, "You'll feel a pinch. That's all. You'll be fine."

A little disappointed—was he hoping for more drama?—Firi said, "Do it."

Lace held the little knife with one hand, Firi's wrist with the other. Firi automatically closed his eyes, bowed his head.

He felt the cut first as pressure, then after a few long seconds, a sharp sting on top of a deep ache. His body tensed even more and jerked a little. He felt Lace let up with the knife; his own breathing had stopped.

He did not dare open his eyes but stood very still as the warm water lapped around them. He could hear the shattering sound of the nearby falls, the surging purrs of crickets in the surrounding foliage, and the vampire's slow, steady breaths.

His hand in Lace's palm seemed weightless, unattached, until he felt the velvet lips move against his skin and the light lapping of a tentative tongue. The mouth was cool, moist as it moved over his wrist, the lips drawing on it, lightly pulling.

He gasped as streams of pleasure tingled all over his body, inside and out.

In response, Lace's now free arm curved about Firi's waist, drawing him close until their upper bodies touched and the top of Firi's head bumped Lace's shoulder.

He couldn't move, could only press closer as he felt the vampire drink.

A rush came over him so powerful he saw tiny lights at the edges of his closed eyelids. He realized he was biting hard at his lower lip and let up. It throbbed and his mouth opened in a small 'o' as he sucked at the air.

Lace smelled of tea-leaves and the heat of a summer wind.

He pressed his head closer to the vampire, almost as if to root under his arm, and let out a small groan.

Lace's arm around him loosened, then tightened, but the mouth on his wrist kept up its pressure, gentle but strong. There was no pain anymore.

His body floated; his toes curled against soft, wet sand. Everything seemed alive inside him, electric, fine-tuned.

His feet came up and his lower body started to float back. The arm around his waist shifted, the hand now lower on Firi's hip, cupping him there.

He heard sounds. The word "oh" over and over and realized it was his own voice uncontrollably reacting to the intensity of this sharing, the intimacy.

The lips let up. The tongue softly dabbed but he still felt no pain. He lifted his head to see Lace straighten.

Hands now at his sides, Firi could only look at him with wonder, their bodies still in contact as the warm water continually seeped between them.

Firi gasped once but did not break eye contact. Lace licked his lips, pink and damp, not red as Firi expected, but it had only been a small cut, not messy.

Lace leaned closer.

When those pink lips gently touched his own, he completely stopped breathing.

Lace had said the sharing of the autumn wine would make him dizzy. *Dizzy?* he thought. ***This** is dizzy!*

He wasn't sure what to do. He remembered his protest. *I'm not a child!* But in this moment he felt so young, unsure, enraptured and lost at the same time.

His limp arms now moved as if of their own accord, up and curving, around Lace's waist until he found himself holding onto him as if for his very life.

Too abruptly, Lace drew back. Firi's fingers slipped against his smooth back, trying to grasp. He didn't want him to pull away. Not right now. Not ever.

But Lace pushed him back with a delicate strength and brought his arm between them. Suddenly, Firi found the vampire's wrist in his face, saw a seeping gold cut there right before it was pressed to his mouth.

All he could think was, *Like honey and stars.*

The vampire's blood permeated his mouth. There were no long, loud gulps, just soft sips as it spread over his tongue, up the roof of his mouth and down his throat with the texture of rain.

It was like the vampire was melting into him.

The blood going into him heightened all his senses even more. Sound jumped to a higher volume, and scents lingered as he breathed through his nose: roses somewhere, loam on leaves, and a distant snow-cold hint of coming winter.

His body flamed everywhere. He thought surely the waters around them must be bubbling. They buoyed him up as if he had no weight at all. Maybe he had no weight now. Maybe he could fly.

The blood was like a sudden addiction, tart and heady. His mind saw explosions of light, kaleidoscope images of skies and lands set in semi-precious stones. He saw topaz suns. Aquamarine moons. Amethyst winds.

Too soon Lace took his wrist away. Firi nearly yelled but it came out a loud groan. Lace pulled him close again and kissed the groan from his lips, but that didn't stop the inarticulate sounds from continuing to burble up his throat.

Lace's hands were on his hips again, then lower. He felt the fingers pull at the cloth to his underwear.

Firi tensed, tossed his head back.

Lace looked all hazy, blue-lit around the edges. He wondered what he looked like to Lace.

"Beautiful," Lace answered as if reading his thoughts. And maybe he was. Firi felt the link between them like a tender slice of light in his mind.

Lace tugged his underwear again. "These," he said, "are in the way."

"If you touch me..."

"Shh," Lace kissed him before he could finish. But the thought completed in their minds. *I'll explode.*

He felt the cloth ripped away and himself instantly naked and free in the water, skin blazing, his blood on fire.

Lace pushed against him and he realized the black-band loincloth was gone as well. He could feel him. All of Lace pressing against him. To even think about that made him crazed.

Firi tasted whole universes in Lace's next kiss. No time, just glory. He was lifted, brought to the brink of transformation again and again.

His breathing came heavy, labored.

Some time later, after Lace had steered them to another alcove in the lagoon, less rocky, even more serene, he curved his hands under Firi's buttocks and brought him up onto a mossy bank.

Lace licked the water clean from Firi's chest. His vampire hands moved up and down his sides. He nuzzled Firi's groin.

Firi cried out. He was so sensitive. Embarrassed, even as he started to curl up.

Lace said, "Everything natural is beautiful." He held Firi in place and licked him there, all up and down his erection, taunting him.

Firi nearly choked on the pleasure. "But I can't hold…"

Lace moved up quickly and kissed his mouth again. When he let up he said, "The taste of youth is so sweet."

Firi's eyes rolled up. "I can't hold on."

"Then," Lace replied, smiling wide, "this will take but a moment."

A long moment or a short moment? But he realized he didn't care as warm breath, tongue and lips were upon him, taking him into tight pleasure, suckling at his essence, another kind of autumn wine.

He came on the thin winds, still damp from the water, droplets of the spring still clinging to his shoulders, to his nipples, and gathered in the hollow of his stomach. It was a rolling pleasure that pulsed from him, on and on. It seemed he would never recover.

Soon Lace was holding him again, kissing him, and it was natural to curl into the embrace, their legs entwined.

He thought he slept. For a few minutes. Or a few seconds at least. He woke with his hand between Lace's legs, and stroked and stroked until the pearly fluids filled his palm. Now Lace's head was buried against Firi's shoulder as the vampire panted and moaned. Firi reached up and touched the long leaf-brown and black hair.

They kissed under the three moons for what seemed like hours and the goblin trees watched as their lovemaking continued far into the night.

He napped again, off and on. Once he woke to see Lace standing naked in the shallows of the spring, head thrown back, hands raised as if in communion with the sky. He was completely uninhibited, open, erect, his silhouette immense and beautiful.

Firi rose from their moss bed and waded into the little pool, kneeling before him in the shallow waters. He kissed the muscled thighs, stroked the engorged flesh very lightly, then brought it to his mouth.

It was the first time he'd done this to Lace. Even after everything, he'd been still afraid, shy. And Lace had never demanded a thing from him. Now he wanted this power. He wanted to feel it intimately like this, suck on it, drink this final drink in its throbbing ecstasy.

Lace tasted of the lightly seared salt of stars. Of dreams long-buried in galaxies made of rain. Firi swallowed everything he had to give. Wanting more.

The vampire came with a howl, and fell back into the shallows boneless, drained. Firi crawled toward him, splashing, and moved on top of him. They wrestled and rolled like children at a swimming hole. Laughing playfully. Kissing lightly, then deeply, then moving together again, languid for a time, then restless.

Lace suckled Firi again and his young body pumped and pumped as if he were losing his heart.

They could not get enough of each other. That and the swell of the blood they'd shared, and the three moons overhead. All of it conspired to create an orgy out of the entire beautiful night.

They did not drink more of each other's blood, but Firi could not forget the wonder of that, the flavor, the invigoration of it. If he felt vibrant and strong before, the feeling was now ten-fold.

They dragged themselves once again from the warm, spring waters and fell together, arm in arm, on their velvet moss bed near bending ferns and blue grasses. Again they curled into each other and fell asleep.

Firi dreamed of big windows filled with meteors. Of oracles made of blown glass. Of satin beds between the stars where he and Lace slept among the photons and ions of space.

In the dream, Lace spoke softly to him, telling him sweet things at first, but then the stories turned to war and violence and uncontainable grief.

"I need this link with you, Firi. I need you, Halfling child, for I am about to do something I cannot un-do. I am about to commit an act for which even eternity is not enough time to repent. My mind may fracture, may well not survive the trauma. Our kind can go into comas for thousands of years, losing all sense of self. I do not want that to happen. My link with you, precious human, will keep me grounded if nothing else, and maybe if you ever feel so inclined, you will find me again one day, and we will be free to love as nature intends."

Firi opened his eyes and found himself fully dressed, lying in the old meadow grasses. *What?* Had this only been a dream?

He sat up, hands in the dirt, and as he put his weight on them one wrist throbbed. He looked down and saw in the dim moonlight a line there, a slowly healing cut. As he pressed his weight forward to stand, he shook his head. Damp hair brushed his neck, making his skin shiver in the low breeze.

He felt sated but hot at the same time, still tingly all over. What they had done! The wonders.

And now it was over.

"Lace," he said aloud to the air.

No answer. Just wind.

And the darkness hunched and desolate behind him.

*

Chapter Seven

The bond between them: a pungent ghost-autumn, a slow burn in a lamp made of crystal and silver, three moons called Raven, Bleak and Wise.

It was as if the wind walked beside him every hour. Every day. As the weeks passed Firi saw the world grow from a childhood bedroom, home, meadow, passing friendships one makes in a bustling schoolroom to feel less alone, to a more adult world of open vistas, endless city sprawls, depthless possibility. Firi's body changed. His muscles strengthened, rippling beneath skin that shone in his mirror like burnished copper. He grew his hair longer. It contained a wild black sheen, like a hallucinogenic night, like the skies that shrouded them the night he and Lace had spent at the fae spring.

His heart galloped with every second of life, missing Lace constantly, but sure he would see him again one day. Lace was the strongest, the oldest of his kind. He would not be caught. Firi knew this. And he would be back.

Firi's new self, though lonely for love, glowed. He became quick and energetic in every task. Everything was clear. His mind opened. He smartly passed all tests for future education. Several colleges he'd applied to after seeing Lace offered scholarships and letters of acceptance.

His parents, who in the past had silently accepted their more withdrawn and shy child as possibly amounting to an average life with an average education, were happy he had finally blossomed, if a little late. They were proud of him and let him know it.

If they only knew. Sometimes he wanted to just blurt out: *It was a vampire who awakened me. Created me. They are the most beautiful and glorious and powerful creatures of the Earth!*

But of course he couldn't. He would be considered a traitor to say such things, a hopeless madman, shunned.

Romanticizing the enemy. There was an old word for it. Stockholm Syndrome. A term used a lot in the beginning of the war when vampire devotees from classic fiction and movie days were more vocal, before the literature was burned, the films destroyed, the laws passed making it illegal to write about vampires in any way except for appropriate news media war coverage. If the older generations remembered any of the fictional classical characters with any hint of dying fondness, they remained silent.

One could actually be imprisoned for glorifying the monster-myth.

Though the world was clear and limitless to Firi now, it was still a much darker one than he had ever wished for as a child. Except for the bond he shared with Lace, a constant tingling in his mind and body, he would've been but a shadow upon it.

Sometimes he would still hear Lace's voice. As if maybe, impossibly, they could still communicate on rare nights when the wind blew warm and sweet and night flowers offered their candy scents.

He would burn so hotly then.

He would hear Lace say, "You are strong. You are beautiful. Firi, the last of the Halflings. You are the one."

*

Home for the winter holiday after his first semester at college, Firi was sitting on the couch in the living room of his childhood home when the news broke.

The official word was that vampires were now almost completely extinct. Firi knew otherwise, so whenever news of the war came on the TV, with reports of how the vampire threat was taken care of, he grew disgusted and left the room.

But this night the news was different.

Reports came in about a military base on the outskirts of Firi's town that had been attacked and raided by the last remaining vampires at large.

This time there was rare film footage which showed dozens of human bodies scattered across the yard of a fenced compound. Some looked to have been beheaded. The scene was graphic and bloody.

Something bright and shiny in Firi's mind turned to bodily pain, like a dulled knife under his ribs. For a moment he couldn't breathe.

In his mind he saw Lace standing in the shallows of the spring where they'd shared so much, his body in silhouette as if sculpted from the dark itself, muscles tight and flexed against the parchment of the sky, arms raised in supplication, organ erect. Within that image a memory shifted loose and edged into the forefront of his thoughts.

He now remembered that before he'd gone to Lace and knelt before him in supplication that night, Lace had been speaking to him. Voice soft and resonant. Shaky but devout.

How had he forgotten what Lace had been saying?

Lace had been speaking while Firi had been lost in recent passions, dozing in the fresh night.

"I take the strength within me for what I must do." It was as if Lace spoke to the invisible energies around them. "I take from land and air and space. Trees and water and the fire of the stars. And from my Halfling mate, Firi, who is human and my enemy, but also ally and lover, I take the blood and the seed."

"I'm not your enemy," Firi had whispered.

He didn't think Lace had heard him, but Lace had replied, "You are human. Your family is human. Your world is human. They seek to destroy us from fear alone, for we are peaceful creatures, natural to our realm and yours."

"I don't want you destroyed. And you know I won't tell anyone about you."

"I know. We are linked. You cannot help but be loyal. But you will still hear stories in your future and find that what you know about me and what is reality might contradict themselves, and you will be aggrieved."

Firi smiled at the word "aggrieved." "I think I can handle it. Lace, I'm on your side."

"There are things I must do. And these things will change me. Change the link that is between us. I will shatter myself to succeed in my quest if I must. If that happens, I will retreat in my mind. I may be captured. I may be sent into the deepest sea or the hottest volcano. I will never die, but I will not walk this Earth again until the seas dry up and the volcanoes cool. In that time, I and all of us will be in hibernation, shattered, burnt, flayed, or drowned. Our minds will come to rest in the Sea of Sentient Dreaming. It will place a great weight on your mind. It will, quite probably, young Firi, drive you mad."

Firi had gotten up then, and waded into the warm water. He was about to kneel when Lace put a hand on the side of his cheek. "I'm so sorry this is happening. All of it. But your strength will give me what I need to do to attempt to complete my task."

"If they catch you, you're saying I will feel you suffer?"

"Yes."

"They can't catch you, Lace. You're the oldest, the strongest. I'll help you hide. I'll--"

"Shh." A firm hand covered Firi's mouth. "If they don't catch me and do away with me, you will one day find me again. You will sense me and come to me in whatever condition I will be in. That is the best case scenario I can offer. The best hope. Again, I'm sorry."

Firi dropped to his knees. "I pledge to you that I will find you. Everything I am is yours. Lace, I love you." He'd buried his face against the vampire's stomach.

"You'll be a strong one, Firi. Try to remember that. Try not to allow our link to harm your mind. And I will do what I can to protect you from the worst of my thoughts should the time come when I will enter the suffering for tens of thousands of years."

Now Firi sat on the couch watching the news and thought: *How could I have forgotten that moment?*

Why was it only now coming back to him?

He heard Lace's resonant voice in his head: *Everything is a story, a dream.*

He could not remember Lace ever saying that to him before. Was this voice a new communication? He searched the bond between them. As he did so, pain plunged into him starting first in his chest, then shivering its way throughout his body, strongest in his heart and head.

Firi's mother turned to look at him. "Firi, are you all right? Are you feeling sick, sweetheart?"

He quickly made up an excuse. "I think I may be coming down with the flu."

"Well, off to bed with you, then."

*

He had wept all day and all night. And it wasn't just from pain. He knew Lace was in danger. He knew Lace had been either injured or caught.

His parents thought it was merely a fever, the winter flu. It had been going around. Firi had rarely been sick a day in his life. He had taken no precautions against this flu, no vaccines, no shots and they gently reprimanded him for it. But after Lace, he knew he didn't need them.

And anyway, it was not the flu.

But he told his parents and everyone else that it was.

The image of the slaughtered bodies in the compound on the news kept flashing at him. He knew instinctively and through the link that it was Lace's doing.

He kept hearing Lace's voice in his head from that reclaimed conversation. *You will be aggrieved.*

Lace: so old, so gentle, so wise. Tender in every way as if made from the trees, the land, the river, and the very stars themselves. As if made from love.

There are things I must do. And these things will change me.

He could not even imagine a broken, violent, murderous, vengeful Lace.

But that's what it felt like in his mind when he mentally touched the bond. Despair. Rage. Agony.

He slept and woke, slept again. He ate nothing, which worried his parents who kept dutifully giving him flu remedies he threw away or flushed down the toilet.

He stared for hours at the blank white ceiling of his still-childish room, watching a mobile of plastic stars glimmer in the winter light.

The pain in his body came and went like chills, or cramps. The desperate grief in his mind never waned. It said: *If I have to, I will kill you all to gain back and protect forever what I love.*

Firi's mind tore.

The wind that had been walking at his side for months was now more of an insolent rush of storm lost upon the soul of night.

*

Chapter Eight

Firi did not get out of bed for two weeks that winter. Christmas holidays came and went. He roused himself only enough to sit for an hour at a family dinner.

His parents made excuses for him that he'd been ill with the flu. He knew they were worried and he hated worrying them.

So after a few weeks he forced himself to get up, go outside, eat, pretend that he wasn't as hollow and anxious inside as he felt.

He walked every day for hours, through the silver quieter days of December and on into the snowflaked wilder winds of January. He didn't answer calls from his friends who, after a while, stopped calling.

He didn't go back to college.

He took to wearing all white, white jeans, white shirts and sweaters with long sleeves he pulled over his wrists and fingers, balling the edges in his fists.

He walked through freezing temperatures that chromed his eyelashes and never felt the cold.

Sometimes he thought he felt Lace walking beside him like a disembodied sphere of amber heat. Through the chills of the north he would smell honey-glazed pollens, warm waterfalls, the cool velvet mint of moss. Because of Lace, he knew what it was like to taste the night, as if the very stars themselves had all fallen into his eyes and mouth.

He failed to notice hunger and thirst, but forced himself to remember to take a small shoulder pack with him on his wanderings, packed with a sandwich or crackers and cheese, a thermos of hot tea.

Still, he grew thin, but also hard limbed, muscles sinewy beneath his numb skin. He became a specter all in white wandering the snow with his black hair rippling behind him like a shadow always faithful, always following.

When he came home he usually went straight to his room. Sometimes he'd sit in the dark and think about Lace, only Lace, for hours at a time.

Lace's words would come back to him then: *You will be aggrieved.* And, *Our minds will come to rest in the Sea of Sentient Dreaming. It will place a great weight on your mind. It will, quite probably, young Firi, drive you mad.*

He knew Lace wasn't dead.

He knew it was far, far worse.

Sometimes he would access his computer, peruse old books online that contained heavy, strange fragmented philosophies, books from old times, surreal classics, anything that he might open at random, read a passage and assimilate into his own insular world. Poetry. Dream journals. Ouija board channelings. He searched for odd words and topics and turned up interesting things.

He tried to keep a journal of his own, written in a made up code, but he rarely wrote in it and then only short phrases that came as if from distance itself: *...my double is at the window...the suicide of clouds makes rain...gold and violet towns constructed of weeds...river of dark wings...owls on a cold star...*

He couldn't hold any one thought for long.

One day, he opened a page of blank lines and wrote: *L was right. I am fucked. I am "aggrieved."*

His parents wanted to send him to a doctor. He wouldn't go. When they became impatient with him he would remain silent as if listening to their wisdoms and demands. Then he would turn quietly and go back into his confining, childhood room, lock the door and sit in the dark.

He watched cobwebs form in the corners.

Whenever his mind would try to determine what really might have happened at the military compound he would come up against an obsidian wall tall as space, wide as the world.

He could still *feel* Lace, but he could get no images of that one major event. All he saw was the repeated news feed, the field of bloody bodies, the chain and razor wire fence, the shadows of a large building in the background. All he could hear was the silence of the film recording death and carnage. A silence that filled up his mind with an eerie wail worse than the loudest, open sound.

He could still feel Lace's presence through their link, but that was all.

One day in the middle of January when everything was at its grayest, the sky, the meadows and the roads heavy and ponderous, he dragged himself up from his somber mental hovel and, instead of going for a walk, asked his parents if he could borrow the car.

They were grateful for any sign of life from him. His mother, who worked nights and his father who worked half-time in his office in their home, were both present that day. They willingly gave him the keys. They asked where he was going.

He lied. "I need some new clothes. Maybe I'll see a movie with a friend."

They gave him money.

His father said, "Get some new boots. You've worn out the ones you have with all that walking you do."

His mother said, "And a warmer jacket, sweetie. I don't want you to relapse with the flu again. You've only just begun to look stronger." She gently brushed his long hair back from his shoulder, her thumb caressing the line of his jaw. His heart leapt at their kindness. Did he even deserve it?

If they ever found out he was a traitor to his own race—

He denied the thought, refused to finish it.

He took the jingling loop of keys and went out into the cold, unlocked the car and got in.

Then he drove. He did not go to any store.

For awhile he went in circles through the town, past familiar landmarks, his old school, and restaurants lined with white lights making them look like iced-cake cottages. He drove to the town square, around the courthouse with its rose red roof. He drove down roads thickly lined with giant evergreens that gave one the impression of heading down a long, frosted tunnel. His town was beautiful, evidential proof that humans could make lovely things, that the good in them could be roused and shine forth. He looked at the town and could not believe that within it, and others like it, there also existed a hate and fear reflecting no beauty at all but only a warping of sanity for which there seemed no cure. You couldn't tell that fact just by looking. When the vampires needed a place to come due to the shrinkage of their own realm, he saw how easily they might've been tricked into thinking the human world, a world of vast inventions and metropolises, quaint little townships, art and music, might be a welcoming and friendly place.

Was it all really only a façade to hide the beasts within?

Questions and more questions pierced his mind.

He finally found himself along the outskirts where the hills drew up, and the tree-line thinned.

Over one white mountain and then another, he drove. He came to the lonelier cabins of shyer folk, of hermits or rogues—who could tell one from the other?—and then even they were left behind.

He turned down one of those back roads usually dangerous in winter, but this one was safely plowed for now, the drifts at the edges like blackened silver in the wintry half-light. Some drifts loomed high as eight feet in places, walls of ice in abstract shapes that twisted like ominous sentinels haunting the way in.

About a mile in, he began to see some signs warning of **Private Property** and others stating **Property Owned by GSD Army.**

Firi ignored them. What would the damned army do anyway, shoot him? A citizen? A human?

The day was dark and his headlights were on. They made amber glares in the ice on the road.

He could see the compound in the distance now, silent, snowy, eerie. Yellow lights lined a square, dark building of several stories. He'd expected it to be bigger.

A gate blocked the road. Beside it stood a small glass kiosk. It was lit from inside by a single white light. The silhouette of a man sat within, fiddling with a computer.

Firi looked up into the thick trees and saw cameras.

Slowly he approached the kiosk.

All around the compound stood a twelve foot high fence topped with double spirals of razor-wire. He suspected the fence rooted deep into the ground as well. No one was getting in. Or out. Unless they could come up from the center of the Earth. Or fly.

He tried to sense Lace through their bond. Still, all he could feel was a vague life-force, an essence of evening and autumn and silver clouds.

At least there was that much.

The man in the kiosk came out as he approached. He was dressed in a blue uniform and wore a thick brown coat with lambskin lapels and collars. A blue cap covered his head. He waved at Firi's car, forcing him to stop about ten feet from the gate.

Firi opened his window as the man, hand on his side-arm, came around the front of the car and walked up to his door.

"I think I got turned around back there."

"This is a non-public area. Sir, you need to turn your car around. You cannot go any further."

"Oh, sorry. Army, right?"

"Yes, sir."

"Wow, that's crazy 'cause I was just thinking about joining. I'm almost nineteen. College drop-out. I need a job."

"You should enlist, then. Young men and women are always needed."

"How old were you when you enlisted?"

The man's hand did not leave his side-arm, but his face visibly relaxed. "Nineteen. It offered good training and good benefits. I couldn't ask for more."

"Wow, thank you for talking to me. But this place— What is it?"

"Army testing. That's all I can say."

"It's familiar. Was it on the news a few weeks ago? Vampires attacked, right? You guys are heroes."

"I'm not at liberty to say more, sir. You need to turn your car around now."

"Sure thing. Thank you. I'm going to think about enlisting."

The man nodded briskly. "That's good, kid. Now move along."

"Have a nice day."

The entire time they were talking, all Firi could feel was a slow burn building inside his chest. His body was hot, sweaty, nauseated.

Slowly, he made a u-turn, the car's tires crunching in the frozen snow. He did not want to leave. He wanted to beat the guard at the gate to a pulp, crash the gate and find Lace. He didn't know how he knew it, but Lace was in that compound. Somewhere.

He had not yet gone to the Land of Sentient Dreaming. He was not that distant or fragmented. Not yet.

Firi had to force himself to drive away knowing he was leaving behind the most valued thing in his life.

He yelled into the car's silence, air and sound rushing from his throat in abject frustration.

It was a mile back to the road. It was the longest mile he'd ever experienced, gliding by gargoyle-ish ice-henges and silent peaks walling off the trees and wild land. He felt trapped in ice. Surrounded. He wanted to scream again. Cry.

That was when the beginnings of his plan formed.

He would join the army.

He would become a highly trained guard. The best guard anyone ever saw. He would work out. He would grow bigger. And he would get a job at this compound. Then they would have to let him in.

He would then find the truth about what had actually happened at the compound. And he would find Lace. That he vowed. If it took him months or years, he would find him. After that, whatever he had to do to free him, he would do it. No matter the obstacles. Or the risks.

A little voice inside him asked: *Even if you find out Lace is a murderer?*

His lips set in a grim line. He nodded to himself. Then he said aloud to the road, the ice, the slate skies, "I will free him. No matter what."

He remembered the hot spring, and the gentle ritual of sharing blood. Lace had not been bloodthirsty in any definition of that word. He remembered how soft Lace's lips were, the ecstasy of his kisses. How gentle he'd been with Firi. How utterly devout. Firi had loved and been loved beyond his imaginings. He shared a link with Lace through the sharing of the autumn wine. He felt that superior tranquility.

He could not believe that Lace was a murderer. Even after Lace had told him he might be forced to do things that would fracture his soul, Firi still refused to believe. If violence had happened, it had to be self-defense.

Though Lace had called humans "enemy," Firi could not imagine him tearing apart human flesh, ripping heads from bodies. That scene from the news could not be Lace's doing. And if it was, then there had to be some explanation. Somewhere, somehow there were secrets and mysteries to be unraveled. And he would stop at nothing to unravel them.

*

The night before Firi went into the army, he cut off all his rippling black hair leaving only a half-inch cropped look.

In the mirror he looked older, more hard-edged.

It was madness, what he was about to do. He was a college dropout. A worthless kid.

But he had seen Lace standing in a lavender-sky draped wood amidst snapdragons and serene sorcery. He could not forget.

His heart knew what it had to do.

When he went to bed that night, he had a strange dream.

The three moons, Raven, Bleak and Wise dipped low in a soft purple sky, showing only their curved edges, one after the other. They were like three canoes following in a row, or three commas typed upon the setting night.

On wings of snow, he flew to the middle moon, Bleak, where a black city stood against a backdrop of giant, fang-shaped, pale rocks.

He entered the silhouette city through a tarnished silver gate, moved along a black-ribbon avenue bisecting land which held a choppy, dancing river of shadows on one side, and a deep forest of elder green on the other side, ageless in its ever-presence.

He thought he heard running in that forest as if something galloped on tough hooves.

Moon-deer? Alien satyrs?

He walked toward the big structures away from the foreign wilderness, and the only light seemed to be two candles in the clouds, the sister moons fore and aft, Raven rising as Wise set.

He smelled char on the air, as if something dank smoldered in damp dirt. It smelled like downtown big city gutters, and ancient rain.

The street was slightly slippery. Moon-mold? Slime of gothic origins?

The towers were steepled and as he approached they appeared as a grouping of steel rockets ready to blast up and away. The ground shuddered.

Before he could get close enough to touch the shiny surface of the nearest rocket, a light walked, wavering in the gray wind. The light grew as it dawned without bringing the day, and became a figure emerging as if formed directly from the shade, cloaked and billowy. It held an old-fashioned lantern housing a burning curl of orange flame.

It said, "You are not one of us."

"I'm visiting." Firi heard his voice as if it came from afar.

"This is the World of the Dead. You are not dead."

"Are you?" he asked.

The figure pushed back the hood of the cloak. Its face was heart-shaped, with owl-eyes and little tufts coming out of its hair like ears. Something moved behind the being within the folds of the cloak. As Firi looked closer, he saw a flash of white, a shimmer of feathers. Wings!

The being stared at him with great, green eyes and he was enveloped in its beauty.

"If you are not dead, you are here for a reason," it said.

"I'm looking for someone," Firi admitted. "A man. No. Not a man. Lace."

"I do not know the name."

"He's like you, maybe, but without the wings."

"There are many beings of many worlds. Some have wings. Some do not."

"On my world, we call beings like Lace vampires. Their world is shrinking and so they breached ours. My people sought to destroy them all."

"But of course vampires cannot be destroyed. Surely you know this. Sometimes they move on, if they have the need. If they have the time."

"Move on?"

"To another energy plane, another way of being."

"I don't think the vampires who came into my world have had the time to accomplish that," Firi said.

"Then you must find these lost souls," it said. "Find the door to let them out."

"I don't know how to do that. But maybe if I can find Lace, he can find the door."

The owl creature's eyes seemed to sink into him, as if a green sea encased him. "Your Lace may have already attempted this and failed. If you are here now it is because you have a way you have not found yet. A process, a new angle, a key."

Frustrated at the riddles, Firi asked, "But what is it?"

The creature's solemn gaze searched him up and down. It said, "You are remarkable in the things you have not yet done."

The dark city rumbled. The rocky ground under Firi's feet shuddered, then moved in a sort of liquid wave. He started to fall but his body rose up toward a shiny, black sky. Stars pressed in on him.

Firi woke with the warmth of tears on his cheeks.

*

Chapter Nine

Firi excelled in boot camp. His muscles grew thicker. He stood taller than all the other women and men. He did everything that was asked of him faster, better and stronger than the others in his unit.

When it came time for military placement, he'd ranked top in his class. This allowed him the privilege of choosing what he wanted to do.

He chose security.

He studied hard and practiced hard, becoming the best in his job. No one could beat him in combat skills. He joined an elite squad guarding high ranking officials and dignitaries.

The official word was that all the vampires of the world had been caught and dealt with. Firi knew better and so did the marshals, generals and colonels he guarded. His clearance allowed him to be one of several elite bodyguards at hushed briefings and secret meetings. They spoke of vampires held captive for research purposes. They spoke of containment through force and pharmaceuticals. They even discussed outrageous plans to create controlled vampire armies through magical serums and transfusions, though nothing had yet been put into action.

They could not know Firi's thoughts, that he believed they were out of their minds, that they understood Lace's people not at all.

The did not know that Firi could feel Lace through a psychic connection, that he could see the jade and lavender skies of his world when he closed his eyes, that he could smell the fresh golden scent of him sweet as honey as if Lace stood right next to him night and day.

He knew exactly where Lace was. Simply, he had to get there. But that proved not to be simple at all.

He had to earn his way to the top of the elite. Then he had to put in requests for a position at the secret base outside his hometown several times before anyone took a moment's notice.

When he met with his boss, a lieutenant colonel, for future job placement, the woman asked, "Why would you want to work with the Blueguard?"

He smiled at her and said, "It pays well. And it's near where my parents live, my childhood home."

"Homesick?" She did not smile when she asked the question.

He could smell the wind of Lace's world on his own skin, river-scent and moss, taffy-autumn winds with an edge of smoke. How could she not notice herself?

In the military he'd constantly had exams and blood tests and no one had ever said his came up looking different. And yet Lace had called him a Halfling. What did that really mean? Was it only a mental or psychic difference? Was his uniqueness just so well hidden that it didn't show up on regular tests?

"Of course the Blueguard would welcome someone with your talents, but there's not much action to be seen there."

"But it's an important job and they need people with high clearance."

"The clearance isn't an issue. All is in order. But with your intelligence and experience, and your physical qualifications alone, you'd be over-qualified. And bored, I'm afraid. There'd also be a slight pay-cut at first until the new job probation period is over, then the pay raise you're after will go into affect. Six months at that facility before you're assessed for that pay-grade bump. I really can't recommend—"

"I know all that," he interrupted quietly. "I'm willing to take on those terms." He shrugged and gave her a warm smile. "It's my home town."

She let out a heavy breath. "That's your reason? Or maybe you have a girl back home?"

"Maybe."

"All right, then. I'll put the transfer on the record. You'll hear back within a few days. I know you'll do a good job."

When she rose to finish the meeting, he stood. They saluted each other.

It had taken him two years to finally get where he wanted to be. He only hoped it wasn't two years too long.

*

Before Firi could even start his new job at the GSD secret complex near his old hometown, there were short classes and briefings to attend. He watched videos and read reports about what it was, exactly, he was guarding, and the special rules he needed to follow with this very special prisoner.

It was stated plainly that the prisoner he was to guard was a vampire, despite news broadcasts stating that vampires were nearly extinct.

Already Firi knew this for the lie it was.

Guards were never to speak to any prisoners except to give orders and commands. They were instructed not to have any cuts or open wounds on display for the prisoners.

That would have been almost impossible since their uniforms covered every inch of their bodies except for hands and face. Even their shirts under their blue jackets were turtlenecks.

They were instructed to be armed at readiness for self-defense, since these prisoners of war were mass murderers, very strong and capable of terrible killing feats. The strengths of vampires, the briefings stated, allowed them to tear limbs from human bodies as if they were no more than plastic dolls.

The vampire prisoners, it was said, despite their apparent docility, were drinkers of human blood and the dangers of so-long unfed vampires could not be defined severely enough.

Firi had already signed document after document stating he could never talk about what he saw in the compound to anyone outside his security clearance ranking. The penalty for talking about "state secrets" was a swift sentencing of life in prison.

*

Firi had no one outside the military he would even want to talk to about his job. He was estranged from all his friends at school. He saw his parents only once a year. Even though he was stationed closer to home now, he lived in a small apartment on the compound. His co-workers became the group he socialized with. The compound housed a small bar, a theatre, and a cafeteria/restaurant. He could buy whatever he wanted online and have it delivered. He had little reason to leave the heavily fenced and guarded area, and now that he was closer than ever to Lace, he didn't want to leave.

He requested to be on Lace's specific guard detail and his request was granted.

The official file about Lace, a small part of which had been reported over two years previously in the world media, was that he had gone rogue and had massacred more than a dozen soldiers just inside the very compound where he was now imprisoned.

The reports he read in his briefings gave much the same story. *"Twelve men died at the hands of the vampire Lace,"* he read.

Further details were included. The date. The time of day.

The report stated, *"Twelve men from the infirmary, recovering from an outbreak of the flu, had been brought into a*

*courtyard area to partake of fresh air and relax in the summer
sunshine. Without warning, a vampire had breached the security
fences and attacked the men, dismembering and killing them all. The
nurses attending the sick men were also all killed. Assistance came
too late. Military Police came upon the massacre minutes after it
happened to find the attendants and the patients all dead and the
vampire on his knees, hands behind his back, head bent in the
submissive posture of surrender. No shots were fired. The vampire
was taken into custody to be questioned and studied before imminent
disposal."*

This also described only a partial truth. With his
security clearance, Firi had access to files involving vampires
who had been imprisoned before Lace was caught, and
detailing medical testing of their blood on live human guinea
pigs. He knew the sick men who died in the massacre that
fateful day were part of that vampire blood research.

What he didn't know was why Lace would do such a
thing as murder all those people. His mind wouldn't allow
him to believe it. The Lace he knew had been a peace-loving
being, gentle and kind. He had even stated that his empathic
response to others made war and violence almost unheard of
for his kind. Almost.

Was it possible, as the reports stated, that Lace had
gone rogue? Had he become insane somehow, and murdered
men for reasons no one would ever know?

It seemed improbable. There had to be much more to
this story, and Firi was determined to find out.

*

Chapter Ten

The first time Firi saw Lace in the prison cell he did not fear for Lace's life, since Lace could not actually die, but he did fear for his sanity. The thought came to him that he might be connected to a quite mad, and now violent, alien, telepathic being.

By the end of the first day of work, the more he saw and experienced of the secret military prison, the more he wondered if he had the strength to continue to the next hour, the next sunrise.

It began easily, despite his nerves, his apprehension at finally being reunited with the one being who'd occupied his thoughts non-stop for nearly eleven years.

After an initial orientation to learn his way around the large facility, he reported for duty and an eight-hour shift as he would with any other job. He was instructed to an office on the second floor where he met the colonel of the facility, Evan Kado.

The colonel was a boss unlike any Firi had worked for before in the military. While this project was top secret and important enough to require round-the-clock guards with security clearance, and the support of an entire base, the man greeted Firi with ease and demanded to be called "Evan." Everyone else was referred to by their rank and last name. That was the rule. But the colonel responded to nothing other than his first name.

Evan had a casual office, with plush chairs and a leather couch. A small table against one wall held assorted flasks and wine bottles, bottles of orange juice on ice in metal bins, plates of muffins and donuts, clean glasses and a bowl of fruit. Firi later learned Evan always offered his unique hospitality to anyone who entered the premises, even the cleaning crew. If you indicated you were hungry, he would have entire meals brought up. He talked of movies he had recently seen. He was knowledgeable of sports, computer games, ground-breaking scientific discoveries and current events.

The first thing he said to Firi, after making sure he was comfortable with a glass of juice and a pastry, was, "Know anything about rocket science?"

Firi wasn't sure what to say. Lace knew about stuff like that. Firi sometimes dreamed of the mathematics of the stars, and twice now he'd dreamed of a city on a moon called Bleak. Lace said he had been transformed by people from an alien race, people who came in ships from "out there."

Firi shook his head no.

"You're security, of course." Evan said. Without waiting for a response, he continued, "But you wouldn't be here if you weren't the brightest of your profession. The elite."

Firi said, "Top of my class in fire arms, hand to hand combat, surveillance, reconnaissance. And I can drive anything from a forklift to an 18-wheeler. But not a rocketship." He let his lips curve up in a slight smile.

"No. I suppose not that." Evan lifted a glass of orange juice to his mouth and drank. He was not sitting at his desk, but rather perched on the edge of it, the picture of a man at home despite the sterility of the place, and the guard kiosks and prison walls that surrounded it.

"I think we are on the verge of breaking through," Evan said, setting his glass aside. "Don't you?"

Frowning, Firi asked, "Breaking through to what?"

"Why, the stars. Or the very gods themselves."

So, he was going to be working for a crackpot or a genius; sometimes it was hard to tell the difference. He'd not expected this. And this wasn't the Air Force. It could either be a stroke of luck for him and Lace, or an unknown variable that could lead to potential problems no one, even the smartest guy, might predict.

"Well," Firi said, "We've got space stations, and remotes on Mars."

"I'm not talking about robot surveyors. I'm talking about people. We'll be sending people soon enough, you know. To other planets."

"Yeah. Some day."

Evan smiled and nodded. "Sooner than you think, maybe." He winked.

"Does this have something to do with my job?"

Evan tilted his head back and assessed him as if he could see more of Firi beyond the blue uniform, at the greater distance of one inch more. "Everything is connected."

Lace had said something similar to him once. "Yes, sir. I do believe in that, sir."

"Call me Evan. I don't answer to 'sir'."

"Yes, s... Evan."

Evan turned his head to the wall, exhaled a deep breath, and said, "Now. To your job. You know you will be guarding a very dangerous subject. It's nothing you can ever speak of outside these walls. And you may only talk to your co-workers about them within these walls, and only as it pertains to doing your job. Even though you all live within the grounds of this facility, you are not to discuss your job in off hours in your apartment, the store, the bar, the commissary or cafeteria. Do you understand?"

"Perfectly." He remembered not to add "sir."

"In his current state, the main subject you will be guarding is not an immediate threat. But in other circumstances, he is very dangerous. You should understand he is one of the last vampires in captivity. He is here for research purposes. Do not ever underestimate him."

"I won't."

"You are well-informed of the massacre that happened here over two years ago, of course. But the details you've learned up to now have been... let's say embellished. You do not need to know all of them. But you should know that this vampire, whom we call Lace, is responsible. It was reported in the media that the dead were officers of this facility. In a way, they were. But not officers. Corpsmen. Military prisoners who volunteered to be test subjects for certain experiments being conducted here in lieu of court-martial. Think of them as patients. You should know this so you will understand why this vampire is kept as he is, in his state, and in complete isolation."

Firi nodded. "Should I have a more accurate, detailed report? I'd like to be as informed as possible as to what really happened."

"You don't need to know any more than the fact that this prisoner, and the others we have here, are kept for research purposes. The nature of the main research is to find a cure for vampirism. You don't need to understand any more than that."

"A cure? But I thought vampirism couldn't be caught by... by us humans."

"We want to make sure it remains that way, of course. And so we study the creature who is our enemy, look for ways to reverse their own mutations."

"Mutations?"

"If we can make them normal, we can render them harmless should more invade from whatever hellish dimension they came through."

"So the cure, if you make one, will be your future weapon if more beings invade and more vampire/human wars occur." He stated it as a fact, not a question.

"I see you're a quick thinker, and this is why we need our best guards to have top security clearance. You will be witness to uncomfortable scenes. And we need to be kept informed of any changes in any prisoners, but most especially Lace, who has undergone more treatments than any other prisoner, and that will also be your job. To observe. To be the eyes and ears of any developments in behavior as you keep watch."

Firi kept himself very still, his breathing controlled and even. Inside he was raging. Angry. And afraid for Lace's well-being. Though Lace could never die, he could feel pain. He could suffer. "Understood," he replied softly.

The congenial Evan smiled, showed flashing white teeth in a demeanor that looked every part the hero of this war. A hero who was winning.

Firi's stomach contracted in revulsion.

But his resolve to do the job, his conviction to his plan to help Lace, gave him strength to keep his act together.

When he left his shoulders were taught, his mouth grim. He realized his hands had formed into fists. He consciously relaxed his fingers, walking briskly to the guard's office to report for duty.

*

The guard's office had tan walls and a kind of sick yellow light that made everything dour, serious. The floors in the prison wing were all tile. You could hear the footsteps of anyone approaching from yards away. A faint, tangy scent, like burnt dust, edged the air. And bleach.

That was where Firi met Chaz. Chaz was several years older than Firi but had only been working there for a year, was to show him the ropes.

Chaz was bright and blond, husky, short but strong. He wasn't smart but he wasn't as glib or rude as other men Firi had trained and worked with. He looked like he'd be tough in a fight, but he was soft-spoken, even overly friendly as if he hungered for outside stimulation.

Firi shivered. The place seemed filled with echoes. Already he knew a person could brim with loneliness just from being in this atmosphere day after day. Other guards in the room watched them with shuttered interest, though their body language, stiff and closed in, communicated a shut down of emotion, as Chaz began explaining the routines.

The job seemed easy. The stress seemed high.

"It's a lot of standing," Chaz explained. "You get used to it."

"I did that a lot in my other jobs," Firi replied.

"The halls are mostly empty, not much going on except in the mornings when Evan comes to do his interrogations, and experiments. It gets boring. But you're not allowed to do anything. You can't have cells or tablets. You can't be distracted. If you're caught, you're put on cleaning duty. Or fired."

"I read the job description. And all the regulations."

Chaz gave him a half-smile. "Most guys are lazy even if they are the so-called elite in this job. They think they can get away with stuff. But there're cameras everywhere."

"I see that." Firi looked up at the ceilings of the guard offices, and out the glass windows to the hall beyond. Black half-globes lined the walls on both sides, one every three or four feet.

"And just so you know, sound is wired into the cameras. Remember, anything you say is being overheard and recorded. If you ever get some days of computer duty, you'll see that human eyes are watching at the various junctures at all times." He grimaced and shrugged. "Well, as much as humanly possibly. Sometimes guards fall asleep. And sometimes you have to glance away just to save your sanity."

"If not much is going on, the brain does get bored," Firi said.

"You won't be as bored in the mornings. Speaking of that, you do get frequent breaks. One ten minute break every two hours. At the four hour mark, you get an hour lunch to get your breath back, and fulfill your need for stimulation. There's a basketball court just outside the lunchroom. And a jogging trail. And a TV in the break room. You can have your tablets and phones in there, too. You can go downstairs to the gym if you like. But keep track of the time. Evan notices if guards make a habit of being late, even if it's only one minute."

"Got it."

"It's usually the buddy system for the area you're assigned to. I'll be with you today, and other days, too, probably. So you don't need to wait for relief to get your breaks. We take turns. Lunch will be different. Two replacements will come to relieve us. We'll take our lunches together. They do it that way so we stick together throughout the day, make a team. Evan believes camaraderie is developed if people take meals together." He fiddled in his pocket for the keys to the door to the hallway. "He wants no one to feel left behind or alone. 'The lone wolf is the most dangerous wolf', he likes to say. Safety is in the pack. He wants trusts to form."

Firi laughed impulsively. "Ah, he doesn't trust us completely; he wants us to be good spies for each other."

Chaz frowned. "No. I mean, no, I never really thought of it like that."

Firi backed up. "Yeah, I was just kidding. It's about having each other's back."

"Yeah. That's it exactly." But Chaz's eyebrows remained narrowed as he opened the hall door. "You'll be getting your own set of keys by tomorrow. You'll stick with me all day today anyway."

"What about our breaks?"

"I have an extra key to the hall door and lunchroom. Ready?"

"Let's go."

As they walked down the hallway, Chaz's voice remained low, almost a whisper. "Our assignment is Lace. He's the main prisoner, and the most dangerous, though I've never seen him lift a hand toward anyone in aggression of any kind. Still… orders are orders. He's considered a threat."

"I understand."

"He's always quiet except during interrogation or when he's with the doctor."

"The doctor?"

"You'll see. I've grown fond of having this duty. Lace is easy to handle… so far. And he's a mystery. He's polite. Well-mannered. Just don't offer him clothes other than the threadbare ones he's wearing. That upsets him. He throws them back at us. But he doesn't require food or water. Nothing. If I didn't know he was an evil, dangerous vampire, I'd think he was an angel." He laughed softly. "He's stunning when you first see him. Overwhelmingly handsome, I guess you could say. This job…" He sighed. "It's easy as pie, this job."

"But Evan said never to underestimate him," Firi said, pretending to be surprised at Chaz's observations.

"Exactly. And that's why we're here. And of course because of what happened two years ago. I wasn't here, then. I never saw it, never saw the massacre. But if it happened once, it could happen again. We are what will prevent any potential future evil outbursts from ending in a body count."

Firi did not like Chaz's repeated use of the word "evil." But he knew Chaz could only understand the situation in the way he'd been taught.

The prison seemed pristine. It wasn't the usual kind, with open bars. This was a closed prison, more like a hospital, where all the cells had one door. Each door they passed walking down the hall had a small window in it, more a slit, actually, too small to even pass a hand through. But that slit had thick-paned glass in it. A guard could peer in at a prisoner without even having to breathe the same air they did. Every cell was very private. Firi heard no sound coming from any of them. The windows were too high for him to see inside without walking up to the door. He noticed no eyes peeking out at them.

The silences from behind each door lent an otherworldly chill to the empty passageway.

Chaz stopped, finally, at one of the doors midway down the corridor, taking his keys in his hand.

"Be alert," he said, "whenever a door is being unlocked. In this case the prisoner is chained, but the routine must be followed."

Firi stood on the left side of the door, hand on his firearm.

When the door opened a scent drifted out, a brief burning on the air as if someone close by was baking something sweet, cookies or a cake.

Firi knew that scent. It was an essence of the other realm, Lace's world of lavender stars and purple-green skies, of lagoons like blue topaz surrounded by old-man troll-trees and emerald ivy. A world that rolled beneath three moons.

Chaz said, "Clear."

Firi came to stand in the doorway. Though he kept himself still, his face neutral, all the air in his lungs stopped flowing. His body froze. For a moment he also thought he'd gone deaf. An eerie whirring—his pulse?—filled his head. A fluttering like wings scattered over him and inside his chest and belly. His skin heated, then went cold.

Lace lay on a narrow prison bed. The bed was covered with a blue blanket. Lace lay on his side dressed in threadbare black trousers and a billowy but ancient-looking white shirt. His hair feathered across a thin, white pillow, reflecting all the shades of dead leaves in late fall, restless browns mixed with strands of lost black, the depths of it glossy even under the harsh fluorescents. Lace had not been free for two years, yet he showed no ill-effects. His skin looked rich with health, his face golden.

Chaz frowned as he looked him over, but he was also smiling. "Have you ever seen a vampire before?"

Firi tried to take a breath and couldn't. He slowly shook his head, the lie easy enough even if he still didn't have his voice.

"Your first time… the beauty can shock you. Don't let it fool you, though."

At that moment, Lace opened glowing eyes. The vampire's gaze came to focus on Firi.

He stayed frozen on the threshold of the cell, not moving, not wanting to show recognition in any way. He hoped Lace would be as stoic.

His worry faded quickly when he saw no comprehension or acknowledgment in Lace's expression. Only winter on a face as closed and quiet as if it still slept, the same winter that now coursed through Firi's veins.

Horrified, he realized Lace did not know him.

"This is Lace," Chaz was saying.

Firi only pretended to listen as he stepped backward into the hall, severing the eye contact, breaking his own heart in the process. Yet his mind still felt the connection to Lace like a tremor, a living conduit of sparkling energy as if fireflies buzzed him out the corner of his eye.

He swallowed dryly, and forced himself to take a slow breath.

"A little overwhelming at first," Chaz said, coming toward the door. "I know." He came out and locked it behind him.

For the next two hours, they stood in the hall at near-attention, and spoke only when necessary. Another rule: no chatter on the job. The only communication allowed was that which was required to do the job and convey information pertaining to the prisoner.

At the two hour mark, when it was still only 10 A.M., Chaz told Firi to take the first break.

Firi took the extra key and went back the way they'd come, down the echoing hall, his footsteps almost too loud, and in through the glassed-in security room. From there he entered the lunchroom and went straight to the rest rooms. He locked himself in a stall for the entire ten minutes.

Face in his hands, he failed to hold back two years worth of tears.

Chapter Eleven

Firi never got used to seeing Lace tortured with whatever drugs they were giving him to try to change his blood from bronze to red. Seeing him strapped down to the bed, watching as the various serums went into his body, and hearing his screams always threatened to blank his mind. He feared he'd pass out on duty and be immediately fired.

He thought about everything he had accomplished to get this far, to see Lace in a top security facility face to face. Yet it was not enough. Despite learning the routines, the prison layout, Firi still had formed no plan. He was helpless. Useless. And Lace himself was unable to assist, his strength sapped, his memory all but gone.

Firi made few friends, kept mostly to himself. Two other guards, Ivana and his orientation guide, Chaz, were his closest pals. He had lunch with both of them nearly every day, and drinks at night if he was supremely bored enough to go out drinking, a pastime he hated.

Bright, blond Chaz may have been short, but he was husky and strong. Firi had seen him lift 200 pounds easily over his shoulders. He wasn't overly smart, but he wasn't as glib or rude as some of the other people Firi worked with. Ivana was broader than Firi, who was muscular but had remained lean, and she was almost as tall. She had blue, almond-shaped eyes with very dark lashes that made her face look, despite her size, almost under-age. In fact, she was older than Firi, nearing 30, and had once, in a sparring practice, thrown him so hard to the floor he lost his breath. She always grinned when she hurt someone in sparring classes. She didn't care. She liked three things: Firi, Chaz, and dark beer. About the job guarding vampires, she was indifferent. She said she took the job for the elevation in her pay grade. She was saving so she could have her own business.

"What do you want to do, open a security firm?" Firi asked her.

"I want to run my own private prison."

"And you'll be the warden?"

"Of course."

She was strange but funny. Firi didn't really like her but she liked him and Chaz and she entertained them with crazy stories about being a bodyguard for various celebrities before she was arrested for beating the crap out of a fan and remanded to jail where a judge told her he wouldn't impose a two year jail sentence if she willingly joined the military to help win the vampire war.

She had strange plans for her private prison. "I'll have my own dungeon," she told them.

Chaz asked, "What are you going to do, torture your prisoners there?"

"Oh no," she replied. "It'll be for me and my most trusted friends. Strictly for sex stuff."

Chaz had gone purple with embarrassment. Firi merely smiled.

They were all friends of a sort, but each withdrawn in their own way, harboring secrets but none, Firi decided, so earth-shattering as his own.

They never shared secrets. Not really. Ivana's tales were braggings, and many of them quite obviously embellished. She did not reveal her true self in them. She was a fiction to herself, trying too hard to impress. Chaz was more shy. They were all introverts in their own way, but Chaz drew strength from concentration and practice, while Ivana was all bravado, and Firi fueled himself with anger and secret love. Sometimes Firi thought everyone could see it in him, that he broadcasted tension and anxiety everywhere he went. But no one ever said anything, or seemed to notice. His secret remained safe.

The three formed a loose clique. Sometimes they shared meals in the evenings. Sometimes they got drunk. They sought each other out in the gym for exercise and practice sessions, and on the gun range. But after a few months, Firi still could not say they were close.

Officially, all the guards at the facility worked for Place Holding Tank 101. That was the unobtrusive title on the compound's address and on their paycheck deposits. It was a name to throw outsiders off its true importance.

Firi and his guard-mates called it the Winter Prison because the snow never completely melted even in the summer.

But it was a lot more than a prison. While the prison took up the entire basement floor, the research department inhabited the entire top floor two stories above the basement. None of the guards Firi knew ever went to that floor to the locked labs. He saw technicians in white coats come and go, and that floor had its own small guard unit with its own separate lunch room and locker room.

Every guard who worked in the facility in any capacity had signed detailed contracts, contracts which had required dozens of pages of signatures, and an entire afternoon to complete. So many clauses about secrecy and the strictness of it, along with pages of threats of imprisonment should anything from within the complex ever be revealed to the outside world. To be chosen to work in the Winter Prison, they were the elite.

Because of that, Firi, Ivana and Chaz rarely discussed work except in the vaguest sense when they were off-duty. If any part of the job bothered them, they were not free to say so to each other. And really, they had no reason to complain. Their pay and benefits were excellent. And vampires being tortured? Not a concern since they were, of course, the enemy.

No one ever suspected Firi, with his Halfling blood, had a link to the supposedly most dangerous vampire of all time.

Every night he dreamed of three moons.
Every day he oversaw Lace.
He was exactly where he wanted to be.
But he had no plan.

*

Something jarred Firi, winged and golden-eyed. He was sliding down a cloud. He was dreaming.

A voice said, "They must be killed. They must all be killed."

Firi woke, turning in the sweat-soaked sheets.

The wind outside his small apartment on the prison grounds rattled the bedroom window, moaned like a ghost.

He could smell the fresh snowfall on the air even through his closed shutters. Crisp. Sharp. Decembered.

For several minutes he had no desire to move, or to go to work.

It had taken him two years to find Lace. Now it seemed there was nothing he could do about it. He had no plan and he couldn't even talk to Lace.

What was the point in getting up?

But today was a work day. He needed to go to work. He wanted to go to work. Being close to Lace, even if there was nothing he could do, was the most important thing in his life. On his days off he always pondered and worried, making himself miserable. Seeing Lace hurt and confined was better than never seeing him at all.

He got up, showered and dressed as if in a dream.

He always left his apartment earlier than he needed to, liking to take his time walking. Liking the time alone. He never walked to work with co-workers.

Today the air met him with a chill that made his face ache. He wrapped his scarf tighter, pulled up his hood, and headed into the sparkling ice world of the compound.

Firi watched a raven flop about in the snow. His boots crunched the half-shoveled path. The prison loomed brown in the distance, rising from the glistening whiteness, square windows high up on each level, three rows for three floors and a bottom row for the basement sector. It was huge and silent, a gloomy giant pushing its shadow into him. It could have housed 100 or more, but so far he'd only seen one prisoner in chains. Lace.

The raven gave a pirate-y "arg" and took off with something in its beak, a piece of trash maybe, or a dead twig tunneled from beneath the crystallized ice. It flew up and away, beyond the distant fence line where the razor-wire glittered in the fierce cold sun.

Of the raven's casual freedom, he thought: If only it were that easy.

Firi took the back path, out of the way of the jogging path, away from the other humans. The trail led around the back of the building. Everyone else walked the short avenues that led from the apartments to the facility's front steps and double-locked, camera-eyed doors.

Firi preferred a quiet walk, the silence a welcome, but never a solace.

He felt trapped.

Lace might have been imprisoned, but Firi had frozen himself in place in a job that left him waiting for some magic moment to a call for action that might never come, and left Lace still helpless, suffering, trying to sleep away his pain.

His head felt hot. His face. He had an urge to burrow in the snow and never come up.

Spring in Lace's other-dimensional fairy-world was light-years away. Hazy in Firi's memory now.

He wanted to feel that world's waters curving about his young body, and breathe the silken, sugar-spun air. He wanted to feel Lace's touch again, more than ever, the unburdening of his pent up youthfulness as Lace's lips opened against his own.

He was starting to think it would never happen again. It had only been two months since he'd come here, but it felt like forever. It had been over two years since he'd seen Lace before getting this job.

The careening, wailing wind in his head never stopped. The winter of this place reflected his insides perfectly.

Firi moved slowly, crushing snow crystals underfoot. He heard the raven's privateer voice again off in the distance. Heard wings. But could see nothing but mounds of frosted white and the tall tops of evergreens. The fence sparkled nearer as he wove a circle further from the crouched and waiting building. It was still too early to go in for work.

Something in the forest moved. He stopped.

He pushed back his hood. Cold tufts of wind stole under his blue scarf. Standing still, he listened, straining his senses.

Not a sound but for a ruffle of twitching wind in pine needles.

Who was there? What?

What he saw looked black-caped, or maybe it was just the raven again moving in rhyme with tree shadows to make itself look bigger.

He thought of the cloaked being of Bleak from his dreams. Its sibling moon was named Raven. How could these not be signs? The world contained supernatural elements now. He'd held one in his arms.

He looked up at the white sky and whispered, "How can I help Lace?" His mind strained, putting out a mental call to any supernatural being that might be listening.

For a moment he thought the edges of his vision had turned gold. A castle stormed through mist out the corner of his eye, as if it were alive and growing, building itself tall until it touched the stars. Something passed by the silver coin of sun, and a shadow encased Firi, then soared off.

"Who's there?"

He turned full circle, scanning the pathway and the snow banks. His apartment complex was lost behind a strand of trees. Nothing existed but the whiteness, the forest, the grim, brown prison-giant.

His cheeks tingled in the cold. Wind traced his ears, an invisible caress. The otherworld of Lace's vampire kindred felt so close. The closest he'd felt to it in two years.

For a brief instant, the new winter wind smelled of the dusk-green, minty waters of Lace's spring-warm lagoon. It smelled of fresh bed-linen and May sky. And Lace stood next to him as the water lapped their bodies where skin met skin, where cells embraced.

The image faded in a blink.

What if, he thought, the doors to fairyland, to vampireland… are everywhere?

As if in answer, a single snowflake touched his cheek and melted to a tear.

*

Seeing Lace listless, unremembering, his powers disenchanted was hard enough. Listening to him scream unbearable.

Firi watched as red liquid dripped through tubes into the golden veins of the vampire, wrecking his very nature. It was as if the medics and researchers were filling him up with acid. Lace's lean body convulsed. He told them "No." He yelled. He sobbed. Sometimes—those were the better times—he passed out.

Today, once again, Firi stood guard at the doorway to the infirmary where the experiments on Lace were conducted.

The freshly polished tile floor shone beneath his boots. The polish had a faint soap-sweet scent and he tried to focus on that. He breathed shallowly but still the antiseptic scent of the infirmary overpowered the clean smell in the hall and stung his nose and throat.

He kept telling himself silently, *Let it be over, let it be over.* It was a litany to help him control.

Still, Lace's agony stunned his mind until he saw white flashes in his peripheral vision.

He faced away from the room, standing stiff and alert. He had already seen enough of this. Today he'd been one of the guards to help strap Lace down to the bed, the spongy cuffs tight about his wrists and ankles. He had already seen Lace's body twitch and jerk too many times now, the soft, threadbare clothes he refused to remove stretching, straining, ready to tear as Lace's body convulsed. The black pants, once shiny and silken, were like thin paper now, faded to gray. His white shirt, gathered full at the arms and held together by thin black cord at the neck and mid-chest looked ready to disintegrate against his tawny skin. His bright hair, glossy and long, tangled over his face as he tossed his head in misery.

Firi's hands itched, made fists with the longing to rush to his side, stroke back the over-long bangs and draw his knuckles over his cheek and jaw. He wanted to calm him, help him, tell him that it would all be over soon, that he was here now and had come to take him away.

He could not help him. Yes, he was here. He'd made a career of getting to Lace. But he was as helpless standing before him as he was when he was far away locked in his old room in his parents' house.

The screams of the vampire filled his mind until he thought it would burst.

He thought of the raven on his morning walk, swooping up on black wings, taking its treasure—a twig or pine needle—to freedom. In his mind he pictured the trees where it had vanished, and he saw again before him the sun-struck snow. And then it was as if he were standing in the sharp winter breeze. He saw nothing for a moment but the pure whiteness, the clean relief of it as a landscape for his thoughts.

His mind cooled. The tremor of his heart surrendered.

At the same time, Lace went quiet. The screaming stopped.

The prisoner had passed out.

*

Firi and Chaz supported the near unconscious vampire between them as they dragged him back to his cell. Lace's bodyweight draped warm and heavy against his shoulder and side. His arm wrapped about Lace's back below Chaz's grip, taking more of the burden in his strong arms.

Lace smelled of summer wind and human blood, both beautiful and brackish. Resplendence and nightmare mixed. Lace's body shivered, but not from cold. It was like touching a live wire, the air almost sparking.

Lace was still in pain.

Firi wanted to drop to the floor right then, draw him close. He resented Chaz's presence. He was disgusted that cameras followed their every move.

He kept his eyes focused ahead, his features neutral. If anyone saw him through the camera lenses, or if they walked up to him right at this moment, they would not see his fury, his overwhelming outrage.

Inside Lace's cell, Firi took the weight of the vampire against him and settled him into his bunk as Chaz stood back and said, "Good job. You're strong. You never ever drop him."

Firi looked up through narrowed eyes. For weeks he'd worked with Chaz. This was the first time he'd ever said anything like this to him. "You've dropped him?"

Shrugging, he replied, "Not intentionally." His voice lowered as he glanced over his shoulder, knowing the surveillance system could pick up every word. "Some of us aren't so gentle. Gordi shoves him into his cell without even bothering to enter and put him in his bed. I don't like seeing him on the floor. I don't like doing the job half-assed."

102

"Vampires are evil." Firi tried to keep the hiss out of his voice. "Why should you care?"

"Senseless cruelty creates drama. He's never lifted a hand against us. The least I can do is do my job right by him."

Firi nodded. He watched as the man, the monster, the vampire who had been so kind to him twice in his life shifted in the bed, curling his hands toward his chest, eyelids tightly closed. His breathing came in puffs. His body shivered.

There was nothing else Firi could do.

"Come on," Chaz instructed impatiently. "We're not allowed to linger and you know it."

Eyes hot, throat dry, Firi turned away from Lace and followed Chaz into the corridor. Chaz locked the door.

Rusty winterlight drifted in the dust-motes of the hall. It was all Firi could see for a moment, air the color of loss slowly swirling in cold flares.

"So?" Chaz said. "Don't think I don't notice how you take your time with him. How you study him."

After a few seconds, he said, "Shouldn't I assess the prisoner? I'm better off knowing what I'm dealing with."

"Yeah. But never let your guard down. You always take a little too long to get him settled. This one is unpredictable. Remember, he massacred a dozen men."

"He has the strength of a kitten. And his feet and hands are chained."

"But he's not like us."

Firi caught Chaz's gaze and held it before saying, "Nope. He isn't."

"Well, I'm just telling you what I see. I've been here longer than you. Don't let his weakness make you forget how dangerous he is."

Firi tried not to roll his eyes.

Chaz tilted his head thoughtfully, then said in an almost whisper, "At first I felt sorry for him, too. But the pain is necessary. What they're doing with him is necessary. For our future. For the future of all humans."

Chapter Twelve

Firi managed to figure out the routine well enough so that some days he was able to check on Lace without anyone really noticing.

He saw the way clear one day when he had gone on a break and run into Ivana outside. The day was silver and the smoke from her cigarette curled up and blended with the air. She'd glanced at him casually and said, "I'm not supposed to be here. You won't tell, will you?"

"Of course not," he'd quickly replied "You're my friend."

Over the course of several days, he noted her extra breaks and started sending his partners on their breaks during those times.

So twice a day, when Ivana took her unscheduled and unauthorized smoke breaks, he could look in on Lace and nobody said a word.

He began to talk to him a little bit every day.

At first, it didn't seem to help. The hints he gave Lace, what little he knew about who Lace was, and his situation, were forgotten after the medical treatments. The side affects of those treatments were, Firi decided, what had induced the amnesia in the first place. The treatments were daily. Everything Firi did to try to help Lace recover was, the next day, destroyed.

Evan would come and interview him, Lace would fail every interview, and new treatments would begin.

The only light Firi saw in the entire proceeding was that Lace's personality, when he did speak, retained a strength, a curiosity and a determination to try to do whatever was being asked of him. In those moments, Firi recognized the vampire he'd met when he was ten, and the wise, self-determined man and lover he'd met again at eighteen.

His entire body longed to rush to action. He wanted to take Lace and escape. Sometimes he dreamed of killing everyone on the base, taking them all on and winning, then running with Lace into the snowy forest where they'd cross the portal together to his slowly shrinking dimension.

At night, dreaming of his idea for rescuing Lace, he'd wake damp and shaking, knowing that was no kind of plan, that he was no murderer anymore than Lace was, massacre or not.

He had to be patient.

Once again he stood in the cold, tiled corridor, watching Chaz leave for a ten minute break. He unlocked Lace's cell door and entered. Scents of autumn smoke, cider and honey assailed him. The fragrances of Lace's beautiful world infused his skin, his hair.

The cameras recorded everything, but if Ivana did not report anything out of the ordinary, no one would look at the footage.

He went to the bunk where Lace lay sleeping. He touched him lightly on the shoulder and the vampire's flashing green-gold eyes opened.

"My name is Firi. Do you remember me?"

"I see you every day," Lace said quietly. "I remember your name when you tell me."

"I'm here to help you. I want you to try to remember that. Keep it in your mind no matter what the day brings. Please try."

"Who am I? What have I done?"

"Your name is Lace." He reached out and brushed just the tips of his fingers lightly across Lace's temple, brushing back a stripe of dark copper hair, mixing it with the darker layers underneath. "We've met before. I know you don't remember, but please keep trying."

"Firi." Lace's eyes watched as Firi took his hand away. "It sounds familiar but..."

"Shh. Everything here is recorded. Everything. I have to go now. I'll be back later. And tomorrow."

He hated turning his back on him, hated the empty, desperate look in such a normally powerful being. Lace's gaze brimmed with questions. He heard him stir in the bunk. He quickly stepped into the hall and shut the door before he could look back, before his heart could break any harder. His heart hummed; his pulse burned in his veins. He breathed through his nose, forcing himself to calm. Forcing himself not to think about the daily treatments, the tortures, and the screams.

Day in and day out he did his job.

And watched.

The turning point came on the day that Lace announced for the first time that he was hungry.

Firi watched as he ate real food for the first time since he'd been made into a supernatural being over a thousand years ago. Listened as Lace talked calmly and politely to Evan in the deserted prison cafeteria. Assisted when Lace asked for newer clothes, and more blankets to ward off the winter chill he had never felt.

Lace was becoming human.

This was the agenda of the treatments. Making Lace mortal. But why? To Firi it would've made more sense if the research being conducted was about immortality and prolonging human life, putting the magic of agelessness into the blood, not taking it out.

The idea of it, Lace as a human, went against every instinct Firi had for protecting his friend. The memory of them sharing their blood with each other kept replaying in Firi's mind.

*

Firi watched the play of green-tinged morning light on the thin gray carpet of his bedroom floor. The curtains were open half-way. Silver rectangles dappled the room.

He sat on the edge of his bed, shirt off, right arm stretched out in front of him. He held a razor blade to the edge of his skin just below the inside of his elbow. He held his breath and cut deep. Blood welled in garnet beads. It wasn't enough. He pressed deeper until it trickled in several rivulets on either side of his arm. He took a damp cloth from beside him and cleaned the wound, then pressed a bandage firmly in place.

The cut stung.

The pinching pain reminded him of when he was ten, and then eighteen. He bent his arm and a sense of conviction tightened his stance. He put on his white undershirt, then the blue, button-up uniform shirt.

He stood. The bandage against his skin felt slightly damp. That was what he wanted.

*

The morning after Lace announced he was hungry, when Firi and Chaz went into Lace's cell to escort him into the hall, there was no moment for Firi to be alone with him. Together they walked Lace to the interview room, chained him to the chair, and went to stand at their posts by the door.

Firi refused to look directly at Lace. If their eyes met he feared he would show emotion. Any emotion would be too much emotion. He did not want to alert anyone that he and Lace had any connection.

Still, out the corner of his eye he saw Lace glance his way a couple of times. He could not discern the look on his face. He didn't dare acknowledge him in front of Chaz and all the room's cameras.

The corner of his right palm rested gently against his weapon. He stood tall, chin up.

Today when Evan entered the room he was not alone. Close at his back came a tall man of indeterminate age, with straight black hair cut in a "V" in back, long over the ears, not a usual military cut at all. His face was light brown with high cheekbones and soft indentations at the corners of his mouth. His dark eyes glittered as he took in the room, ignoring the guards, then focusing on Lace. He wore a white uniform with many colorful pins denoting a Colonel's rank. Firi did not recognize the other ornaments, and could not place the unit or base he might've been visiting from.

Lace and the visitor held gazes for a long moment, then the dark-haired man smiled and said, "You don't remember me, do you." He did not phrase it as a question.

Lace's eyebrows narrowed in a tiny frown. "Should I?"

Firi liked that Lace had not lost his strong personality despite having no memory.

Evan intervened. "Lace, this is Colonel Varae. He's visiting from Virginia."

Instead of politely acknowledging the greeting, Lace said, "Why?"

"Well," Evan said, "we've had a breakthrough with your condition. Your need to eat, bathe, eliminate."

"So something was wrong with me before that and now it's fixed," Lace commented.

"Somewhat."

"I don't seem to have any memory beyond these walls, or this day. Will that be fixed?" Lace asked.

Evan smiled. Colonel Varae did not.

Evan said, "One thing at a time."

Both men took chairs at the table before Lace. The interrogation began.

Firi listened, as he always did, but today the cut at his elbow reminded him of his own personal agenda. A hot energy coiled inside him that he hadn't felt in weeks.

108

Lace said, "I don't know why I'm here. This is obviously a prison of some sort. Have I done something terrible?"

This was how it always started. In this room, Lace always questioned Evan about why he was locked up. And Evan always asked Lace to try to write down something he might remember.

Today, Lace answered many questions with questions of his own. He was given paper and crayons. He did not pick them up but shook his head, staring only at Evan as he said, "I don't remember anything to write. Not even my name."

Firi observed that neither of the humans seemed annoyed by Lace's memory loss. Or surprised. Colonel Varae's body language was almost smug, and he exchanged many glances with Evan that seemed to communicate a hidden knowledge between them. Or possibly distrust.

Despite being more "human" on this day, Lace did not display any human symptoms such as sweating, restlessness, or impatience. If he felt emotion, he didn't show it.

From the moment he'd come to work at this compound, Firi had wondered if Lace's amnesia was a desired effect of his treatments, or an unexpected detail. He was not allowed to ask.

When they finished, both men stood. Firi saw the Colonel turn and look at Lace. Lace met his eyes and Firi saw Lace's first reaction of the day. The muscles around his eyes hardened. This was not a natural glance of curiosity but something more. Recognition? If so, that meant Lace was lying about his memory today.

Who was this visitor?

Colonel Varae inhaled, a shallow, soft sniff, and turned toward the door.

The bandage on Firi's arm began to itch.

Firi and Chaz unlocked Lace's chains from the chair and escorted him into the corridor where he overheard Varae say, "I want to observe today's treatment."

"Of course," Evan replied.

Lace's body tensed, a response so subtle Firi doubted anyone without a blood-bond to the vampire would have been able to observe it.

He knew the torture that awaited Lace, but could say nothing to reassure him. He tried to project only calming energy as he walked beside him. His instinct to protect Lace was, yet again, quelled.

As Lace was strapped to the hospital bed once again, Firi had to focus not to close his eyes and turn away. He stood in place at the doorway and stared straight ahead as the yells turned to screams.

He didn't think he breathed once during the entire procedure.

Colonel Varae watched passively, but toward the end he turned to Evan and asked, "Can I touch him?"

"Why?"

"I want to see if he reacts to my presence."

Evan nodded.

Shocked at this new tactic, Firi couldn't help but shift his gaze to the bed. Lace's head was bent back, his long, multi-shaded hair hanging over the head of the mattress and frame. The scent of the room was antiseptic, sharp, so unlike the pumpkin, powdered sugar aroma of Lace's cell.

Varae approached Lace and stared down at him. Lace seemed oblivious. But when the Colonel put his hand in the center of the vampire's chest, Lace's breath caught. The screaming stopped for a moment. Lace's eyes opened and he recoiled at what he saw. His body, tightly tied, tried to move away but he was helpless. Tears streamed down his temples and into his sideburns. His pink lips parted. His mouth opened. He yelled something that sounded like another language.

Firi realized his hands had become fists.

"There," Varae said, nodding to Lace. "It's just going to get better from here on out, isn't it?"

Lace's eyes rolled back. He sobbed once, shaking his head back and forth as if to say 'No'. Then his eyelids shut and his entire body went still.

"He's passed out," the doctor stated.

Though the poison continued to pulse into Lace's veins through the I.V., the sharp fragrance subsided. The air turned crisp as an autumn day. Firi smelled leaf and loam and roses as Lace finally rested.

He swallowed in instant relief.

Varae turned at that very moment and stared at him. Firi's heart slammed his chest in surprise.

Varae's eyes flicked away and he said, "Who is that tall guard with the dark hair?"

Evan said, "One of the newer ones. Excellent reviews. There've been no problems with him whatsoever."

The Colonel crossed his arms over his chest and said, "I want to talk to him. Bring him to your office this afternoon."

"Of course."

On their way back to Lace's cell, Firi took all of Lace's weight on his shoulder. The vampire could barely walk but the doctor wanted him mobile to see how quickly Lace overcame the effects, which was why they so often did not use a gurney.

Firi said to Chaz, "I got him," as he led Lace to his bed. Chaz stood by the door, arms crossed.

Firi laid Lace gently onto the mattress and pulled the pillow under his head. He pulled a dark blue blanket up and over his body and quickly brushed Lace's hair back from his forehead, soft as he remembered.

"Why are you so kind to me?" Lace asked in a shaky voice.

Keeping his voice soft, Firi replied, "Just doing my job."

"I know you, don't I?" Lace asked tiredly.

"Shhh..."

"And that other man..."

"Shhh. Don't speak. Just rest." Firi felt the tape of his bandage pull at the delicate cuts on his arm. Right now Chaz was hovering. He could sense the other guard's impatience. They needed to leave the cell, lock the door and take up their proper locations.

Lace said, "Please don't leave."

Firi straightened. "I'm sorry."

He closed the door to the cell, locked it and joined Chaz in the corridor.

Chaz was frowning at him when he turned away from the door.

"What?" Firi asked.

"So why are you so nice to him? It's not really your job."

Firi frowned. "I'm not. I just don't see the point in hurting him further. You yourself said the same thing the first day I was here. He hasn't done anything to hurt us."

"Only killed a dozen men."

Firi did not reply.

"Why do you think Colonel Varae wants to talk to you?" Chaz asked.

Firi shrugged.

"I've been on the case the longest. Why doesn't he want to talk to me?"

"I don't know."

Chaz scowled and looked away. They did not speak for an hour until it was time for their breaks.

*

Firi told himself he wasn't nervous as he waited outside Evan's office where Colonel Varae was to meet him. He ignored the couch against the wall by the door even though its brown faux leather looked smooth, the cushions plump and soft. He stood stiff and tall, hands clasped behind

112

his back, breath coming in slow puffs. The air smelled slightly of stale coffee and floor cleaner.

In his mind he saw Lace screaming and then Colonel Varae touch him, palm down, in the center of the chest. For a second Lace had seemed to struggle against not only the poison in his veins, but the stranger's touch as well. Then he had passed out.

Firi blinked, as if that action could take away the image. But the vision of Lace strapped down and suffering never left him. He moved forward every day with no plan, and a waning hope that he could do anything to help Lace.

The cuts on his arm stung afresh.

The door to the office opened.

Firi saw white snowscapes through the window behind Evan's desk. For a moment the walls of the room melted away and he was in the middle of an icy field that sloped toward a dark, emerald forest. The sky curved white striped with lavender bands. He smelled sweet cider and autumn glow.

Evan said, "Firi, please come in."

The walls resurrected themselves. Two men stood beyond the doorway. Firi blinked, pushing his bangs from his eyes. Over the weeks, his hair had grown faster than he realized. He kept forgetting to make an appointment with the barber.

He entered the room, breath held.

Evan sat on the front edge of his own desk. Colonel Varae stood to his right at the end of the desk. Two half-finished cups of coffee sat on Evan's desk. Against the wall was the familiar buffet of snacks, water, coffee and alcohol.

None was offered to Firi.

"You may sit if you like," Evan said, motioning with one hand toward a chair.

Firi eyed it, realizing that the two men would literally tower over him if he took a seat. "Thank you. I'm comfortable standing."

Colonel Varae's eyebrows narrowed slightly.

"That's fine." Evan smiled. "Normally the procedure is to ask you for a written report of all your observations on Lace. But the Colonel here wished to speak to you personally about him."

"I'll do my best to answer any questions, sirs," Firi replied, keeping his eyes on Evan. For some reason, Varae made the small hairs rise on Firi's arms and legs. He had to force himself to look in the Colonel's direction.

Varae started right in. "I'd like to know if you observed anything different in Lace before the changes that occurred yesterday."

"No, sir."

"So before he stated he was hungry and cold, nothing had changed?"

"Not that I noticed, sir."

"Does he ever speak to you?"

"He asks questions. Sometimes."

"Such as?"

"Several times he has asked if he is a criminal, if he has done something bad."

"What else?"

"Sometimes he asks how long he's been here."

"Do you answer?"

"We're not allowed to give him any information."

"So you say nothing."

Firi inhaled slowly, keeping his eyes on Varae's face but not looking directly into the dark gaze. "I tell him we are not allowed to answer his questions, sir."

"Does he ever indicate that he remembers the past, his own past, when you are with him?"

"No, sir."

"Not even his name?"

"I… I don't know, sir. Maybe."

Varae shifted his stance. "Since the change, now that he feels hunger and cold and a desire to bathe and produce other bodily functions, does he show any sign of improved memory?"

"Not that I have seen, sir."

Varae asked him a few more questions. Firi could tell he was not giving the answers the other man was seeking. He didn't care. He wasn't about to give these men anything about Lace that he didn't need to.

But now the Colonel switched to a different tactic. He began to ask Firi about himself and the job. How did he like working here? Was he ever shocked at the things he saw? Did he understand the sensitive nature of this establishment and the important research being conducted?

Firi wasn't sure how to answer. He remembered that being honest was actually his best defense. Remembering lies once told in the past, keeping track of them, was too difficult.

He couldn't help but think he was being interviewed. But for what? Or could this be a review, a test of some sort to see how he was working out? But no, his instincts told him this was about Lace. All about Lace. And Colonel Varae knew a lot more than he was saying.

And so he told the Colonel he was shocked at first, but he liked the job. He understood that research for defense purposes was top secret and that he was never to discuss it with anyone.

Firi decided to ask a question of his own. "Colonel, sir, if I may ask. Is the prisoner more or less of a threat now since the change has happened to him?" His heart fluttered. He wondered where such bold directness came from.

The Colonel looked startled at the question. He answered anyway. "Less of a threat, I should think. He's becoming human."

Firi didn't dare breathe for fear of giving away any emotion. This was definitely not a good thing, but they seemed to think it was. His fingers wanted to curl into fists but he held his hands loose and still by his sides. He wanted to yell, to shout. He wanted to ask, *To what purpose?* He kept silent.

But why would they want to make an immortal mortal? Surely learning about immortality would be the great experiment.

And then he realized it. They were learning about that as well. Everything here was designed for learning about Lace, what he was made of, how he ticked.

In the medical ward's brightness, Varae had been dark-edged, slick, an interloper with an almost craggy countenance. Here, in the softer light of Evan's office, he looked ten years younger. His hair, blacker than Firi's own wavy locks, was so straight the ends drifted, wispy in the dry air.

Something about this guy... He didn't seem old enough to be a Colonel. And yet his demeanor was huge, crackling, clearly the oldest and wisest essence in the room.

Finally they locked eyes, and Firi felt the verging of other times in that look, a sense of impressed age upon the air as if another scene enfolded the one they currently stood within, dust, ruin, black trees with no leaves. He heard it, felt it, tasted the ash in the air. Someone ran through the dead forest weeping, the stars burning to dust around him.

"You understand," Varae was saying, as if from far away, "even though Lace is becoming human this does not dispel his threat."

Firi pressed his lips together, nodded, then said tightly, "Yes, sir."

What was he sensing? It couldn't be. But he had to ask himself, silent, wavering, recoiling in a kind of disgusted wonder, was this man, this Colonel a Halfling like himself?

He looked to Evan, who was nodding casually, seemingly oblivious, unconcerned. Did Evan know?

"You can go now," Evan said.

Firi turned. As he exited, it seemed ten degrees cooler outside the office. His skin crawled, shivered. He realized he had been holding his breath.

116

He needed a plan and he needed it now because instinct told him time was running out. Both for Lace and for him.

*

Chapter Thirteen

Firi's breath made ghosts on the breeze. He stood under the amber streetlight. The street gleamed like blackened silver, shining with haloes as the bus drove up.

He entered the warm air of the vehicle with a slight pause, his mind running over the list of things he'd accomplished on his day off and the first day in two months that he'd left the base.

The unmarked copper-gray car with rust spots on the fenders that he'd just bought for cash from a shifty guy in tattered clothes now sat back among snowdrifts amid soft pines several yards from the most deserted spot of the road. The location was a two mile walk from the compound.

A wad of cash, most of his money saved from two years of work, lay buried in plastic inside a locked tin box under a red rock twenty yards from the car.

In the trunk of the car he'd packed water, blankets, clothes and food. Snack foods in tins and sealed plastic wrap. Candy bars, nuts, jerky for himself and for Lace if Lace's change had made him human enough to need to eat.

If he could manage to get Lace out of the compound and make it to the car, at least they had the means to run.

He paid the bus fee and sat in the front seat. The bus was mostly empty. He took the ride to the center of town arriving at the exact time he'd planned.

Ivana and Chaz met him at a noisy restaurant for dinner, thinking he'd just come from a day spent visiting his parents.

Ivana embraced him, her long dark hair down about her shoulders for once, then Chaz, broad-shouldered and smiling underneath a parka and hood. Firi forced a smile before saying casually, "Brr. Only two seasons in this town.

Winter and July." He rubbed one hand up his right, jacketed arm, feeling the cuts under his shirtsleeve throb as he pressed down, some fresh, some older that itched as they healed.

Guards rarely left the facility. When they did, they usually opted for social activity: nightclubs, eating out, movies, shopping, even so-called massage parlors. Chaz and Ivana eagerly shared their day with Firi and he relaxed, letting them talk, hearing about every third word of their download.

When they were ready to go home for the night, Ivana drove. She was the only one of the three of them who had a car.

They drove by the area where Firi had hid his new, unlicensed car. He glanced out the window to make sure nothing revealed its location. He'd even made sure to use a pine branch to wipe his footprints and the car tracks from the snow. That part of the highway's shoulder looked as wild and untouched as the rest.

"You're quiet tonight, Firi," Chaz said from the front seat.

"Big day. Just tired."

"You're too young to be tired this early," Ivana observed.

The darkness of the forest swept by them, along with flashes through the trees of occasional cabin lights as they got further and further from town. Firi saw sunless evergreen, dark as loss upon endless black shadows stacked all the way to the sky. The hurdles he faced seemed as great. "Sometimes I think I'm too young for any of this."

"What do you mean?" Ivana asked.

"The job. The war."

"The war is over," Chaz said.

"So we've been told," Firi replied.

"As for the job," Ivana added, "you can take the two of us down to the mat in about five seconds. You're trained for this, but you're a natural, too. It's who you are."

Firi laughed but did not feel amused. "I'm twenty-one. Who knows who they are at twenty-one?"

His comment was met with silence.

Finally, Chaz said softly, "It's the vampire. I know we're not supposed to talk about the job outside of work, but people I know over the past couple years say being around their kind for long periods, or getting too close to them physically can do things. You know. To the mind."

"What kinds of things?" Firi asked. "I didn't read any of this in the reports." Evan had never mentioned the possibility that Lace could affect people this way. Lace himself had never told Firi he might be able to affect people who weren't known to him, who had not shared the autumn wine, who weren't Halflings.

"No one talks about it except when they're really, really drunk. But I've heard a few stories. It hasn't affected me but some guards have mentioned having weird dreams after touching the… the thing. They get, you know, jumpy."

"I've heard the same stories," Ivana said. "But I've never been in the same room with him so I don't know. But the others…"

"Others?" Firi sat up straight in the back seat, suddenly wide awake.

"I've been here longer than the both of you. There were more once," Ivana said. "Before even Chaz got here. Vampires as well as human prisoners."

"Why would there be human prisoners in a top secret military compound? Were they terrorists, or traitors?" Evan had told him there had been humans for the lab testing. But he wanted to know what Chaz and Ivana might have heard.

"Convicts. From the state pen. And the military prisons. The story's classified."

"Isn't everything?" Chaz quipped.

"I've never seen human prisoners here."

"That's because they're all dead." Ivana sighed loudly. "Fuck it, I shouldn't be saying this. But they're the ones Lace killed. All twelve of them. The other vampires? I don't know what happened to them. I never saw them taken away. I've heard they're still here. Still in their cells sleeping. Deep in their self-induced comas or something. No one talks much but you pick up pieces of the story here and there. That's what I know."

Firi leaned over the front seat between Ivana and Chaz. "I thought Lace killed soldiers. Guards from the infirmary who were recovering from the flu. I thought the massacre was a battle."

Ivana's voice dropped low. "That's what the official report we all got said. But a lot of guards and nursing staff died that day. And they weren't sick. The humans killed them. It was afterward that Lace killed the humans from the labs. Of course that's not how the story got reported on the news. And that's not the story we were told coming to work that day. I didn't see it. It happened on my day off. I was called back to work an emergency shift."

"Why would the humans kill their own nurses and the guards? A riot? Were they trying to escape?"

"We were told the vampire did it. All of it. Vampires are the enemy after all, and highly dangerous. But I was friends with one guard who saw it go down on the monitors was ordered to doctor the camera footage. He said they blamed it all on Lace, but the convicts were the actual monsters. You know they were experimenting on them, right?"

"No," Firi and Chaz said in unison. But Firi did know. And now the story was unfolding much clearer in his mind.

"Yeah. Feeding them some concoction made from vampire blood or something. They changed, but not like the real vampires in the other cells. They stopped eating food, even stopped sleeping. I saw them sometimes, when they were taken out into the yard for air and sun. They seemed complacent, almost drugged. My friend said the massacre was sudden. They were all in the exercise yard sitting mostly,

121

quiet, peaceful, and without warning all of them turned on
their guards, ripping them to shreds in seconds, drinking from
their mangled bodies. Drinking their blood. It seemed to make
them crazier. Then Lace came."

"Came from where?" Firi asked.

"I don't know."

"Wasn't he locked up?"

"He wasn't a prisoner at that time. He just appeared in
the yard. He killed all the humans. They found him with all
the bodies, covered in blood. The cameras caught it all, but
only a few people saw that true footage before my friend
edited it and destroyed the truth. The media were shown only
the vampire surrounded by bodies with blood all over him."
Ivana paused. "Hey, you guys aren't gonna tell anyone any of
this, are you?"

Both Firi and Chaz shook their heads 'no'.

Firi said, "Thanks for telling us. I've always wondered
what happened that day. I hear Evan question Lace every day.
Lace can't remember. He always insinuates that Lace is evil,
that he did something so horrible it caused his amnesia. I
couldn't help but be curious."

"You guys, really, tell no one you know this. Just
knowing any of this… I feel like it could put us in danger. So
you gotta promise."

Chaz said, "We signed the same contract you did, Ive.
No talking to anyone outside of work."

"We're not even supposed to talk about the job with
each other," Firi mumbled. "But your secret's safe. We all
have the same clearances. We all know the dangers of talking
about the job to anyone. Your story is just that, a story."

"Good." Ivana turned the car down the side road that
led to the complex. "Can we all talk about something else
now?"

Drifts of snow sparkled in the car headlights. Firi heard
Chaz say something about a new movie they all wanted to see
next week. The guard's voice faded as his mind spun with

questions. What had this military special unit been doing...
and were still doing? Experimenting on people? Making
monsters of human beings? Was this why Lace had come
here? Firi thought back to a day almost three years ago when
Lace had taken him to his alluring and beautiful alien
dimension where they had shared essences, a bond, and so
much more. What had Lace said to him? He pressed his
fingertips to his forehead, thinking. *There are things I must do.
And these things will change me,* Lace had said. *You will be
aggrieved.*

Somehow Lace had known what was going on, known
about the military experiments. He had walked straight into
the lair, the lion's den. Firi had always believed he had done it
to save lives. Now he knew for sure. Lace was no mass
murderer. Lace had come to keep the murders from
happening. He'd arrived too late. And he'd been caught. By
Evan. By Colonel Varae, whoever he was. And perhaps by
other men even more insidious. Men with power. Humans
who wanted vampire-fairy power for themselves and were
determined to simply take it.

*

Part Three

Lace

Chapter Fourteen

Hungry. Thirsty. Tired. Lace's eyes ached.

Cold shadows poked him.

The blanket scratched.

His bladder was full.

Mortal whining had found him once again after a thousand years.

Lace shut his eyes, remembering the edges of the night's final dream. Remembering everything else as well.

Blood in his mouth, full, tart, rich. Wind dusting the red scene with sparkling flakes of snow. Silver flashes of guns. The golden nets that caught him and would not break even from the frenzied clawing of vampire strength.

Through the weave of the nets, after it was all too late, he saw bodies all around him. Some in pieces. The ones in uniform he had not touched. But the ones in prison garb, the monsters who had become eaten from within, their minds slashed by angry blood-bound poison... those he killed. They could not be allowed to live in their thirsting anguish, beings stripped of the bonds of self, of safety, of love. They knew only pain and ravaging. Appetite drove their zombie-hood.

Lace had done them a favor.

That day drew down all the shadows of all the years that encroached upon his home realm. When he closed his eyes he saw the three moons of his world rise in three silver frowns, saw the sky close down upon the once bright lands, as if time itself were running faster, running out, his "Earth" replaced with mayhem, madness, incarceration.

The owl-man stood apart from him, beautiful and burning against a lavender sky, wings beating like black storms caught upon his back. He said, "Conquering must be done through love, or destruction is imminent."

And he remembered in the dream and in reality the day he was made, how the lakes and rivers ran pink with blood as the survivors of his people were transformed. Not everyone had survived the coming of the owl-men, but their alien grief and their love saved as many as they could. The owl-man who sewed himself inside him, soul-mate and heart-god, gave him everything he had. He entered Lace through skin, bone and mind, and left a thousand pieces of himself even as he stepped away, re-boarding his star-craft and heading back to the moons, the stars.

Now he spoke again in Lace's mind, in the dream, in reality. "Re-find your power and you will succeed."

Lace said aloud, "But I didn't come here to conquer."

The owl-man replied, "We all flee dying worlds to conquer the next ones. You are no different." He leaned toward Lace, pulling back his dark hood revealing the most beautiful face he'd ever seen, young and noble, green-tinged skin and hair like wild fields in autumn. His eyes were dark as voids, endlessly cold and kind, his lips full and plush. He kissed Lace on the mouth hot and claiming, deep. He reached out and pulled Lace against him and Lace let his arms come up and encircle his maker in return. He thought he would weep. He couldn't help but respond.

His maker pulled back a fraction of an inch. "I love you," he said, "most of all."

The power inside him opened light as air, heavy as a galaxy. It bloomed in awe, outrage, submission, devotion, aggression. It was blazing, icy, stony, liquid, hopeless, fated, sensuous, sexual.

One moment, one kiss, a consummation of fire and lust and the ultimate driven, sharp pain of love.

The owl-man left him like that, spent but still longing, craving. And there was nothing he could do but grieve and live in the beauty of what the intruders had left behind.

Lace felt the cold mat underneath his body, the sting in the air of his cell, and woke fully now to all his memories.

Slowly, he opened his eyes to a sharp anguish of light.

And there stood Firi before him, leaning slightly downward, hand raised as if to touch him on the side of the head or face.

He remembered this prison guard all too well. He wasn't sure why he was suddenly remembering so much. Something different had happened in the past day.

Lace smelled blood on the young man. And a hidden power he wanted to smile at.

He himself felt so weak. The humanness they had infected him with here in this prison clung throughout his system. It made him so thirsty.

Softly, Firi said, "Do you remember me?"

Lace replied, "Yes. You are Firi. What happened to your beautiful hair?"

He watched Firi almost smile at the question, as Firi opened his mouth to answer but no words came out. Beneath the blue sleeve of the Halfling's uniform, he could almost see the blood welling from the many cuts he sensed. His tongue moved against his teeth as if he could already taste them. Even as human-ness was trying to claim him, he still craved that sweet Halfling blood, that healing blood. "Are you injured?"

"No." Firi turned his hand over, frowning as he tried to understand. "I missed you so much." The young man's eyes misted. "Do you need blood?"

"Yes."

"But… are you even still yourself… a vampire?"

"No."

"It's okay." Firi folded his sleeve up and Lace saw the small bandages that covered his skin. The salty, acrid scent strengthened.

Firi said, "Take. We have only a moment."

Lace reached out and took his arm, ripped off one bandage and put his lips to the skin just above the wrist, then his teeth. Firi gasped.

Lace felt his small fangs puncture the soft skin, let the red liquid coat his mouth. This was different from when Firi was ten and then eighteen. This was needed on a much higher scale. Firi tensed in his grip but did not move away. Lace swallowed in ecstasy, sip after sweet sip, until Firi said, "I don't want to be caught."

Reluctantly, Lace let go of his arm, pulled back. A furious energy shot through him. It was as if he'd been thirsting in a desert forever and this was the first drop of blessed rain. The blood from the Halfling was both soothing, like honey, and invigorating, like a drug. He took images from the blood as well, saw Firi's plan, the car in the wood, the supplies and the money. He wanted more blood, more information, but there was no time. He made a decision. "We will be leaving this place tonight. Are you ready?" He had to force the words around the still-savored sweetness in his throat.

"What? Tonight?" Firi looked scared but determined.

"Your plan. I saw it. You have a car."

"How are you remembering everything so suddenly? It's not just my blood. You knew me when you woke. What's different?" Firi kept his voice to a whisper.

"I don't know. Everything is different now. And you should also know that Colonel Varae is not who he appears to be."

"I sensed that. Who is he? Do you know him? Is he dangerous?"

"Very. But that's another tale." It was hard for him to focus even with beautiful Firi standing before him. The room kept wavering, or vibrating. Something was off. His body felt fiery and unstable.

"I want to know everything you remember," Firi said, "but we don't have time."

"No. We don't."

Firi looked so tense. Blood trickled down his arm. Lace touched his sleeve, pulled it down over the self-inflicted injuries.

Firi stared at his now covered arm and said, "I did it for you. All of it."

"I know." The power of Firi—he wanted to devour it. He had to fight hard for control. Something was very wrong with him, but at least he remembered everything now.

"And now I am ready to leave."

"Just like that?"

"Just like that." *Firi, my young love.* He wanted to reach out to him. He didn't dare.

Firi said, "You can't just get up and walk out."

"That is my plan."

"But not right now. We can't…"

"Now." Lace sat up. The blanket fell away. He wore green cotton hospital trousers and a pullover cotton shirt. He was unhappy with the look and the feel but there was nothing he could do about that. As for the winter temperatures outside, as an immortal they would not have affected him but as an almost human now he would be cold. He folded the blanket in his lap and reached for his boots, the chains on his hands chiming. His ankles were also bound,

"We need time to…"

Lace interrupted him a second time. "It must be now or it will be too late."

"But the guards. You have to get past too many. There's the guardroom and three locked doors. All the cameras. Then the locked gate at the kiosk and security outside."

"I know the set up from your blood. I see it all. I can handle it."

"But in your human form you cannot only be injured, you can be killed," Firi insisted.

Lace looked up and softened his gaze. "Thanks to your blood, Firi, I'm mending. It will just take some time."

"Then let's wait!" he whispered.

"No. My body won't be able to take another treatment without even more serious damage, as well as consequences to this place, maybe even to you. It must be now." He paused, hearing the guard outside the door—Chaz—fishing on his belt for his keys. "It's too late anyway. Our conversation has already drawn attention."

As he spoke, he heard the keys at his cell door, the snap of the lock.

Firi turned as Chaz pushed the door open. "Chaz, everything's fine," Firi began.

Lace watched his human lover jerk back as the alarms sounded. He stood quickly, raising his arms out and apart, breaking the chain that held him. As he stepped forward, the chain at his ankles gave way. Relieved that his strength, augmented by Firi's blood, had almost fully returned, he lunged at Chaz.

"No, don't!" Firi yelled.

Lace touched the man on the chest, palm down. Chaz collapsed in his arms. He turned to Firi, quickly placing the man on the floor. "I wasn't going to kill him."

Firi nodded rapidly, but he was breathing hard.

"You have to trust me."

"I do, but…" Firi stared at the broken chains on the floor. "How'd you do that? They're made of the same stuff as the golden nets your kind can't break."

"I don't know. The chemicals in the metals must not work on me in my current state. I'm more human now, but my strength is still enough."

How he wanted to take Firi in his arms right then. Drink him to soulful contentment and grow stronger. Through the fear and shock and alertness, the exquisite loyalty of the boy shone like sylvan gold, and despite the glorious hair being gone except for dark, shining bangs grown long, Firi's beauty still trumped that of the most beautiful fairies he had known in centuries.

The appetite inside him yawned wide. It was luscious. It was dangerous. He forced himself past Chaz and out the door, knowing Firi would follow. The alarm pierced the air of the corridor, a high pitched shriek accompanied by all the lights flashing in quick succession. The strobe effect made their movements appear out of sync with time, but that was only because Lace moved so fast, and Firi ran to keep up with him.

Firi had his keys in hand, but Lace had taken Chaz's for himself. He didn't wait for Firi to take the lead and had never expected that. Of the two of them, Firi was in more danger now, still the weaker. Lace had to take all the guards down before they had a chance to fire. Lace might still take a bullet and live, but Firi might be injured beyond help.

Like the moonstorm winds of his realm whipping through forest and dale, Lace flew to the door at the end of the corridor. He had it open even before the guards behind it could react. His body whipped about them so fast, he knew they were seeing only a whirl of gray, a ghost triumphing over each and every one as he tapped chest after chest. Some weapons went off, but they faltered, bullets hitting one window and the ceiling above.

Firi was still safe, trailing behind in the flashing, screeching corridor. He had only now made it to the guard room.

Behind another glass wall, an armed guard aimed her weapon. Lace had not seen her quickly enough, but he leapt aside and her aim missed.

"Ivana!" Firi yelled.

Lace dived through the security glass, which was harder than it looked. It cracked in giant chunks, leaving deep, stinging scratches along Lace's shoulders and arms. He felt a graze at his temple and red-gold blood dripped into his left eye.

He caught Ivana as her weapon discharged a second time. Her yell was cut off as his touch to her chest crumpled her to the floor. Then he was through the second door to the lunch room, and onto the next set of guards.

Behind him, Firi was hissing. "Shit. Shit!" Still, he followed.

Lace smiled as he took on the next group.

They came to the third locked door, the alarm still sounding in ear-splitting fullness around them. Beyond, he could see nothing. But he knew they were there. More guards. More elite security. It was Firi he worried about, not himself.

He could hear him in his mind through their bond. *Are they dead? Are they all dead?*

"They're only unconscious," he said aloud. "Stay here!"

"No."

"I said stay!"

Firi's mind and thoughts were utterly distracting. The boy had excellent focus and training but the collage of his emotions leaked psychically into Lace's thoughts, plunging him into spectrums of longing and loneliness, dreams of Lace in every guise, sexual aches, devotion, awe.

If he wanted to describe Firi poetically, he would've used words such as henna and angel, sorcerer and cinnamon. His brain rolled in the irrational confusion of images. Snow sculptures of vultures. Icy falling stars. Moons of indifference. Moons of shadows that spoke to his heart. A city of bone. A man in a hood.

Lace drew back at the Firi-shared vision of the shadowed figure, the cape, the hump beneath the flowing material that could have been wings. Had the owl-man visited Firi? Or was it all some coincidental dream?

No time to ask now.

But they had much to discuss in the future. His tongue pressed against his teeth, longing for more of Firi's blood, the way it spoke to him, the language of its oceanic salt, the tartness of its tides. His body wanted to do anything to accomplish getting to the essence of the boy.

Only a fine edge of sanity held him back. Or maybe it was the pureness of simple love. Either way, he could have ripped Firi limb from limb to get at what he wanted, but he could no more kill him than he could kill himself.

Precious Firi. The boy of his wishes. Prince of inward, breathless love. Indefinable. Pathway to memory, to purity. The main ingredient of the journey to once again reach full immortality. Firi was his heart.

He would not lose him in this fight. He needed him to understand his own vulnerability; he needed him to stay.

But Firi was right behind him, breathing hard.

"I know you can't see them," Lace said, "but I can feel them beyond this door, waiting for us to come through. I can deal with it. You will only get yourself shot."

Firi finally backed away, saying, "Okay, I'll use the door for cover."

It was the best Lace was going to get from him. Firi would fight, but at least he would stay back.

Lace unlocked the door. He let himself go and knew the speeds at which he could glide would look to mortal eyes as if a silver wind whirled about the room.

He found the first ones behind the pillars in the lobby. They sank at his brief touches to their chests. The others were at two side exits, and more by the front door.

Above them, the second floor and the ones above remained silent. They had protocols when any prisoner escape alarm went off to lock themselves away, disable the elevators.

Firi never got off a shot. The shots from the guards that rang in the lobby went wild into the walls, and out on the front steps bullets flew into the sky.

He and Firi walked out before back up Jeeps containing more soldiers could arrive.

Firi started toward the outside gate, the entrance. Their breaths made clouds of fog in front of their faces. Lace still clutched a blanket under one arm, but he did not yet feel the cold. He could smell the sting of it in the air, though, and

132

distant hearths, burred pine, the gasoline of approaching vehicles. It was a combination of the mortal winter world. War. And fear.

Lace turned. "This way. We'll go over the fence."

"We can't climb it. It's electrified."

"I said we'll go over it."

"What?"

Lace was running before he could answer. There simply was no time for questions. He trusted Firi to follow, and sped up when he heard the snowy crunch of loyal footsteps behind him.

They ran behind the building and into a field of white. There were no trees except those beyond the fence-line, so they stood out. Lace used his fairy senses, mutilated from the poison they had given him over so much time, but still far better than mortal senses, trying to ascertain if they were being watched or, worse, followed.

He sensed more guards in the building on the first floor, but they were confused and posed no instant threat. He felt more eyes upon them from the second floor. He glanced up at one window, saw a rifle. Then another window. Another rifle.

"Hurry!" He reached behind him and grabbed Firi's sleeve, pulling him forward.

He glanced back. There was nothing he could do except keep going. Then his eyes squinted at a flash. He waited for the sight of breaking glass, and the sound wave to reach them, the weapon's retort. He grabbed Firi harder, pulling them both down to the ground.

No bullets came at them. No resounding shockwave.

He glanced up. The windows were secure, the rifles gone, and he no longer felt the eyes.

"Come on." He hauled Firi up and they sprinted to the fence. "Put your arms around me."

Firi holstered his gun. Lace still had his blanket under his arm. He reached with his free arm and pulled Firi to him. Firi put his arms around his shoulders.

Lace jumped.

Firi let out a little yell as they shot up and over the fence.

Lace landed gracefully, knees bent, but Firi bounced in his arms. His grip loosened and Firi fell straight back onto his ass in the snow.

Lace looked back over his shoulder. "We had help."

"What?"

He leaned down and pulled Firi up to a standing position. "No time. Come on."

"This way!" Now Firi was adamant about leading. "I have a car hidden two miles away. Can you make it?"

"Can you?" Lace asked.

"I'm fine!"

The snow already rose to their knees. Lace thought two miles wasn't too far unless you were trying to slog through fresh powder on top of slippery ice. Unless you were a tortured vampire fairy who was again rapidly running out of energy. Putting all the guards to sleep, the escape, and the leap over the complex's fence had sapped him.

Firi now made headway into the woods, moving quicker than he could. He pushed himself hard to keep up. Their trail would be found soon. There was no way to cover it. They would be hunted. Hopefully just not before they reached Firi's secreted vehicle. If they could get to a portal, like the one in the field behind Firi's parents' house, Lace could lead them to his realm where he could rest and heal.

His head ached.

His bladder was still full.

And his feet were beginning to feel the iciness upon which he walked, the ache of it creeping up from his toes to his ankles.

Firi's stride cut the path and Lace followed in his wake as closely as possible. Low branches of pine trees brushed his face. Ice fell from them onto his head and shoulders, making its way down his shirt which he only now noticed was torn at the sleeves from his jump through the security glass. He did not feel the cuts on his flesh the glass had made, but there was red-tinged mortal blood all over him, so unusual to see, and he realized it must be covering one side of his face as well from the cut on his head.

He drew the blanket around him and forged on. Under the thickest over-growth the path was clearer where the snow couldn't reach. In the deepest shadows it was colder but easier to move and not leave so blatant a trail for pursuers to follow.

When the trees thinned out again, Lace was breathing harder. The snow deepened and he immediately fell, the blanket sliding from his shoulders.

Firi turned and kicked his way through the drifts toward him. "Lace!"

He felt warm hands on his arms pulling him up and leaned into the strength. How many times now had this boy saved him?

"One foot forward," Firi said softly, his arm under his.

Lace struggled about two steps before his legs gave way again.

Firi's arms tightened around him. "We need to rest. But it's still far."

"Maybe for a minute." Lace had not felt so weak in uncounted centuries.

Firi gently let him down. They were surrounded by white on white, ice and cold. The blanket did little to protect him from the immediate chill that went through him as he sat and rested on the ground.

Firi came under him, supporting his head and back against his chest, his warm body making Lace feel almost colder, shiver harder. Then Lace watched as Firi pulled up his sleeve revealing the reddened cuts on his bare flesh, some still with small bandages across them. "Take more from me. It's fine." One cut looked fresh and shining where Lace's fangs had earlier scraped it raw. Lace could not resist.

He placed his lips upon the sweet skin and tasted dusk, starlight, home.

The immediate world blackened around the edges and he went straight into the memory of Firi at eighteen at the fairy pool where he had taken him to share the autumn wine. Beautiful Firi, long dark hair damp and shining in the triple moonlight, naked body slick from the fragrant waters. A flash of the whites of his eyes, arm upraised, curved over his head, Firi opened to him. Lace's memory of the satin texture of his skin against his cheek and chin as he nuzzled him, came with all the senses. Firi tasted of mulled wine, and the summery fields of his home. He could hear the tremble in Firi's veins as he laid his head upon his young chest. That drumming fervor of excited arousal. Where the moonlight edged and surrounded him, his skin turned gold. Where the shadows brushed him, it was ash-dark, lean, and hard as marble. And the genitals, so lovely, tight and straining. When he put his mouth there he could feel that Firi had never done this before with another. Firi's organ jumped and grew even tighter, stiffer. The flavors, the scents. Lace grew empowered from them, from the syrups of Firi's leaking essence. When the boy had come in his arms he cried out in such a beautiful voice it sent an ache through Lace's soul that he could still feel in the memory, fresh and churning.

A hand at his head, pushing.

A tug against his lips.

A rasping voice. "Lace. Lace! Stop!"

Immediately he felt Firi's pain through the renewed blood-bond. How long had he been drinking?

Firi was panting. He leaned down, looking Lace directly in the eye. So close he could feel his warm breath on his cheek. "I want to give you everything but we have to get out of here."

"Yes." *Yes, of course.* Time was of the essence and he had lost himself. They could not afford that right now. Later. Later for everything.

"Do you think you can stand now? Can you walk?"

Lace closed his eyes, reassessed his body. A flush of heat flowed through him. He no longer felt his headache or the pain of a full bladder. In fact, he was partially aroused.

With Firi's help he managed to stand. Take a first step.

The blood was strength. Essence of Firi was his drug of choice. He was not even close to his full strength or power, still all-too human, but he knew he could make it now. "Let's go."

He grabbed up his blanket as he stood. Firi had an arm around him but he didn't need the support anymore.

Together, briskly, they started moving again. Firi, still strong even after some blood loss, ploughed through drifts and pushed back tree branches as they made their way deeper into the forest.

It was hard work. Their breaths came in silver-white clouds.

Even with Firi's blood and newfound strength, Lace's feet were numb now.

Between breaths, Lace said, "When did you get the car?"

"Only a couple days ago."

His eyebrows rose. "Lucky timing then."

"I don't know. It was just an overwhelmingly urgent feeling that I should do it. I got money, too."

Lace inwardly smiled. They wouldn't need money if they could get to a portal. "All that based on a feeling?"

"I couldn't sleep thinking about it. I knew I had to do it fast."

They plunged ahead. Snow crackled, collapsed, fell away in soft wet clumps. Pine needles brushed their hair, poked sharply at their faces.

As they traveled, Lace's thoughts tangled, then scattered, memories falling like leaves about him, images like stained glass breaking apart and flying away in abstract garnet, citrine and sapphire shapes. Halflings, he thought, might have random gifts like foresight, precognition. Maybe Firi knew this moment was coming, building in his subconscious mind, giving him that sense of urgency to take constructive actions for their escape from the complex.

But there was also another reason for Firi's actions burning in his mind, tapping its foot, a shadow moving upward in his vision, alien and elegant and damning.

"It's not much further." Firi's deep voice interrupted him, strained from trying to run through snow.

The words were more than welcome. It seemed they had been going forever.

Sounds had changed the further they went. It wasn't just the occasional car, he could hear the asphalt ribbon of road winding through the wood, rootless, stone, and smell the essence of the cut into the very earth itself with its oil and tar.

"I hear the road," Lace said. *Civilization.* Although technically they were miles from any house. And two miles from the complex, which he could still feel like a heavy giant stirring, rotating its huge head and trying to see with all its faceted eyes. He had not detected any cameras in the wood, but they might be anywhere along the road. Just because they reached the car would not necessarily ensure safety. There would no doubt already be marked and unmarked military vehicles patrolling every street and every side road.

The best hope: no one knew what kind of car Firi had.

"They might have roadblocks everywhere," Lace murmured aloud.

"I didn't think of that," Firi said, suddenly slowing down.

"If we can get to a portal…"

"Okay, but the one by my parents' house might not work. If they know it's me who helped you, and I'm sure they do by now, there could be patrols watching them even now." He looked suddenly scared.

"It's all right, Firi, I know many portals."

"Close by?"

"No, but we'll make do. Is it much further?"

"Just through these trees, I think."

They sloshed through more snow and low-hanging branches. Lace kept himself on his numb feet and upright, thanks to Firi's blood. But he still wasn't right. He was far from right.

He heard a sound of exclamation from Firi. The boy moved faster ahead. "I see it! Come on!"

Lace let out a long breath of relief at the same time he heard Firi hiss, "Stop!"

Lace had been staring at the ground, trying to see if his frozen feet really were still there. He looked up to see Firi with his left hand held up and his body frozen.

But it was too late. They'd been seen. And Lace knew exactly by whom.

"About time you guys showed up," said a drawling voice from the shadows.

Lace came up behind Firi to see Colonel Varae, the one who'd been in the room during his last interview with Evan, leaning against a coppery brown rust-bucket of a car parked just off the road, far enough so it couldn't be seen, in the snowy wood.

"Lace," the taller man said, his lanky frame straightening from where he had been leaning against the side of the car.

"Var."

"Lace, who is he?" Firi asked desperately. "I thought he was a Colonel…"

"It's okay. I think." He paused as he and Var locked eyes. "He's one of us."

"One of us?" Firi echoed.

Var wore dark trousers and shirt. He had an open black, soft-looking jacket lined with sheep's wool but Lace knew it was for show only. He didn't need it. He would not have felt the winter cold at all.

The last time he'd seen Var was in their home realm. It had been too many years to count. Var's perfectly straight black hair had flowed long enough to cover his lower back.

They had not socialized in over a century. But in the deep past they had been lovers once, hot and fervid, their cries written in the ink of stars. Outside of that, their thoughts on everything were contradictory, opposite. They argued in their every utterance. They'd never gotten along.

Lace was more the nature fairy, perhaps a farmer at heart.

Var was less than elemental. He wanted chrome and forged technologies. He was a rocket man. One day he intended to go to the stars and kill all the owl-men who'd come and taken over his world. Taken his loved ones away. He was a man bent on revenge.

Var moved forward from the clearing, approaching Lace and Firi. "I've sent them all off-track, but we still don't have time. I know where all the patrols are." He gave a shifty half-smile and shrugged.

Firi, mouth still open in shock, said, "Is he like you?"

Nodding, Lace said, "What did you do to your eyes?" They looked completely human, not a spark of fairy glitter in them.

Var said sarcastically, "You've heard of contacts, haven't you?"

Still, to Lace, he looked different. How could the humans not see that he was an immortal? It was in his bearing, his scent, although Lace could smell how Var had covered the sweetness well with coarse soaps and a bitter, alcohol-smelling aftershave. The way he talked was refined and any of them could speak any of the human languages if they concentrated enough. But how had Var convinced the

140

humans he was a Colonel? How had he insinuated himself into a strict military hierarchy? Also, he looked older, which was impossible in their condition. But to be a Colonel, of course he'd had to age himself. No one would have believed a youthful, thirty year old face in the rank of Colonel.

"I can hear it in your mind, Lace. You have a lot of questions. But right now we should get going. And you don't look so well."

"I'm fine," Lace replied.

"He's not," Firi said.

Var turned to look at the human. "Ah, so this is your Halfling. We have met."

"Yes." Firi's brows were narrowed.

Var said, "He's definitely got the Halfling look."

As they approached the car, Lace watched as Firi ran off to some bushes, moved a somewhat large rock and began to dig. He came away with a box in his hand.

"Money," he said, as if in answer to their stares.

Var said, laughing suddenly, "Oh my dear boy, that is not going to be a problem."

Lace saw Firi's face deepen in color. His lips thinned. Lace said quietly, "Thank you, Firi."

Firi looked at Lace. "Why isn't it a problem?"

Var said, "I've successfully stolen many an identity, making a mortal life here in these last decades. Stealing money to aid in that adventure… that was the easy part."

"How much did you steal?" Lace asked.

"Enough." Var smirked. "A lot. And after you have enough you don't need to steal more to have it multiply. But if you want to go to the home-realm for awhile while you recuperate, we will not be using much of it. But if we need it, it's there, untraceable. I've got cards, I've got cash. Are you guys ready? You don't have phones or anything on you that are traceable, do you?"

"No," they both said in unison.

Firi went to the car and unlocked it. Lace said, "I hope it has heat."

"It does."

Var came forward then, putting his arm under Lace's shoulders. Lace let him, but he was not in any mood to play any of Var's games right now. And he could sense Firi's unease with the whole thing. It wasn't pride that had the boy annoyed, but more propriety. Lace could sense Firi through the blood-bond. The human felt responsible for him and was not going to want to give control of Lace or his needs over to Var. From now on, none of this was going to be easy.

Var's grip was firm but gentle. He opened the back door of the car and propped Lace in the backseat. Then he got in beside him.

Firi just stood there looking at them.

"You drive," Var said to him. "I'll tell you where to go. I already cleared a path to the road."

Lace had little strength to protest. And even less to push Var away like he wanted to.

Firi said nothing but got into the driver's seat. The car started cleanly, a soft purr that was contrary to its rusty, paint-chipped look. Having only sat in the cold for a couple of days, it ran smooth and they were on the road in seconds.

Of course with Var's powers, even if the battery had been dead, Lace knew he could've put his hand on the hood of the car and started it that way with barely a passing thought.

The Var Lace had known in the past had been a mercurial sort of guy. Given to quick mood shifts and highly self-absorbed. But when he gave you his attention, he gave it all. And that was hard to resist.

Var reached around Lace and pulled his blanket closer. He ordered Firi to turn the heat up on high. He said to Lace, "Bend your knees and put your feet on my lap."

His feet were so cold he could barely feel them. Var helped him into position, then gently removed his boots. He put his hands on Lace's stocking-clad feet and held them

142

there. A kindle of warmth surged. Lace's body jerked at the pain/pleasure of the pins and needles.

Var simply said, "You're a fucking mess."

The heat continued to penetrate his frozen flesh. The air in the car grew warmer. Lace started to shake so hard his teeth chattered.

Var looked at him serenely. Lace gazed up front where he saw Firi glancing at them in the review mirror. Then Var put a hand against his chest. Surges of pleasure suffused his body. He remembered:

It was as if his hands took siege of everything they touched. This man before him, dark as the crystal orbs that grew at the bottom of the castle gardens. Emanating grief more than love. He'd absorbed less of the aliens' love in his personal transformation, a random error in their actions that sometimes occurred in their transferences of their immortal gift, and it left him moody, critical, harsh. But in lovemaking, it was as if Var wanted to take into himself the things he was missing, the longings and wishes and hopes he could not help but give up on, disbelieve. It was almost too much for Lace. The way this man consumed him. Heavy as stars and as hot in their scents of urgency, fervor, like burnt wood.

The unbalance in Var always made Lace upset, angry, and moody himself. Aside from sex, they were not good companions.

Once Var had told him, "I want to kill them."

"Kill?" No fairies ever killed. "Kill who?"

"All of them. The ones who came to our world and did this to us."

"They're immortal. How do you kill an immortal?"

"Easy. You make him… or her believe she's mortal again."

Of course Var was always full of non-sequiturs, destructive words, angry gestures. He seemed happiest when he was being cruel. Or when he was with Lace in bed, bent to him and saying, "Yes, like that, harder and don't be nice."

For immortals having spent only a year together, their shared lust was like a one night stand that didn't even last the night.

Dim memories of bright eyes and beauty carved of shadow, full moist lips and rampant cock. Every day he was with Var he woke to his dark-of-the-moons gaze, sleepy fingers, twitching smiles. Var wanted to possess him five, six times a day. The man was not tame-able. He was insatiable.

Now the dark fairy's hand upon the flesh covering his heart only made Lace more listless, sad.

His eyes closed. Darkness soaked him.

*

Chapter Fifteen

He woke to the memory of his lost memory. And the words: *How do you kill an immortal? You make it believe it's mortal again.*

For two years this was what the humans had been doing.

Now he remembered his own amnesia. And he could see that was what the humans, Evan and his kind, were trying to accomplish all along with their painful tests, their poisonous solutions poured intravenously into him.

They wanted to figure out how to kill the immortal intruders upon their world. Their past methods had not worked. Not permanently, at least. An immortal could be distracted and blocked by being buried at sea or thrown into a volcano but eventually they would climb out of their traps and heal. Eventually they would return. If humans could refine a perfect death for them, they could win the war against the influx of alien beings upon their world.

He lay upon a soft mattress covered by a fleece blanket that had designs of Christmas trees and snowflakes on it. It was a blanket Firi had given him some time during this journey, one of the essentials he had packed in the trunk of his new/old car.

He tried to move and realized his body was sore all over. He had a sensation of internal heat and yet his skin was cold.

He could sense he was not yet back in the fairy realm but instead, by the sounds and smells, in an older run-down building run by humans who always looked the other way. A small, edge-of-town motel.

A door opened and slips of light fell over him. He turned his head on the pillow, blinking, and heard Firi say, "He needs me. I can give him what he needs."

Var's patronizing voice replied. "You would run out of what he needs before you ever drew your last breath."

Lace's heart clutched in empathy for what the human was going through. Firi had given everything, including his career and his very existence to help Lace, to save his life. Such amazing loyalty. Devotion. But it was no surprise. Since the age of ten the boy had been his.

Now Firi could not go back to the humans without a warrant forever hanging over his head. Life would never be the same for him.

Lace tried to sit up, the blanket falling partway down to his lap. "Firi, come here."

Immediately, Firi came through the door and was at his side.

Var moved out of the line of vision from the open doorway, his footsteps stalking to the edge of the other room. Lace heard a click. Voices. The television.

"I haven't thanked you for everything."

Firi sat on the side of the bed, slumping against him. "You don't have to. I'd do it again and again and…"

"Shh." Lace took him into his arms. Embraced him. They could never show this kind of emotion in the prison. The most physical contact they'd had in two years had occurred only during the last few weeks; Firi touching Lace on the side of the head, or Firi supporting his weight with one arm after his medical torture treatments.

Firi's arms came around him now, warm and insistent. "I missed you. All the time."

"I know. Me, too. But what I did had to be done."

"The humans? The ones you… you killed?"

"They weren't human. They were monsters. They were very strong. They would've turned on everyone in the complex, then released themselves into your world. Maybe,

146

after a very high death toll, they would've been stopped by your weapons. I could save lives by doing it right then and there, and making sure they were truly dead."

"I know they weren't right, weren't 'human'. I heard the story... not officially, but I knew it was true. I knew you weren't part of the entire massacre of the prisoners and nurses and guards as well. The monsters killed their nurses, and the guards."

Lace gave a small, unhappy laugh. "You're always so willing to believe in me."

"Not 'believe', I *know*," Firi said, holding out his arm, showing Lace the cuts underneath the lifted sleeve. "It's in the blood. Our bond."

Lace smiled, hugging him tighter to his chest, brushing at the now short hair. He remembered those long soft curls, and Firi as a boy so elfin and sweet. "You're extremely receptive. Even for a Halfling. More so than I ever could've imagined."

Firi moved his head up so their faces were less than an inch apart. He whispered. "Let me give you what you need. Var said—"

Lace kissed him, interrupting whatever he was going to tell him Var had said. He already knew anyway. And reluctantly agreed with him. But for right this moment he had Firi, beautiful Firi.

The boy's lips parted under his mouth.

There was no denying the stirrings their kiss brought, dream-deep and beyond conscious desires. Firi was who Lace's soul wanted. And Firi's Halfling soul longed to come to Lace. To home.

That was how the bond worked.

They were a perfectly matched pair.

It took every ounce of will he had left to push Firi back from the kiss, his taste still sweet upon his lips.

Firi's face fell into an unsure smile.

"I want you," Lace said softly, "but you can't give me what I need to heal. Not right now. I'm too sick, still too human, and you're too worn out. You've already given me your blood."

"I don't care. Take whatever more you need."

"You know I won't compromise you any more. It has to be Var." He reached up and stroked Firi's cheek as the smile left that beautiful face.

Eyes downcast, body stiff, Firi said, "I don't want to leave you. Not with... *him.*"

"He's strong. He can give me what I need to be myself again. You want that for me, right?"

The space between Firi's eyebrows creased. Even in his pain, he was lovely.

"H...how long have you two known each other?"

"A long time, but we were together only a very short time."

"You were together? As in--?"

Lace nodded. "It was a short time because, in truth, though we might have loved once, and we have a blood bond, we can't stand each other."

"But he went out of his way to save you."

"Believe me, he has an agenda." He could hear the TV on in the other room but that didn't mean Var wasn't listening in. His senses were even more heightened than Lace's. In every way.

Var was one of the strongest of their kind. And that was why Lace needed him now. Even if he didn't really want him.

"I can't stand the thought of..." Firi began.

"Shh." Lace kissed him again, wanting more, frustrating himself.

When he pulled back, Firi said, "How long will he have to be... be with you? Feeding you?"

"A couple days, perhaps. I don't know for sure."

The boy's eyes sparked with tears. "I want you to send him away."

"I know. But when this is over it'll be you and me. I promise."

Firi gave him a shaky smile. "Always on the run." It was not a question.

"Perhaps."

"That's okay. Anything is okay as long as I'm with you."

For a few minutes they sat together embraced on the bed. Lace wanted to breathe Firi in, all of him, and bask in that intimacy. It helped him, but it wasn't what he really needed right now. Firi had fed him twice. The first time he used all the strength Firi gave him to subdue the guards in the secret complex. The second time he'd imbibed less, and just getting through the snowy woods took all the effort he had.

If he was to properly heal, he needed more.

He thought of Var in the other room, sitting, waiting. A fairy made of blackest suns, blackest voids, blackest depressions. Maybe the assessment was a bit extreme, unfair, but Var had a side to him that was breathlessly dark. It could be invigorating and bitter at the same time. Var was an irritation that slowly worked its way into the flesh and mind. Exciting, yes, but liable to bite as easy as kiss. And the affliction of shadows across Var's heart could leave mirror-shadows across the hearts of those who crossed his path.

One could not deny the reasoning behind Var's anger, but it was no way to live, especially if one's life was never-ending.

The fact that Var did not choose his pessimism didn't make it easier to deal with him.

After awhile, Firi moved. He put his palm to Lace's face. "You feel hot. Does it hurt?"

"A little." In actuality, it hurt a lot. His head pounded. He saw silvery haloes around everything in the room, including Firi. His limbs ached as if he'd been tied into contorted positions for days. His stomach seemed made of knives. His mouth felt as if it were filled with sand.

He barely noticed it when Firi moved over the side of the bed and stood.

Lace slumped back onto the pillows.

Chapter Sixteen

He must've fallen back to sleep because he had no sense of time passing, and he had not heard Firi leave the room.

He opened his eyes. Warmth emanated from a long-limbed form leaning against the headboard next to him. The darkness of Var was like a cloud on the air. Full of wind and fury and rain.

Lace blinked him more into focus and saw him flipping a tiny silver knife over and under his fingers as if he were performing a magic trick.

"Where's Firi?" Lace asked tiredly.

Var's dark eyes shifted. He looked down at Lace with a combination of remoteness and fondness only Var could manage. "Awake now?"

"Was I asleep?"

"He's in the other room. He'll be fine."

But he's not fine with this, Lace thought.

"So," Var said, holding the thin, short knife steady now, brushing it lightly across the skin of his own wrist. "Where shall we begin?"

The thirst in Lace was an aberration. He hadn't felt this much in need since the owl-man first transformed him. He stared wordlessly at the pulse just beneath the surface of the flesh of Var's arm. He could smell the nectar of the other fairy's blood, already taste the dark burnt sugar of it, knowing how the texture, like honey, would melt down his throat.

He had so many questions he wanted to ask Var but no strength to speak them. What had he been doing all these years? How had become a Colonel? And why?

Var shifted in the bed, his body brushing Lace's blanket, his weight pressing into his side. He lifted his wrist and the knife and began to make a cut. As he split his own skin, he showed no response of pain. He spoke and his voice was very clear. "Take all that you need. For as long as you need. All I ask is you give me what I need in return."

Because they'd shared the autumn wine before, though that was long ago, Lace knew exactly to what he was referring.

He was in no position to deny any of Var's demands. He'd be in even less of a position very soon to deny his own desires that enflamed him whenever he drank the blood of his own kind. It was only natural, of course.

His vision dimmed. Strangely, he felt hot tears. "Agreed."

Var finished making the cut, set the knife aside, and reached his free arm underneath Lace's head, pulling him close to his chest. Voice low, he said, "What was done to you can be undone."

Var smelled truly not of himself, of human aftershave and man-made shampoo. The scent of laundry detergent still lingered on the soft black shirt he wore. But the fairy's body was warm, hard, strong. Still Var. All of it was distracting from what he truly wanted.

Golden blood began to seep from the cut, and Lace's throat began to ache.

"What are you waiting for?" A low chuckle.

Lace reached up to touch his hand, then grabbed harder, bringing the wrist, the split skin, then the blood to his lips. The moment he took the first sip his vision reeled. His mind spun. Then, all he knew was the sweetness, the bliss, the dark ache of his healing, and pleasure building and building as he drank. His thoughts soared and fell.

Var always complained that he did not like the grass biting into his skin, or the leaves falling on him, tangling in his hair. While Lace loved making love in the open air, in front of all of nature under the lavender sky and the stars, Var preferred a feather bed, soft flannels, velvets, Elvin cotton. He wanted four walls, no wind, no rain, no sun. He demanded pillows and warmth and comfort. He wanted luxury. And he did not want to share Lace with anyone, and most certainly not with the spirit of nature itself.

He liked to tease Lace, dark body lying back against white sheets with just an edge of the top-sheet over his groin. He would stretch his muscled arms back, over his head, shut his eyes, twisting slightly under the sheet, letting it fall a little, letting it show off his edges, his curved muscles, his deeper ardent shadows. He could be enticing as an angel, seductive as an incubus.

Lace felt the fairy-blood flow into him more rapidly, the fountain of it going down his throat so gratifying he could only crave more.

Var. How had he forgotten the nectar of him so void-edged, spiced, so delightfully contrary and wicked?

They had always argued. Day in. Day out. But the sex had been incandescent. Obsessive.

Now he drank the essence of Var and no longer cared who had split up with whom, or why.

The moons rose red in the window. Eager hands stroked. Thirsting mouths suckled. Open bodies invited. The fevers of the flesh rose and fell all night long, every night for the year they were together as a couple.

They did not talk much when they made love, save utterances of encouragement or awe, and so while their voices might continually argue during the day, at night their bodies only wanted to agree.

Memories flashed from one hundred years ago.

Lace's body became fervent, enflamed. His veins grew hot and all the aches in his muscles, his stomach, and his head began to vanish. The mist in his mind cleared. Still he drank. He opened his eyes.

Var was there, close and beguiling like the devil himself. Irresistible. Over the edge of his fist above where Lace's lips still pulled, their eyes locked. As if speaking through an echo, Var said, "Had enough yet?"

No. He had not. But Var's lips were parted and moist, his face beautiful, open. Slowly, Lace let up on the suction of the wrist, tasting only with his tongue now, his grip on Var's hand easing. He lifted his face. He could feel the gold of Var still coating his lips.

Var leaned in and licked at Lace, stole a taste of himself.

A yearning ache twisted through his body and pooled at his abdomen, the ecstatic pain of arousal. So fierce his hips came up off the bed as his body surrounded Var, pulling him closer.

The soft licking at his lips from Var became a rough kiss that penetrated more than mouths. It invaded the mind. The war of pleasure had begun and there would be no losers now.

Their bodies scrambled to get even closer. Hands pushed at the cloth of shirts at their backs, at waistbands, tugging, pulling, sometimes tearing.

Var's hairless skin was like silk. Slightly moist. Intensely hot. Lace ran his palms up and down Var's sides and chest and still his hands wanted more.

Var touched him in return, a sensation like the sun drowsing all over his body until he simply wanted to melt into pure salt and ivory light. He felt his pants being yanked away and Var coming to lie between his legs, kissing anything and everything he could reach. The side of his hip. The top of his thigh.

Nights of gossamer and fog. Rolling through the gray, cat-soft shadows, bodies tangled together in searing hedonism. How they had once feasted on sensuality, heedless, lost.

A tongue left a stripe of wet across his belly just below his navel.

Lace pushed himself up into Var's space, wanting even more connection. Wanting to feel him everywhere. He was rampant. Seeking. Needing more contact.

A passing thought of Firi sent a pang of indecision through his heart.

Var touched him softly on the chest. "What you need. This."

154

The promise he'd made to Var and the promise he'd made to Firi seemed at cross purposes. But he had to keep one promise to keep the other.

Sharing the autumn wine, the completion of the task and the ceremony required an exchange.

Var was not interested in blood.

Lace spread his legs and Var's hands slid beneath him to cup his buttocks. He nuzzled the inside of his thigh. Lace's erection, full and taut, grazed Var's cheek.

Var said, "Always so willing."

Lace said, "Always so infuriating."

The soft responding chuckle vibrated against his most sensitive skin.

Var licked the root first, then swathed his tongue up the shaft. He licked lightly at the burgeoning tip before smiling lips closed around it.

Lace's eyes rolled up.

Var sucked the head into his mouth, his tongue remembering everything that Lace had so loved. And more.

Whirl of stars. Dark velvet lover lapping at his shore.

The universe expanded. Contracted. He wanted something to hold but Var was too close and too far away at the same time. His heart opened wide.

I need to hold onto something…

Var came up off him before he was through and moved up until he was crouched over him. "You think too much." He pulled Lace into his arms and kissed him. "There. Was that what you wanted?"

Making love. Var was pretty damn good at it. He was teasing him now. Something about the kissing and the way Var's fingers folded into his hair was the answer.

Lace had always thought back then, when they were lovers, *He lives his life grim and hard, taking, demanding.* That was Var. Always hating the beings who had come to transform them because his parents and siblings had not survived. Nor had his wife and children. Bitter, shallow, snide. Always scheming. A dark thought on a sunny day. Disapproval of the way their kind had become lazy sun-worshippers and philosophical dreamers. Passive, gentle creatures of a crystal realm which Var despised.

And then there was this. Var so present, so conversant in the ways of the body. So eager. It was as if the darkness in him made the sex even more appealing. And when Var coaxed, when his voice turned low in the throes of passion, Lace became the craving itself, everything the deeper body wanted, the soul.

Now Var nipped at his lips, then licked his way back down Lace's body, taking him in his mouth again. It was demanding. Simple. Who couldn't admire that?

Lace bucked. The way that mouth moved over him, then up and down, sliding, repeating. The drug of it suffused him. His mind went back to ancient streets and swaying lanterns. He floated in his simple dream. The lanterns became stars and he went up. They nestled in his hair, on his face. Minutes. Hours. Eons.

Var produced a fluency within his body for the language of pure ardor. The torment of longing. The ambition of love.

Ambition. Var had that in abundance.

Var touched him with his hands. On the thighs, the stomach, the base of his cock and the fleshy sac beneath it. He cupped his hands beneath him again, squeezing his ass, and holding him as he fed.

Lace could feel himself growing lighter and the dizzying sensation that he was close to breaking apart washed over him. He climbed that ecstatic peak as Var's tongue did amazing calisthenics against his rigid flesh. The lips pulled. The mouth contained him, so hard, so wet and urgent.

When he was filled up to the breaking point, everything spilled over. He let go with a cry.

This was the wine Var wanted. Always.

Did he think it bound them closer than blood? Maybe he was right.

Var drank and drank. Lace gave everything that had been held back for so long in the prison cell. He was awake now for the first time in years. And Var's tongue and lips were so good in everything they were doing. He kept coming, his breath frozen, caught in his lungs at the repeating ecstasy.

Var would often fall asleep on top of him, his long hair spilling around them, delicate, dark strands draping over Lace's chest.

...those miles of nighttimes overhead, their world never getting older and the two of them young forever, never to die. The streets of time were theirs for the taking. They could live forever in magic forests, linger in meditative visions in rustic cabins with hand-woven rugs on oaken floors and wade in wavering candlelight that painted the walls in tides of iridescent light. They could glut on reverie and poetry, end of summer breezes and night-rain. Laugh and cry for no reason. They needed nothing but love, dream-basking their life in perfect contentment.

Except for the simple fact that Var was never content.

He pulled Var down onto him, then rolled them both over until they were on their sides. He kissed him, his hand snaking around his neck to pull the dark fairy closer. Their legs entwined. Var's erection pressed against his stomach.

He thought he was entirely spent, at least for the moment, but the flutter inside him came on again as they rolled on the bed, kissing.

Lace let his hand slide down Var's back, over his waist and between his legs. Fingers stroked up the stiff shaft of his cock. Their kiss broke. Var tilted his head back, groaning. Lace held him that way, hand moving slowly as he watched Var's throat undulate as if he fought for every breath.

Lace rolled onto his back again, spreading his legs, leading Var between them once more.

Var pulled himself up on his strong arms, looking down at him. "You are more yourself already," he rasped. He sniffed. "And you don't have that human stink now."

"Stop talking so much," Lace said, reaching down between them, lifting his legs and wrapping them about Var's waist. He continued to tease him with his body until Var gave in and began stroking him low, one finger entering him with ease. As fairies, they did not need fancy oils or other accessories. Lace was damp when he wanted to be for sex, self-lubricating.

The finger drew away and Var positioned himself. The entry was smooth and slow. Silken. Stretching him and filling him up with the loveliest of sensations. How he loved this. And Var was a master. His depleted organ began to fill again.

They were immortal but ephemeral. Ancient and new. The owl-men had made them into myths. Time to celebrate.

Var thrust himself in, out, in. All the way.

…they howled in the night like human wolves…

Lace twisted and turned, impaled upon him, wanting more.

…like fairy tales come true…

Their eyes met, held. Sparkling green/silver to glossy black. As if the years had never come between them.

…like forever-children of the mystic glade…

Var fucked him long past coherency. Insensate.

They both came in a turmoil of hurtling pleasure and mingling essence. It was no longer a healing task. Intimacy could not be denied.

Always in the wake of all-night caresses, Lace would insist on opening the window so the silver petals of the realm fell on the sheets about them.

They collapsed back onto the bed together, a heap of arms and legs and slippery, moist heat. Breathing each other's breaths. Their mouths still wide open, still trying to catch air. Var's cock remained inside him, joining them. Lace's body sucked at it, still wanting him there. Something it remembered but he had not. Until now.

That realization stunned him. Ashamed, Lace had forgotten how much he had loved him.

They had truly shared the autumn wine. Though they were still in the human realm, Var had brought him home.

Dissolving into each other's dreams, they slept.

Chapter Seventeen

"Do you need more?" That delicate, dark-edged voice of echoes, low and rumbling. It brushed over Lace's skin, ionic.

Lace lay on his back, naked in the thin dawn. He licked a final drop of gold from Var's wrist, the new cut already healing. He could've used his fangs to open him again, but he was doing just fine on the amount he had drunk. For now.

The fairy blood had made him hard again. Made him high. Var's hand moved from Lace's mouth to his stomach, fingers drawing lazy circles there.

Lace stretched, bent his knees and let his legs fall open.

Var petted him absently, cupped and stroked his balls until Lace was taut and trembling, ready to give the liquid Var wanted in return.

The dark head moved down between his legs. The licks lapped at the leaking fluid from the tip of his erection. The hot mouth lowered.

Everything broke apart only to be put back together better than ever.

Var drank from him, making soft, wet noises that sent him reeling. Then he felt the strong arms flip him over and a probing tongue on his backside. Var lifted his head, pulled him up at the hips and impaled him. The way Var filled him, his perfect size and girth, the weight on his back, drove him crazy. He pushed back as Var thrust forward.

It was just like old times when they couldn't get enough of each other.

Var's arms came around his waist. He leaned down and pressed his face to Lace's shoulders and neck, rubbing. Leaving wet kisses on his spine. Lace shivered. Wanted more.

Var moved faster. Their gasping breaths synchronized. They were in perfect rhythm.

As an immortal one could do this all the time and not grow tired. They slept when they wanted to. They slept because they loved to share each other's dreams.

But now this frenzy. It was all. Sharing liquids did that to them. The blood. The semen. Demon-elixir or tonic of seraphs. It didn't matter which. It was their wine of choice. Gave new meaning to the word "cocktail."

Right before he came, Var said, "Tell me your new Halfling could ever give you this." He pulled out, pushed in deep, and Lace could not stop the moan in his throat. "He probably comes as soon as the tip of his little cylinder is inside you. " Var touched the deepest pleasure organ deep inside over and over, making it last. "It's sweet when the young ones do that, isn't it?"

Words got tangled in his throat. He wanted to argue. Tell Var he could teach Firi, tease Var about how much fun that would be. He wanted to defend Firi. His Halfling was sweet, yes, and very young, but of the gourmet variety to be sure.

As if reading his mind, Var thrust again and said, "Hmm, he seems teachable, though. Can I watch?" An unintelligible sound came on his exhaled breath. He leaned his weight on Lace's back, gasping again.

Lace felt the liquid pulses, the throbs of the cock deep inside him.

He decided, though, that no matter how good Var was at this, right now he talked too much.

*

He lay underneath the hot flesh of the dark fairy. Var was heavy, but not too heavy.

He slept for maybe five minutes before they did it all over again, staring into each other's eyes.

Var looked young again, no longer playing "Colonel," face chiseled and tanned, eyes dark as storms.

Var said, after awhile and another rest, "I didn't know it was you who had been captured. At least, not at first."

Lace rolled over. His hip touched Var's hip. Var's hand lay as if forgotten on his chest. Covers thrown back, they were naked to the air. "How long have you infiltrated the mortal militaries?"

"From the beginning."

"Which beginning?"

"Before the official start of the war. Fifteen years or so."

"That long! Why?" Lace asked.

"They have technologies I'm interested in," he said vaguely.

"And no one noticed you were... different?"

"What? Do I have a tail or something? No they didn't notice because I'm not out dancing in circles and singing in the forest bringing attention to myself!"

Lace wanted to say, *Neither do the rest of us!* He held back the response. He didn't want to go back to old times again in that way. Not this soon. Arguing and arguing.

Var continued, "It didn't come to my attention who they were experimenting on until very recently."

"You knew about the experiments, though? That our kind was being held and used for... treatments?"

"Knew about it? I'm on the board that sanctioned it." He gave a snide laugh.

Lace lifted himself up on his elbow and Var's hand slid away. "You planned this?"

"Hell, yeah."

For a moment Lace was speechless. Then he said, "Hurting your brothers and sisters?"

"Has it been that long since we knew each other? Have you forgotten everything about me? Or maybe you never knew me at all," Var complained.

It had been a century since he'd even seen Var. A hundred years ago was not long to an immortal, but long enough to forget some things. Some of them came streaming back.

Var arguing for revenge against their makers. Talking about laying waste to the moons and beyond. Always muttering to naysayers, "I'll find a way. I have forever to do it."

Var refusing to talk about the past, furious when Lace had found out he'd had a family, a young wife and two daughters, and asked him about it. He'd said, "You mention them again and I'll kill you." He had pushed Lace aside and left for a week. After he returned, he refused to say where he'd gone.

"You wanted to learn about a method to successfully destroy an immortal," Lace said. "So you infiltrated the humans to get that?"

Var shrugged. "You got it. It had nothing to do with the war."

"I suffered for over two years."

"Yeah, I know. It was only a couple weeks ago that I found out it was you. I came to help as fast as I could. Don't I get credit for that?"

Lace looked aside at the bare motel wall and the flimsy curtains over the tiny window.

Var exhaled loudly. "I wouldn't have left you for so long alone if I had known. Lace." He raised his hand from his chest and brushed the edge of his palm against Lace's long, shining hair. "I wouldn't have wanted to see you hurt." He stroked along the side of his cheek. "Not ever."

Of course Lace believed him. Var could be cruel, vengeful and quick to anger. But he had once loved Lace. Maybe he still did. Outside the bedroom, they did not get along, but they had not parted enemies.

Lace still had no words. His eyes were hurting. The walls of the room blurred.

Var moved over him until he straddled him. Naked and alive. Skin shimmering all over. Lace felt him hovering, saw out the corner of his eye that Var's head was bowed, his eyelids were half-closed, his mouth down-turned. He'd seen Var sad before, even when he would deny it. *"I'm not hurt and I'm not sad,"* he would say. *"Angry. That's what I am. It's not the same thing."*

Lace turned his full attention to him. That face, half-closed now, was not angry at all. "I believe you. I know you came to help me."

Var said quietly, "I'm sorry you suffered."

Lace looked at the stiff jaw line, the tight muscles in the neck. He lifted his hands and ran them over the hard, flat chest, down to the narrow hips. The appendage between Var's crouched legs dangled, impressive and beautiful. He touched him there, watching Var's eyelids slowly re-open, seeing a moment's vulnerability there. Maybe even longing.

What a creature Var was, all power and tightly coiled strength. Hewn of the rich earth, the cycles of the night.

"I know you're sorry," Lace finally answered, stroking up the fine cock.

"I came as soon as I found out."

Lace stroked down the shaft again. "I know."

"I ran."

He squeezed a little just below the tip, nodding into Var's eyes.

"The very day I arrived, I made sure I was there for your treatment," Var said as if Lace weren't touching him so intimately.

More stroking.

Now Var's voice caught once. He breathed in and said, "I made sure I was there so I could give you 'the touch' to your chest. Send you to sleep. End your suffering."

Lace cupped the generous balls in his hand. "I remember."

Var stretched up then, bringing his filling cock toward Lace's face. Lace kissed the tip, then licked a moist circle. Gently he sucked the head.

"I know you hate me," Var whispered. Then as Lace took him all the way into his mouth, Var let out a long moan that filled the room, echoing off the drab white walls. He clutched the sides of Lace's head, fingers tangling in his hair.

Lace tasted nectar as if from the sweetest flower. More balm for healing. But this liquid was more rarified, thick, its condensed potency containing as much energy in one feeding as three feedings of blood.

He looked up, watching the beauty of Var, head thrown back, throat exposed, the dampness in his short, dark hair making the ends wispy, dark tendrils curled against his temples, ears, forehead.

Lace felt the powerful cock pulse again. He took the milk and swallowed.

Var sat back on Lace's thighs, cock still half-hard, mouth slack.

Lace just smiled at him. Then shook his head as if coming up from a long and starry dream. In his mind, he said, *No, I don't hate you.* Out loud he said, "Thank you, Var. Thank you for saving me."

Var touched him very lightly on the chest, just enough to send tingles throughout his body. "I do what I can. You're quite welcome."

*

Chapter Eighteen

When they came out of the room together it was another dawn, shadows the color of cola, the light tinged orange. Lace had on new black trousers, a new white shirt, all provided by Var.

Firi lay curled around a pillow on the pull-out couch bed, hands tight to his chest, one fist under his chin.

There was no room service for him here but there were empty jerky and potato chip wrappers on the table. For two days, Firi had subsisted only on snacks, Lace surmised. He would not have gone out and risked being seen with the whole state looking for him.

In sleep his face was scrunched with a deep crease between his soft eyebrows. He looked so tense. Forlorn.

Var caught his eye, winked wickedly, and said, "Shh. Let the baby sleep."

Lace shook his head and turned away. He went to Firi's side and quietly sat on the edge of his bed. The metal frame bit into his thigh. He reached out and put his hand against the side of the young man's face.

Firi stirred, eyelids fluttering. "Lace?" His voice came out sleep muffled, deep. "Are you...?"

"I'm all right. Thanks to you for getting me out of there."

"You did all the work. And... Var." His mouth turned down when he said the name.

Var was at the door unlocking it. He had his cell in hand.

Firi sat up, pointing at Var. "That's traceable!"

Var turned as he opened the door. "Oh, child, don't be scared. I'm the one who's organizing the search for you." He chuckled as he walked outside, letting the motel room door clang shut behind him.

"He's...?" Firi started to speak but his mouth closed. The desperate look he gave Lace came with a frown.

Lace said, "He's trustworthy."

"He doesn't seem like it."

"I know." Their hands clasped on top of the thin, brown motel blanket.

"But he healed you."

"Yes."

"I'm glad for that."

But Lace knew it was hard for Firi to admit that. The motel room walls were thin. He had to have heard at least some of their antics over the past two days.

He knew Firi wanted to be at his side. Firi had earned that spot for himself several times over. But without Var, they both would've been much weaker right now, and possibly even caught.

He could not deny what both men had done for him. And their next move would have to be on the run. While Var was not a wanted criminal, now he and Firi were. They had to get to the fairy realm until this frenzy died down. Until Var could make things safe and decide the next move.

At that thought, Lace realized his mind had just allowed Var to take the lead. He had not wanted that. Still didn't want it.

And what did Firi want? To complete the rescue, run away and live happily ever after? Of course that would be what he wanted, what anyone wanted from a life of turmoil, hardship, and separation from one they loved.

As if reading his mind, Firi said, "So what's next?"

"We get ourselves somewhere safer."

"Your realm?"

"For now. It's dissolving at a rapid rate, but we'll go where the ground is still stable. It will take a few more years before all of it's finally gone."

"You said 'we'." Firi looked down at their entwined hands.

"Hey." Lace pulled his hand away, brought it back to Firi's face. He tilted the boy's chin up. "You think I'd leave you behind?"

"I only know what I think. Not what you think," Firi stated. "I only know I wanted to try to help you. Beyond that… I wouldn't allow myself to think."

"Listen to me, Firi. We shared the autumn wine. The blood-bond. I do not take that lightly."

Firi turned away, pushed back the covers. He was still wearing the blue trousers of his uniform, dark at the hems from when they'd waded through snow and muddy, icy sludge on their long walk through the forest. He also wore a black undershirt. He swung his legs over the other side of the mattress and stood. For a moment he didn't move, only stared at the dimly lit window shade. The motel was quiet. It was still too early for most guests, even early travelers, to rise.

Lace stayed seated on the far side of the bed, the mattress cooling before him. Waiting.

Finally, Firi said in an almost whisper, "I can't take it lightly, either. I literally *can't*. It makes me crazy. I crave you all the time." Those last words came out so soft they were almost lost on the whispering stillness of the morning air.

"Firi…"

He turned, holding up his hand to stop Lace. Quickly, Firi interrupted. "I only want what's best for you. That means anything. Anything at all. What you have to do you should do. I'll help in any way I can, but I don't expect you to just walk into the sunset with me or something."

Lace suppressed a smile. "You don't?"

Firi's eyes grew bright. He pressed his lips tight. "There's Var. I know he's important. To everything that's going down. To you."

"Var is very difficult to ignore. And you probably heard… some things in the last few days between us."

Firi looked down. "It's okay. I'll be okay. You want him."

168

"You're telling me what I want now?"

Firi looked up. "But he's fierce! So strong. You wanted that. Once. And now. I can see it. I did hear..."

Lace looked at him standing tall, stiff, shoulders back and broad with muscle and abundant adulthood. He'd grown at least two inches since Lace had last seen him. His face was chiseled in determination and hurt. The disappointments he'd faced left an edgy shimmer to his gaze. Maybe a little too much like Var's gaze when they'd first met.

"Have you looked at yourself in the mirror lately? You're fierce yourself."

Firi's fingers curled to fists. His eyes were shining now, bright with tears he refused to shed. He'd grown up so much, so fast.

"What if I told you he's not the one I want?"

Firi shook his head in dismay. "After these last few days, I might laugh."

Now he began to wonder how much Firi had heard from the other room. All of what they had done? He remembered just then hearing the TV on late at night, hearing the volume suddenly go up. "I won't lie to you. We have the blood-bond, too, me and Var. But so do you and I."

The words did not seem to help. Firi still looked hurt.

Lace said softly, "He is the past. You are the future."

Firi dropped his head so his chin almost touched his chest. Finally, his eyelids rose. Low, almost sheepish, he said, "That's good. 'Cause I have nowhere else to go."

And the way he gazed from under long dark lashes, the way he held himself, tall but vulnerable, broad but hunched, he was at that moment more breathtakingly handsome than Lace had ever seen him.

After two days of a wild ride with Var, Lace was surprised, yet not surprised at his body. He felt stirrings for Firi as if they were brand new, as if he'd been asleep for years. In a sense, he had been.

He got up and went to him, touching him on the shoulder. Firi turned and Lace put his arms around him. "Listen to me," he said into his ear, "you are with me."

"I..."

"Don't let anyone tell you otherwise. You and me. Do you hear?"

Slowly, Firi's arms came around him. "Yes."

The boy had grown so tall that Lace could no longer see over his head. Firi's shoulders came up to his chin. The Halfling build, like full fairy, was long and lean. Firi had that along with the bulk of muscle he'd trained for to get his security job. That, and brains. He was quite the prize.

*

Var came back inside with hats and coats. No one asked where he'd gotten them. One for each of them.

"If you want to blend with the humans, you have to act like one. They feel the cold, and it's fucking cold out today," he said to Lace. Then he grabbed a handful of Lace's long hair, abruptly twisting it up on top of his head and setting a baseball cap on the thick mound. "I've got spare contacts I'll give you later if we need them. But I expect to be at the realm by this Earth's nightfall. In the meantime..." He reached into his coat pocket and brought out a pair of black sunglasses. "Wear them. I don't care if it's night, or cloudy or what."

He turned to Firi. "Found this in your car." It was the second coat. "Guess you were smart enough to pack it since you left rather quickly with nothing in your hands but Lace."

"That reminds me," Lace said and turned away from them, going back into the little bedroom. The fleecy tree-and-snowflake blanket lay on the floor by the tossed bedspread and bunched up motel blanket. He picked it up and folded it into a square, then put it under his arm. Any gift from Firi was important to him. He did not want to lose it.

170

"Okay," Var said, eyeing him when he returned to the front room. "Is everybody ready?" He squinted at Lace. "Got your blankie?"

"Got your surly mask?" He pushed past the fairy and walked outside.

Firi's car was parked in the spot closest to their door. Barely past sunrise, the grounds of the motel were silent. No traffic passed on the outside street, which was clear of snow. The road ran into desolate woodland in both directions, glimmering like black ribbon with tendrils of mist rising from its surface.

As Lace stepped off the curb, something moved in a whoosh above the street and went up. He raised his eyes and saw a white owl nearly invisible against the silvery sky disappear beyond the tree-line.

As Firi and Var stepped out behind him, it was already gone.

*

The wind blew fierce, dark and extraordinary. Extraordinary, that was, because it was the fairy realm and bad storms had not been known there until recently. Rain and clouds hid the moons.

When they left the motel, Var had gotten behind the wheel of the rusty car before Firi could say a word in protest. He drove for six straight hours, with one stop for a trunk full of food for Firi, into mountains and down toward flatter lands. By a snow patched, treeless mesa he abruptly turned off the road and down a dirt path.

"It's all sand. It doesn't have four-wheel drive. We'll get stuck," Firi said at the very moment the world seemed to turn upside-down.

In a heartbeat they were no longer on the mesa. The cold winter afternoon had immediately turned to dark, whipping air.

"This is wrong," Lace said, watching as twigs and other debris hit the windshield.

"No," argued Var, "this is exactly where I was headed."

"This section isn't safe."

"The storms here still come and go. This part has awhile before it completely dissolves."

"Why here," Lace asked, "and not the Crystal Glade?"

Var turned to look at him as more debris hit the car. "Is that where you hang out? Figures. The sunny side. That's you. You always liked those sugar-plum flowers to make garlands for your hair."

Lace said, "At least the storms haven't reached there, yet."

He scowled. "Do you have a place there to take Firi? No. As I recall, your house is gone."

"You had a house that dissolved?" Firi piped up from the backseat.

"I did."

"I'm sorry you lost your house."

"That's the way of it, kid," Var said. "All of us are losing. That's why we moved to your world. But my house is still standing. You can use it. It's been remodeled to death. It can stand the storms here for a few more years. In other words, the roof's not going to fly off or anything. You can use it for awhile until things calm down a little."

Lace had wanted to smack Var for the comments he made about him and the Crystal Glade, but now that Var was offering the use of his home he could not stay angry. Instead, he said, "I didn't know your house was still standing. What do you mean your roof isn't going to fly off? I remember when it was covered with dripping moss."

"Well, that's been gone a long time. And the gardens are pretty much destroyed. Needs landscaping again." He grinned. "The violets and berry bushes and trumpet trees by the wayside turned to ash ten years ago. But the house is intact."

Suddenly, he turned left and pulled to a stop.

Var said, "There used to be a little stone bridge over a creek in the back, but that's all gone."

It was unusual to hear Var talk this way, of creeks and little stony bridges and violets. Lace did not discern any sadness in his voice, but he felt it in the words.

Var went on. "The Twilight Gardens in Four-Patch Sector have been gone since last year. While you were… indisposed."

Lace said nothing but bowed his head. They'd been a favorite, miles of flawless mixtures of fire and life, frayed blossoms red and pink, dragging along ponds green-gold as river nymph hair.

But the details of what Var had lost in the surrounding grounds and hillsides were moot anyway. Where they were now, all Lace could see was darkness, and the headlights of the car shining on nothing but whirls of wind. Then his eyes slowly adjusted and he saw the form of the house in front of them, square with a peaked roof, and what looked like a turret and a chimney. The sides were dotted with smaller, darker squares that glittered now and again. Windows.

Bent dead trees in the distance provided an eerie background.

Var turned the engine off. The wind howled about them. "It's strong, but it won't carry you away."

Lace nodded. They opened their doors.

The wind may have been fierce but it wasn't cold. It carried dots of moisture in small amounts. Rain.

Before them was a stony path. Little weeds shivered here and there among the rocks. Dead, blackened leaves and petals flurried along the ground. Hissing air danced around them.

They unloaded the car and laden with packages, Var led them through the drunken winds to the front door. The wind thieved Lace's hat. Firi yelled as it went flying by him, tried to make a grab for it and failed. It soared off into the wild night and disappeared.

"Leave it," Var called out. "I have more."

Var had been rich even in the fairy realm, hundreds of years worth of accumulated wealth. Lace never knew how he'd gotten it, nor did he ever ask. But he knew Var was meticulous about his house and kept it well stocked of things: clothes, jewelry, bedding and other finery. While their kind didn't subsist on food, Var kept stores of rare wines and other elixirs. He admired the art of it as well as the flavor. Fairies did love their wine from any source.

Lace on the other hand had always been a bare bones sort. Never a hoarder and no mind for money. Var had called him impractical many times in the period they had known each other, as well as other words that were distasteful to Var such as: idler, dreamer.

Var always had "contacts" and "people." Lace had no interest Var's business. How they'd ever gotten together in the first place, meeting, talking, let alone wanting to spend time together was an oddity. They met through mutual friends at a gathering. They spent more time stealing glances with each other than talking. They wasted no time in getting into each other's bed, experimenting with sex and discovering great physical compatibility. But their personalities, they later realized, too often rubbed each other the wrong way. Because the sex was so good, they had some patience. At first. But over time, despite their physical intimacy and obsession, outside the bedroom they drifted away from each other.

But Lace realized now, after these last two nights, they still had an intense fondness for each other that he'd forgotten. And a kind of loyalty that had never been tested until now. It added up to love, even if they'd never used that word with each other before. All of that was part of the blood-bond, of course, but ran deeper still.

As they all three moved through the front door, the wind tried to follow, one last gust so strong it whipped the breaths from their lungs.

It had been a century or so since Lace had been inside this ornate house.

The foyer was small and dim. Var flipped a switch and wall lanterns came on, iron framed glass lamps with little electric flames inside. There were hooks along one wall for outer wraps, coats and hats. Fairies didn't get cold, but they enjoyed fashion and often wore coats and capes and top hats for fun.

The foyer ended at a mahogany archway through which they proceeded to a vast living room with high beamed ceilings, strong oak crossbeams two feet thick, which was why the house had weathered the centuries and the current storms so well. Windows were draped with chintz and velvet, dark golds and purples on one wall, green and black on another. A giant, black-stoned, circular fireplace with a polished chrome chimney towered in the center of the room. Shelves lined one wall, upon which were elaborate candelabra, abstract glass sculptures that looked hewn from the sun, and rows and rows of black-spined books.

The furniture consisted of rock tables, dusty velvet chairs and couches, and one hammock, strung on thick hemp from two I-hooks in the ceiling. That old hammock was large enough to accommodate two. Lace remembered it well. You could nap within it all right with another person, but sex in that thing was out of the question.

Var led them to the kitchen area which was more like a keeping room, a place for household supplies used for cleaning, linen storage. The area had marble counters and a sink for water. Since their kind didn't need food, the cupboards contained mostly glassware, and endless bottles of wine. There was a refrigerator but no stove.

They all placed their bags and supplies on the counter and Lace looked at the groceries and said to Firi, "I'm sure you're hungry."

Firi shrugged, looking slightly out of place.

"I've never had a human here," Var said in a matter-of-fact voice. "You can cook over the fireplace if you want. Or eat your food cold."

Firi said, "I'll be fine."

"We'll be fine here for awhile, Var. Thank you," Lace said.

Var did not look at him. "No one's using the place so it's not like you're putting anyone out. I had a housekeeper but he went to the human realm about a year ago. Hopefully he's not one of the ones they caught and threw in a volcano, but I don't know. Anyway, it's dusty, I see, but things should be fairly livable. I haven't been here in over ten years."

"It's perfect. And it's very generous," Lace insisted.

"The beddings may need changing, whichever of the rooms you decide to use," Var continued, all business, not giving Lace any personal reaction to his graciousness. "Obviously, keep yourselves indoors unless the weather eases up. The back door sometimes won't close all the way. The wind blows it open if you don't lock it. There's no heat or air, of course. If Firi gets cold, light the fireplace. There's wood in the bin out back. At least I think there's still some in there. If Firi needs a bathroom, I have several but they only contain showers and bathtubs. But in the anteroom are planting pots you can use as chamber pots. There used to be a compost out back the gardener used for dumping roots and weeds, but it's gone now, I think. But you'll figure it out, where to dump it, I mean."

"Thanks," Firi said.

Lace and Var had lived together here for a short time, so Lace knew his way around. He remembered much of it, but some things had been changed, renovated.

Var kept up his list of instructions. "You're welcome to any of the clothes in the closets, whatever fits. There's plenty of towels, sheets, blankets, pillows."

Finally, Lace interrupted him. "You are staying, at least for tonight," he said. "Aren't you?"

"Why should I? You don't need me anymore and I have things to do."

"It's dark out there!" Lace pointed out. "You can't walk in this weather! You'll come out the portal on the mesa in the middle of nowhere."

"I'll take Firi's car. I'll come back to check on you in a few days."

Firi was standing with his shoulders hunched. He looked up at the sound of his name. "Yes. You can take the car," he offered.

"Fine, but we've already been on the road more than six hours. And you did all of the driving. Rest here for the evening and we'll make some plans, at least." Lace was getting exasperated. It was as if Var couldn't wait to leave and some part of him deep inside felt hurt at that.

Var let out a loud breath. "I don't need to sleep. And I've got a search to coordinate. For the two of you."

Lace said, "Just for tonight. And you do need sleep after everything I've put you through."

Finally Var looked at him. Suddenly, he winked. "Think you might miss me if I leave? Very well, then. Just for tonight."

The muscles of his body relaxed. He'd won that battle. He wasn't quite sure why it was so important to him that Var stay, but things were moving quickly and he wanted more time. With him. With Firi. And to reassess his abruptly changed situation; going from a prison cell to freedom to a motel room with Var and Firi and then, finally, Var's house all in three long days was a lot to take in.

Also, while his body was fully healed, he still felt shaky, anxious. That was probably all mental, and to be expected, but having Var around, whether Firi liked it or not, gave a stability to things as they were still unfolding.

"So, who will be sleeping where, and with whom?" Var emphasized that last word with a sly half-smile.

Lace watched Firi's face darken with embarrassment, which was, he knew, exactly the response Var desired with his blunt question.

"Firi and I can take the red room," Lace said calmly, as if discussing nothing more important than the color of grass.

Var grinned. "The red room," he drawled. "My favorite."

Firi said shyly, which was rather endearing on a man of his size, "I'd like to look at the books in the next room. What kinds of books do you have here?"

Var glanced at Firi as if he were a child. "Just like your realm, child. Most of them are novels. I've got some on science, too. But they aren't in any language you could read."

"Oh." Firi looked disappointed.

"Var, you have some in English I recall," Lace said.

"I do?"

Lace turned away and began to unpack some of the bags. There was fresh fruit and bread, bags of crackers and chips, canned nuts, cookies, peanut butter and more. Var had bought it all and he hadn't realized until now how generous he'd been in that regard, too. So much variety of food. He'd been thinking of Firi's well-being with more than just a half-thought.

Lace handed Firi an apple and said, "Keep your strength up."

"I'm not that hungry." But Firi took the apple anyway and bit juicily into it.

Var had disappeared deeper into the house. Lace thought he'd heard him go up the stairs to the bedrooms.

Now that they were alone, he turned to Firi. "We'll be okay here."

Firi nodded.

178

The wind threw itself against the walls and windows. Despite the light inside, the darkness and havoc outside made things dim, ghostly. The wail of the storm added a gothic chill.

Between bites of apple, Firi said, "This is very different from the last time I was in your realm."

"Back then, I took you to my favorite place. It's called Neriad's Glade."

"I remember there were faces in the trees."

Lace nodded. "It's one of my favorite memories."

"And the three moons I saw. I dream about them. Raven. Bleak. Wise."

"You remembered their names?"

"I could never forget. They're like a poem. I tried to find them when we got out of the car but the storm is too thick. Or they haven't risen yet."

"I'm glad I remember that last time we were together now."

Firi ducked his head, hiding a smile.

"Two years with no focus, no grounding. I had no idea even who I was. It was a kind of hell I can't describe."

"I could feel your suffering. Here." He put his fist to his own chest. "Sometimes I couldn't think. Couldn't breathe. I came home for winter break from college. I couldn't go back. I'd walk for hours in the freezing weather. I missed you so much." He glanced around the big room, taking a deep breath. "When I saw the news about the guards who were killed I knew you were involved. I saw images. I was sure. I decided right then I'd do anything to get to you."

"Even though they reported I was the one who massacred them?"

"I just knew that if you did it, it had to be for a reason. When I found out the truth, of course, it all made sense. I knew you wouldn't just kill to... kill."

Lace went to him and put his arms on his shoulders. "I'm sorry you felt all that."

"I'm not. We're together now. That's all that matters." Firi leaned into the embrace.

They stood together in the gleaming light of Var's astonishing and luxurious home, listening to each other's breaths, the wind outside like a madman looking to disturb any moment of peace. It crooned and cried.

Lace put his hand on the back of Firi's head, still unused to the shortness of his soft hair. Firi turned to look at him. Lace smelled the sweetness of the apple on his breath, then touched his lips gently to the human's. A warm and stirring smoothness came like cider into his mouth as Firi opened to him and their tongues met. The kiss was slow at first, tender, delicate as whispers or the fluttering of tiny wings.

When it deepened the sensation of falling swept him and though he was the immortal, the stronger of the two, he had the thought that it was Firi's physical strength that kept him upright. He could feel the firm muscles of the man against him, a surging human warmth, the softness of the leather jacket. Unlike immortals, Firi's cheek was slightly rough from missing his morning shave.

He loved the humanness that was Firi combined with the usual Halfling beauty. Salt and tart mixed with the syrupy scent of an unknown ancestor from long ago.

Firi was a rare drink one could never buy, served only by fate.

They pulled back for breath. Firi's grip about him tightened. "I'm sorry you're losing your world. It's wrong… what the humans, my people are doing," he said.

"My people fought, too, when the owl-men came. It's the natural order of things, of life."

"But you weren't trying to change us. Your people were living in secret, keeping to themselves."

"Are you sure? Maybe some of them weren't. Like Var, maybe some infiltrated at high levels and were caught. Maybe

180

you just don't know all the details. The paranoia among your kind is strong. It's not there for no reason."

"But it's my people who were trying to change you, not the other way around."

"I don't know any more than you at this moment."

"But you're a fairy-king, the strongest of your kind."

Lace smiled. "Fairy-king? Maybe I led you to believe that but not so much. I was a sort of leader once among my people. For awhile I was known. Before I met Var. Before all the destruction, before coming into your world. But not anymore. The dramas of organizing others were too heavy. They actually made me weak. As an immortal you have forever to go through every phase over and over. I did that part and I don't want to do it again. I've been a wanderer. A loner. I prefer staying to myself. At least that's how it was the past century."

"I can't imagine it. It's as if you've lived many lives. Like reincarnation, I guess, but without the dying."

Lace nodded. "Actually, a lot like that, yes."

Firi sighed. He leaned his forehead against Lace's shoulder.

"Are you all right, Firi?"

He turned his head and breathed on Lace's cheek. "What will happen? We can't stay here forever. When we go back will we just hide?"

"Well, we can't do anything in the open. What would you want to do if you could, Firi?"

"Stop the war, of course."

The innocence of babes was pure and even divine. But it was naïve.

"What if what happened to my world happened in yours? When the owl-men came, only ten percent of us survived. Would you risk your parents for that gamble, or fight back, fight us?"

In that moment, with that one simple question, Firi's body language changed. He lifted his head and stared into Lace's eyes. "Fight you? But... no."

Lace reached up and stroked back the curls of his bangs. "Well, not me specifically. But for your way of life."

"But your people haven't tried to do anything."

"Not yet. But it's the law of nature. The stronger always subsumes the weaker. You know that, don't you?"

Footsteps came up behind them. "Giving him lessons in conquering, slavery, colonialism, war? Ah, Lace the teacher now. Precious," Var said. "But hasn't he already had high school history?"

They turned to face their host.

A series of emotions flitted across Firi's face, guilt, insecurity, irritation, determination.

"It's why the humans did what they did to Lace," Var continued casually. He went to the fire place in the center of the room and began stacking logs in the center of the circular hearth.

"You were part of that team," Firi said hesitantly.

"Yes." Var did not look up as he made the fire. "I didn't care how they learned the technology. I wanted it for myself. I'm not finished with my war."

Firi blinked. "But Lace was tortured."

"I didn't know it was him." Var lit the tinder. Slowly it took hold and orange and blue flame spread in a tide under the logs. Lace smelled the oak and its sweet resins. Pale red shadows lit Firi's face.

"So you came," Firi said.

"So smart. You think?" He snarled the words in utter sarcasm. "I don't really care who they test the technology on, but I didn't want that for him."

"But you still want the technology," Lace said.

"Of course." Var sat in a plush chair before the fire and stared into it.

"Why do you want technology that kills your own kind?"

"I have my own agendas and they're none of your concern. Don't worry. I'm not going to use them on Lace or any of his friends."

Lace went to the couch next to it and sat. Firi remained standing by the fireplace, seemingly soaking up the warmth.

It would seem, with Var's words, that he might have a soft spot for the humans. But Lace knew better. He did not care about them or their world save what they could give him to complete his immortal vow to kill his maker, even if it took him another thousand years.

Everything eventually rotted. In one hundred years or less, all the people currently populating the Earth in the human dimension would be bone-dust, and their offspring left to carry on. If no more offspring were had by anyone, they would all vanish as if they had never been, leaving behind only ruins and relics, their stories and their ghosts. Nothing lasted.

But no matter what, the fairies would remain. In the deepest seas or volcanoes, still they could not be killed. Eventually they would put themselves back together again and return. They were not going away. And when they climbed out of those hells, they were going to be pissed off.

The technology Var wanted was the humans' best resource and answer to what they faced. And further still, if they could make themselves immortal and the fairies mortal, they could not only survive, they could win the war. At the expense of all of Lace and Var's kind.

Lace knew Var pretty well. People like him did not care about the outcome of anything so small as a war, even if that war included genocide of one side or the other. He didn't think of himself as some "kind" with a label that defined his identity. Revenge pumped his heart and fed his soul.

No matter which way Lace turned, it seemed he faced an enemy. And a lover.

He said, "I'm trying to figure out why you went into their realm so long ago and infiltrated at the military level. You didn't do it to help our kind though the destruction of our world was already beginning. You've never hidden the fact that you have no love for your own people. But you have no love for the humans, either."

Var said, "Before they came up with the serum they gave to you, I wanted their space technology. I still do want that."

"But it's rudimentary at best."

"For now," Var replied. "I have all the time in the universe for that to improve. And it will. Believe me. Mars will be soon enough, then the nearest planetary system after that. And still further."

"The owl-men came in rockets and starships. But you assume they came from space. Everything's dimensions. You know that."

"The humans are resourceful mortals. They'll figure it out, especially now after... us. Our invasion. We've just given them even more incentive to learn all the faster."

They sat before the fire in silence for awhile.

Firi moved about the room slow and methodical, looking at every item, every knick-knack, touching glasses, chalices, little statues carved from precious gems. He seemed fascinated by the books he couldn't read. He pretended no interest in their discussion, but Lace could tell he had been listening intently.

Firi was a Halfling. His loyalties were split. For now he chose Lace. The loyalty of the blood-bond could be no other way for him. But what did Lace want? To throw in with Var and hope for the best? Maybe blend with humans and save a few of their own kind along the way from a technology that was perhaps far too close to being perfected?

What would be his next plan? He had no idea.

The wind circled in abandon. It could only carry dark omens, no matter which angle it was viewed from.

Var got up and served them all wine. Lace could tell he was restless, that he had really just wanted to go. Now he was sorry he had convinced him to stay.

Firi, also, wandered about the room and would not sit still.

Two of a kind. Both of a darker breed that took voids into their hearts.

He wanted to hold Firi again. He thought of their time in the glade. At the pond.

The glamour of the wine made him light-headed. He heard Var muttering, "Other dimensions. If there are so many, why have we only found one?"

His eyelids slowly closed. Firi answered as if from a distance, "How was our world even discovered in the past? When my ancestor mated with a fairy?"

"No one knows. It was happening even before my time. Somehow, our two worlds are connected..."

Lace's sleepy thoughts echoed, *And no one knows why these winds of destruction are falling from the darkest rooms in the sky to end us.*

He did not remember drifting off to sleep.

*

Chapter Nineteen

The windows rattled.

Var had gone upstairs to sleep, vowing grouchily he would be leaving in the morning but that he would come back within three days.

Firi sat with Lace before the fire which was now burning down to golden cinders. Lace could feel the human's nervousness and pulled him to him.

They began to kiss again and under the leather jacket and shirt, Lace could feel Firi's tautness, his unease with the situation. He jumped every time the wind knocked against the house.

Lace said quietly, nuzzling his jaw, "We'll be fine."

"I just expected to feel safer here, in your realm."

"I know."

"Isn't there anywhere else in the realm that isn't like this?"

"It's gotten worse in the past two years. It's unpredictable. I don't think Var expected to find it quite like this, either." Lace stroked the back of his head and kissed him again. The fire in the circular hearth might've been burning low, but the heat between them was increasing. Even after two years apart, it was so easy with Firi. The boy was young and eager. More mature and serious, too, but still quick to blush.

The taste of Firi was addictive: wine and burning and sharp excitement, the trembling sweetness of his young mouth. It was obvious Firi wanted him in return, wanted him badly, but he held himself back, the hand caught between them a fist in his lap.

After a few more minutes of affectionate kissing, Lace asked, "Do you trust me?"

Firi nodded and did not pull away.

"Are you afraid?"

"No."

But Lace smiled at the tremor in the single voiced word. Perhaps it was simply Firi's youth. He'd been such an innocent child, both at ten and eighteen. As a top military security guard he had worked to make himself look bold, acquired a strength and a stance of no-nonsense, even intimidation. But here he was Lace's Halfling, the one who'd been so generous, without a thought to himself or fear from someone different from his kind.

Firi had been programmed to be wary, to fight, but it hadn't ruined him. And the kid had never believed the human-against-vampire propaganda.

He was a unique find. One of a kind.

Lace wanted to return all the favors Firi had ever done for him. Wanted to take him in his arms and just give until Firi was completely and totally his.

"Let's go upstairs."

Firi nodded and when they got up from the couch they saw the fire was almost gone.

The wooden stairs curved against a raw stone wall. The landing was strewn with hand-woven rugs that looked like swirling oceans of emerald and blue. Lace knew the way and led his lover to the room he'd chosen. The red room.

Inside, a double-wide bed took up most of the space. A room to one side held a shower and a small alcove where Firi could see to his needs. Lace noticed that fresh towels and cloths were in place. When he approached the bed he could see it had been freshly made.

Var was a generous host despite his darker, more selfish shortcomings.

The bed was all shades of crimson and fuchsia, and held a canopy that draped twists of sunset silks. Lace could already imagine the beauty of Firi lying amid such finery.

The walls had artwork on them, rich abstracts in earthen tones, golds, reds, ochre. A gorgeous amber sculpture, about two feet high, stood on the bedside table.

All this, Lace realized, would be lost forever. For it was obvious Var had no designs upon moving any of it to the human realm. Lace suspected he had plenty of things like these and more already in the human world.

Firi disappeared for a minute, then returned, his jacket off, his hair a little dampened, bangs pushed back. The red hues of the room swirled about him.

It was all like a dream and Lace embraced him and took him down by his side on the plush bed. Their arms moved around each other. Firi knew how to move. He was a man and he had known what he wanted for years now.

The world narrowed to two bodies and everywhere they touched was what existed: palms against backs, knee to knee, chest to chest, chin to cheek to lip.

Lace reached between them and began to push away the clothes. Firi's shirt came over his head and his bangs fell forward in glistening curls. His chest was firm, tight, the muscles more graceful than bulky with the clothing removed. The olive skin gleamed. Satiny to the touch.

Lace ran both his hands up over his chest until his palms were flat against him. Firi bit back a grin and arched into the touch.

Two and a half years was a long, long time for a twenty-one year old to wait for this.

Firi had always been lovely. Now he was incandescent. His eyelashes glimmered, and when Firi shut his eyes they made black, soft lines on his cheeks.

His brown eyes shone golden in the soft light. His lips were pink, slightly moist... and that sweet smile.

Lace could not help his desire. He would have admired him even without the blood-bond they shared.

If Firi had been nervous before, now he looked not only relaxed, but half melted into the bed coverings. His dark blue pants hugged his hips. He wore a simple belt, easy for Lace to undo.

Firi just leaned back and let him.

188

Lace's hair brushed Firi's chest. Firi lifted his hand and tangled his fingers in the long, brown-black locks.

Before Lace undid the zipper, he leaned down and kissed Firi in the center of his body just above his bellybutton. He ran his fingers in circles just below it, around and around on the smooth skin, feeling it flutter, feeling the stomach muscles move against his fingertips.

He moved his fingers down, pushing open the zipper, and hooked the waistband. Gave a tug. The cloth slid over the thighs smooth, graceful. There was nothing between them, not even undressing, peeling away cloth, that was awkward. As it should be.

Off came the shoes, the socks, and then the dream of Firi lying naked on satins made of lustrous fire became a reality.

When the heart knows it is complete, in those moments every feature of time is immortal. Lace wanted to touch all of him at once, do everything, be everything for him.

He put one hand on Firi's hip, one on the front of his shoulder, leaned down and kissed him for a long time. Firi smiled into his mouth, opened, took him in, explored with his own tongue.

"You're so beautiful," Lace murmured when he turned his head to breathe. He nuzzled Firi's neck, feeling the burr of a day's worth of beard, loving the roughness juxtaposed to the slickness of the chest, arms, waist, thighs.

He moved his head down, licking ribs, a hip, kissing along the outside of one thigh. Firi took deep breaths, and his skin shivered, but otherwise he did his best to remain still.

Lace ran one hand over his hip, brushed his stomach, watched the reaction in his body as his arousal increased.

Firi turned his head to the side, the pillow pressing against his cheek. His eyes closed tight.

Lace brushed down, down and touched the beautiful power of his erection, then moved his hand between his legs to brush the taut sac underneath.

If there was such a thing as fate, they were drawn together by sheer intensity. Somehow, their bodies just knew.

The curl of hair between Firi's legs shone darkly. Lace bent and nuzzled there, then licked up the underside to the softest skin at the tip.

Firi cried out.

Slowly Lace used his tongue to the best of his skills to moisten, to tease, and Firi responded, twisting his hips, drawing in huge lungfuls of air. When he decided Firi had had enough, he sucked in the head and moved slowly down the length.

Firi whimpered. His body undulated. He was losing control.

Lace knew how to help with that, and went painfully slow at first, taking his time, moving down and then up, licking slowly with his tongue as he kept up the lightest of suckling.

He would own this man. This night. And for every night after if it was up to him. If Firi wanted him. And of course he did. He could taste that now. The Halfling had given up his entire life to save Lace, to be here in this moment so alive, so true.

Firi started to try to speak but it all came garbled. Maybe he said Lace's name. Maybe he said he couldn't take anymore. Maybe he spoke a word or two of devotion. It didn't matter the words. Their language was all wrapped up in this act. He could feel the pleasure building for him. Moved faster, tightened his lips.

Firi tried to grab for him. His hand slid against Lace's head. Then nothing more was said as Firi lifted his hips and went still.

The strong pulses of ecstasy filled Lace's mouth. He drank the wine greedily, drawing strength, bliss, love. Finally he heard the gasps, Firi's wrenching breaths, his moans, as he continued to drink.

The moment passed, but it would lead to more.

He pulled the human to him, cradling him, kissing the top of his head. As Firi curled into his chest, Lace whispered, "You beautiful, beautiful man."

Firi said, into his shoulder, "You still have all your clothes on," and began to paw him.

Lace let him removed his shirt, then his shoes, socks and, lastly, his pants. He leaned back among the pillows and let Firi find his way back to him again. Let him explore with his mouth and hands and body.

Firi moved over him, surprisingly heavy and compelling, and rubbed his whole body against him. He kissed the sides of Lace's face and neck, rubbed his cheek upon his chest. He found a nipple and sucked it taut.

Everything just kept getting more amazing as he held this man in his arms. Locked for so long in a single cell, not able to remember faces, names, or any of his past, Lace had been worse than dead. He'd been entirely lost. To life. To beauty. To love.

Here he was whole again. To have Firi made him the most fortunate being.

Firi moved all over him, nibbled and licked his way across his chest, his belly, his hips. He caressed him tenderly between the legs, hands of heat, hands of grace.

"I love your body," Firi whispered.

He covered him with kisses. Lace had never felt so worshipped. Not even with the effortlessly perfect Var.

Firi licked. He took Lace in his mouth. He caressed his hips. Before Lace could even begin to control himself, he was coming and the fierce winds outside were nothing in comparison to his inner world blowing apart, disintegrating and being rebuilt in a matter of summer-gleaming-magic moments. The art of pleasure rarified. He went down, down, then up, up. And into Firi's arms. His Halfling caught him before he fell completely apart.

They lay together, sometimes kissing, sometimes just listening to the storm. After a small silence, Firi tossed his head back and laughed at seemingly nothing. The enclosed room, all the scarlet shades and that relaxed sound was the perfect moment, sealed in a strong house and safe in each other's arms. Lace looked up at the ceiling and thought: *This I will remember forever.*

Firi's laugh echoed through the room, embedding itself into the walls, the curtains, the very foundation itself.

He still had trouble believing everything Firi had given up just to get to him.

I'm still in the prison, he thought. *Locked in a coma inside a dream that isn't even real.*

Edges of silk brushed his face and Firi lay beside him, the laugh finishing with a low, contented sigh. Lace pulled the covers over them, wrapped his arms around his lover and slept.

*

Layers of satin, chiffon and smooth, olive skin pressed to his side. Dreams of rain and purple leaves and the unworn pages of youth tossed into the sky to become the stars. Two Earths. Three moons. Owl-men from a mysterious third realm.

Dreams of green glades before the coming of the winds.

Firi lay in his arms, head tucked into the crook of his neck. His breath was warm against the skin of his throat.

Lace opened his eyes and heard a second's silence between waking and dream before the reality of the storm outside filled his mind. He had been safe for a time, for the night with Firi in the red room, but the truth was they were not safe at all. The storm would not let up. The fairy realm was ripping itself apart from the core of its continuum outward. It seemed to affect the very sun itself, and the moons which some said were being pulled straight down from the sky.

Old ruined moons, a beautiful blue-green world, all destroyed for nothing. For the sake of time's mortality, the passing of one second to the next leaving nothing secure, nothing saved, held, preserved. He could not help but wonder if the human realm would eventually be affected.

Hearing footsteps on the stairs, he sat up.

Firi still slept soundly beside him.

Lace got up and put on his pants and his shirt, then went barefoot to the cold front landing and looked down on the living room.

Var stood at a side window dressed in a long-sleeved gray shirt and black trousers. The dark green curtains were parted, and he stared out at white nothingness. Dawn had come but it had not brought any color; it only dissipated the edge of the darkness. Now the day was white, edged with a great, sorrowful shadow.

Lace came quietly down the curving stairs and moved past the fireplace to the window.

Var did not look at him but they stood side by side, watching the outside chaos. Finally, Var said, "I'm glad I didn't leave last night."

Lace said, "I know."

"I don't think you're safe here for even one more night. It's all breaking away."

"How long since the sun was last seen over your house?"

"When my housekeeper left it was bad then. Maybe a year. More."

"Then we can't stay."

"I thought this place could buy us time. Buy you time. But we have to go back. Return to the human realm."

Lace merely nodded.

"I have houses there. I simply thought it would be safer for you here." He let out a sound of disgust.

"Firi and I have already resigned to ourselves that we'd mostly live on the road."

"Don't fool yourself. That's the quickest way to get caught. Always on the move... you gamble with the odds of being seen by more people, more law enforcement, hell, more soldiers than any other way. You need to stay in one place, indoors, a low profile."

"Locked away again," Lace said under his breath.

Var turned to frown at him. "You're welcome." He spoke that last sarcastically. "I'm only trying to help you, you ass."

"For awhile we can do that. Stay away from the world. Maybe. But no one can live like that."

Var looked annoyed. "Did I say it would be forever?"

Lace reached out and touched him on the arm. "Var. Thank you. For everything you're doing. It's been a long three days."

"I trust you had a good night's sleep? If you slept..." His lip curled up.

"Yes. We slept." Why was he always placating this guy? "The red room is my favorite. As you know."

Var walked to the center of the living room and looked around. "Well, if there's anything here you want... Only what you two can carry, of course. Let's plan on leaving within the hour."

The room and Var blurred before his eyes. He blinked. Var was losing his house. It was a big deal. The house was centuries old. Of course Var would not be comforted. But Lace felt everything deeply. His own losses. Var's. The sacrifices of Firi. The murders of the monsters he'd been forced to destroy.

The house would be mourned. Var would close it out of his mind, but Lace would be the one who wept.

*

Firi choose books to take with them. Lace took the amber-arc sculpture from the red room.

Var took nothing that anyone could see. Memories, maybe. Perhaps not even those.

194

They packed the food and some wine—all that they could fit in the trunk of Firi's plain, unmarked car.

The morning had more rain in it, gray and frosted, and the wind whipped an ocean-like foam about the ruined grounds. There was a kind of weird, gleaming crack in the sky, silvery, like liquid mercury, a river of something gone very wrong.

It was the worst thing they could see. It meant finality. The end. They had hours at most.

When Lace had first become immortal, after a time he had thought about the ending of his world and what it might be like to outlive even that. He thought it would be tens of thousands of years away, or longer. Not a single millennium.

No one had dreamed this day would come so fast with the hostile human world their only recourse.

Lace pulled his hat down tighter over his head, the second cap Var had given him in two days. He didn't mind the cold but he glanced at Firi, bundled in coat and scarf, who had to be freezing.

They all got into the car, Firi in the back, Lace up front, with Var, of course, taking the pilot's seat. How Var could see where they needed to go to hit the portal at the exact center, Lace wasn't sure. He had walked through a dozen portals. He never drove through them.

He was trying to block the grief from his mind while still saying goodbye to the world of his origin. Goodbye to the green shades and the sugar sweet streams. To lavender and golden skylight. To iridescent oceans and jungles, to unbelievable tundra and diamond-dust sand. To the three steadfast, gothic moons: Raven, Bleak and Wise.

Firi leaned forward from the back seat and put a warm hand on Lace's shoulder. "I wish I could've seen more, been here longer."

Lace nodded wordlessly.

The car moved forward blindly into the weird sleet. Almost immediately, the house vanished behind them. It could not be seen through such thick cascades of frozen cloud and mist.

"How can you even know where you are?" Lace asked.

"I just do," Var said confidently.

"Instinct?"

"I guess so. Whatever you want to call it." And in this hell, as if it was all so natural for him, the habitat of his game, he turned and gave Lace a grin.

The whiteness seemed to waver as the car crept forward. Iced raindrops spattered the windows, the drips reflecting the interior dash lights. It was like being pelted by falling stars.

Whatever they were driving over was uneven and slippery. The car bumped and lurched. Could they even make it? Lace remembered leaving the human realm and driving at least half a mile before seeing Var's house. A half a mile was a long way in a slipping, sliding car going five miles an hour over a wrecked landscape.

Var made an abrupt turn. Everything still looked the same. A mist from behind which spots of blackness seeped through.

He said, "I think I see..." But the car jumped forward and he cut himself off as he swerved, touched the brake once, then pushed hard on the gas. The motion pushed Lace hard into the back of his seat. He heard Firi whisper a curse.

Var turned again. They bumped along for a few seconds, hitting unseen things so hard with the tires it seemed the car would break apart.

A sudden flash of light blinded Lace for half a second. When it was gone he still saw only the white, pelting rain. The haze like churning ghosts. Then the flash returned. Sharper this time. For almost two seconds.

"What is that?" Lace asked.

"The portal. But the car is skirting it."

"I don't remember seeing light like that before."

Again, the broken light cut through the car so bright Lace had to close his eyes.

It had been easy to go through the other way, last night, from the daylight clarity of the human realm and into the darkness. Though the fairy realm's storm hit them hard, it was still more like driving through a night of strong winds. Var knew the way by heart. But going back was harder, through too-thick fog and directionless winds.

This time the light remained for the count of ten. It switched off, but came back strobing, then staying bright as they kept inching forward, the wheels rattling, the car shuddering as if about to die.

Without warning, the car slid to the side and light danced all around them. Lace felt Firi grip the back of his seat. The car fishtailed and then it felt as if they were falling.

The car landed, jerking them forward and the intensity of the brightness actually stung their eyes.

They were all blinking when they came out onto the sandy trail that had led them here, an empty mesa at the edge of a mountain in the human realm where it was just coming up dawn, the sky a pale green above an orange stripe to the east where the sun was budding.

It took a moment for Lace's vision to clear. He blinked away abstract after-images from the portal's bright tunnel. He'd not experienced that before. All his portal passages had been three-step, easy efforts. One moment he would be on one side, then he'd experience a blurry disorientation while taking two steps, and the next moment with his final step he'd be on the other side. No side affects. No blinding, wrenching light.

That was how the portal was in the field behind Firi's parents' house.

Still blinking, half-blinded, he wondered why he was hearing Var swearing under his breath.

Chapter Twenty

The car came to an abrupt halt. Lace was still only focused on the dawn-smeared sky. He was the last one to notice the darker shapes on the sand nearby, like rocks, only shinier. A solid blockage between them and the desert highway.

Too quickly, the shapes took on grim meaning.

Black Jeeps surrounded them. Soldiers stood alongside their vehicles, weapons drawn. They were silhouetted against the early morning like a stain upon an otherwise perfect canvas.

A moment of panic, not for his own life—he could not die—but for Firi, who was most definitely mortal. And for Var to be caught like this, he could not imagine what the consequences would be to his own personal plans and agendas.

All Var had worked for, whether Lace agreed with it or not, would be destroyed. Because of him.

Firi whispered, "Oh my god."

Var's words continued to be unrepeatable.

Lace himself remained utterly mute.

Someone on a loudspeaker system ordered them to exit their vehicle in a loud, tinny voice.

Var said, "Dammit. I recognize at least three of these people. They can't know I'm with you or years of my work will be ruined."

"If we don't get out of the car, they'll probably shoot," Firi said. "I don't recognize any of them yet but I know how they operate."

"Me, too," Var agreed.

Lace said, "Let them imprison us. We'll just escape again."

"They won't make the same mistakes," Var said. "They'll put us away under the sea and we'll be stuck for decades. Or burn us. It will take decades to reconstruct from that as well. Besides, I have a position to maintain at all costs."

The voice on the loudspeaker repeated its demand.

"All costs?" Lace asked. His heart beat faster. He and Var had two totally different ways of dealing with conflict. He did not like Var's ways at all. And he remembered now that was why they'd drifted apart, left each other to live separate lives.

Var looked at him, dark eyes still and cool. "Any cost."

Firi said, "What are you going to do? What can you do?"

"I can say you're my prisoners."

"Sell us out?" Firi's tone rose. "After rescuing us both?"

"Do it if that's what you need to do," Lace said.

"Always so noble," Var said in disgust.

"I'd give you that," Lace said, "because I know you'd help us again. You wouldn't leave us to rot." He realized he was angry at himself because he couldn't help but feel he owed Var for helping him and Firi. He just hadn't realized he'd be paying him back so soon.

"Don't be so sure," Var replied.

The voice over the speaker said, "If you do not comply with our demand, we will open fire on your vehicle."

Lace said, "That's it. I'm surrendering. I don't want Firi hurt."

"They'll hurt me anyway." Firi's voice shook.

"I'll see to it they don't," Var said.

"By making us your prisoners?" Lace asked.

Var didn't answer. He opened his door. Lace opened his. He did not hear Firi move, but hoped he was doing the same.

Var called out to the crowd of uniformed men and their black Jeeps. "Okay! Okay! We're surrendering! Don't shoot! Don't shoot!"

The car was parked facing the searchers head on. Lace and Var revealed themselves simultaneously. Now Lace heard Firi's door open behind him.

"Hands up!"

They all raised their hands to show they were unarmed. Then a voice said, "Colonel Varae?"

Lace said quickly, "He caught me and was transporting me back to the facility."

The man who spoke Var's human name stepped forward. It was Evan. Frowning. Looking from Var to Lace and then to Firi.

"This soldier, one of your guards, was helping me," Var said, indicating Firi with a tilt of his head.

"But you came through the portal just now. We saw you."

"Yes, we did."

"And Firi is seen on all the camera footage helping Lace escape."

"Yes, they were together. I followed them both."

"But humans don't know where the fairy portals are. We've searched and never found them."

"I followed Lace and Firi through this one."

Evan took another step closer. "Without updating us? Without back up?"

"I had no time."

Lace saw Var twitch. The darker fairy was the best liar he knew, but this lie was getting thin. Thinner. It had started out transparent. Var stood up straighter. "Take these men into custody now," he ordered.

No one moved.

Evan said, "With all due respect to your rank, sir, anyone who comes through a fairy portal to Earth is to be immediately arrested. I will have to take *you* into custody. You'll be debriefed and if all is well, let go."

Var's shoulders tightened. Lace watched him, taken out of reality for a moment in utter fascination at the energy of him, how he exuded himself past the boundaries of his physical body and into the space surrounding them. He was a palpable presence, and the other men behind Evan were focused only on him.

He said, "Of course I'll be debriefed. But taking me into custody will not be necessary."

Evan was the only one not to be deterred. He had a personality of his own that was larger than life. Lace was all too familiar with it from the endless days he spent with the man in the interrogation cell. Evan did not ruffle easily.

Smiling, Evan said, "It's policy. I'm sorry but it can't be avoided. You're with these two criminals. They are not cuffed or otherwise detained. You can see how it looks, sir."

"They came willingly." It was a weak retort and Lace knew Var knew it.

"All right. But the policy—" He did not finish his sentence. Instead, he turned his attention on Firi.

"What a disappointment you turned out to be."

Firi said nothing. Lace wanted to reach out to him. But he did not move.

"A human helping a vampire? What could make someone--?" He swallowed as if he'd tasted something bad. "It's deplorable. An atrocity. Do you know what happens to humans like you? And what do you think your friends will go through? Ivana and Chaz. Guilt by association. They'll be dishonorably discharged if not brought up on charges for collusion themselves."

To Lace's surprise, Firi took a single step forward and said through gritted teeth, "Go to hell."

Someone behind Evan called out, "Vampire-lover!" More voices joined that one until there was a chorus of lewd yells.

"Enough!" Var shouted.

Lace said loudly, "We surrender. Take us in. What more do you want?"

"We want all vampire blood-suckers dead!" Someone shouted.

Var continued. "I told you they came with me peacefully. The guard Firi helped me convince the vampire to come with us. So let's go. Get this over with."

Evan raised his weapon again. "On the ground."

Lace fell forward on his knees, his hands still raised. Firi knelt beside him.

Var still stood in front of the car Firi had purchased such a short time ago. Their escape car.

"Var…" Lace started, then stopped. He could see the stiffness in his back, the dominant posture. Var was not going to easily kneel, not for anyone.

"Colonel," Evan said, the words slow and even. "On. The. Ground."

"You think you have authority over me?" Var's voice was low. You could practically see the words come out of his mouth, black, deadly, dangerous.

"In this situation, I have the back up. I'm bringing you in."

"You think I don't have back up?"

"I don't see any."

"You don't see it?" Var teased.

Now Evan's eyebrows lowered. If he wasn't suspicious before, he was now.

"Var," Lace said under his breath, barely a whisper.

Firi's breath came fast and shaky.

The sun bulged against the distant mountain range to the east, blood-orange. Far-off in the valley a bird screeched. Maybe an owl. An image Lace dreamed of often, but not with any hope. Not anymore. After a thousand years no trace of the aliens could be found. They had no way to go to the stars to

202

look. And the only other realm they'd ever known of was the human one.

Maybe two stubborn, commanding species were never meant to live together. Maybe that was why the owl-men had left as quickly as they came, even after Lace's people, the survivors, were transformed. They left because they'd created beings as powerful as themselves, and both species could not occupy the same space.

Evan's voice echoed through the green air. "On the ground."

Var was not going down. Lace realized it too late. Everything Var had said, including words of surrender, had been lies from the outset. Var was set to fight.

Oh god… no.

He heard Evan say, as if from far away, "I will order my men to shoot."

"I'm afraid that won't be possible," Var said calmly.

"And why not?"

"I'm faster."

*

In the vanishing glow of oncoming night, Var was as beautiful a being as he'd ever seen. Standing before the floor-to-ceiling window, he was cut of the void itself. His long hair became the dark reaches of beyond. No one could grasp him. He would not allow a deeper mental touch. Physical, yes. He allowed that. Sex was easy with Var. He was so good at it. But he still set himself apart. In his eyes, even when they were conjoined, he drifted. Their bond from sharing the autumn wine told Lace this. Not in words, but in the haunting strains of emptiness that played about his heart after he was with Var.

The ecstasy of love-making was always supreme, but afterwards the hollowness inside came more from just craving or continued desire. That was Var's grief and Lace could not share it.

Var would not allow it. Var held himself bitter. Separate. A strong determination no fairy could ever hope to break.

He was the loveliness of a night flower that had been picked too soon, murdered and left to a slow withering in a jar of lukewarm water.

Lace wanted to save him, press him between the pages of his mind.

Var would not be caught like that, nor in any other way. Ever. It made him unpredictable. Some called that dangerous.

It made him capable of anything darkly necessary, without compunction or second thoughts.

What Lace knew, and Var did not, was that every cruel thing Var did only hurt himself more deeply. Only bruised the soul more.

For people like Var, there was never hope of returning from that long lost dark.

The night rolled over them both, revealing itself but hiding them each from the other.

*

I'm faster.

The words echoed on the morning air, meaningless to the humans, communicating all-encompassing disaster to Lace.

Var stood with his fingers curled into fists. The energy rushed off his skin in blue streaks, invisible to human eyes but not to fairy.

He knew without any doubt what Var was about to do.

Lace moved before he could even think, and the red horizon tipped as he lunged toward Var with a cry that broke free of his throat with his entire will behind it.

"Noooo..."

I'm faster.

It was true. Var was superior. And Lace? Well, Lace was simply not fast enough.

204

*

Var said, "Leave me." He moved to the door and opened it, wincing at the golden sun, the world in its outdoor glamour that Lace so loved.

"Come with me," Lace said.

"Leave!" came the command again. "Just get out!"

A bit annoyed, Lace said, "Fine. You want to be alone, then be alone."

"I want you gone; that's what I want."

Lace touched him on the curve of his elbow. Var moved away from the touch. "The fuck you think you're doing?"

Lace laughed. "You're not really kicking me out."

"I am."

Still smiling, he said Var's name in the tone he knew Var could not resist.

Unmoved, Var said, "You're always trying to change me. Fix me. I didn't ask for that. I don't now. You think there's something in me to save? That you, in your prick-arrogant assumptions can make better, oh, soothe away the fucked up rough spots?" His voice had gotten sarcastically high-pitched, sickly shrewd. "I don't want that. I don't want you."

They always fought. Sometimes words were harsh. This time Lace did not want to look, see the difference. How lost Var was. How enamored of his identity as being only skeletal remains. A reanimated set of cells and blood and something beating that might once have been called a heart.

He didn't cry as he walked out, hearing the door slam and lock behind him.

He didn't cry until months later when he realized what they'd both lost.

*

He felt the punctures before he heard the pops. In his shoulder, thigh, chest. The zinging pain. The shattering. The recoil from his body's shock at being hit took him down before his hands could reach their target. His hat went flying. Sand crunched against his hands and cheek. His fingertips had grazed the edge of Var's coat, unfelt, useless, one more failure in his repertoire with Var.

Firi cried out, a shattering shriek that rent the air.

He leapt up to go to Lace when another pop came and Firi came down with a hard, fast grunt.

Var became a blur of midnight blue.

Lace blinked. Trying to follow what was happening with his eyes. To watch the horror.

Firi lay against his side, struggling in confusion, trying to speak. Firi. His love. He could feel the hit in the Halfling's side, not life-threatening but still painful. Shocking.

And all he wanted to do was protect him. But something wasn't right. He couldn't move.

And then there was Var.

Moving through the Jeeps parked all in a row. Fast as a dark wind. The darkest. Six men, all holding their weapons up but unable to do anything with them. Or anything about Var, who went quickly from one to the other to the other, snapping their necks. Letting them fall.

They had no idea what had hit them. They had not even had time to blink. Now they slumped in lifeless sacks of military grade uniforms on a day the fairy realm was beating itself to death with unleashed power, on a day when the sky of Earth was just turning to light pink and the world began anew.

"Firi," Lace managed to say. His body felt heavier than the sun. His fingers moved slightly, clutching grit.

A shadow came over him and he looked up. Six feet away, Var crouched over the final man who knelt in the sand weaponless now, one arm twisted to the breaking point behind his back.

Evan kicked once at the sand. He said, "You're one of them." He looked up at Var, blond hair pink-tinged from

206

sunrise, mouth agape at the tall man, the Colonel who matched him in rank, and who now held him in his grip.

The land was desolate around them. A plain swept by time.

They were but tiny creatures upon it swatting at each other.

Var said calmly, "Well, sometimes. It's a funny story."

"But you're peaceful beings. You don't kill." He tried to glance behind him, but Var had him in too strong a grip. "You can't kill me."

"Well, I don't know about myself, but Lace is peaceful, and knowing that, you still did what you did to him."

"You were on the committee that sanctioned it!"

"Hmm, yes. It is a very interesting technology."

"Var," Lace tried to speak. He saw all the dead men and knew that one more would not bother the dark fairy. "Don't."

Of course he was ignored.

Firi was trying to speak, listen to what was going on around them, and reach for Lace all at the same time. He could feel the boy straining not to pass out.

Evan said, "Why?"

Var just looked at him. Then he said, "I don't think you're really a bad man."

"I'm not."

Var gave a little smile. "But I am." He put his hand gently on the back of the human's neck.

Lace heard a crack, heard Firi give a tiny whimper. He closed his eyes but the dawn bled through his lids, so much red.

*

He saw Var several times after he'd left for good. In the big olden city north of the Urgent Sea. Hurrying through the crowds.

Disappearing into buildings the color of clouds. Losing himself. Vanishing. Always distant. Then gone.

After awhile, Lace turned away from any thoughts of him. Var was lost for good.

Until he met Colonel Varae—

*

He couldn't move. He saw red in the sand. *Firi!*

But the boy was moving, not dead.

Lace gasped as he felt arms move under and around him, lifting him from the ground. He tried to reach out. He didn't want to be taken from Firi.

He thought he heard Var say, "Now look what you've done. Always getting yourself into these scrapes lately. Lucky I'm around."

"Var…" He wanted to tell him… what? To leave him and Firi here, walk away? That he could not be a party to these murders? Always on the run now? The wrong focus for this evil war?

But too late. He already was. Guest and main course. Var was shoving him into the car's rear seat.

And anyway, Lace had the wrong focus for over two years now. He had no reputation to save. The humans already thought he was a vicious murderer. The instigator of a famous massacre, the banner for the human's war.

"Good thing I have an unlimited supply of the autumn wine," he heard Var say.

He couldn't even lift his head. He'd been shot three times. One of the bullets must've hit his spine. That was why he couldn't move yet. It was healing too slowly.

He could see in the window's reflection Var move over Firi, help him stand. The two men came to the car, Firi's head so low his chin touched his chest.

After Var got Firi into the front seat, he left the car and walked away. Lace let his eyes close again. He didn't know for how long, but after a haze of gray nothingness, he heard Firi talking.

Firi was saying, "He took them away. He took them away."

"What?" Lace asked.

"He drove off in one of the Jeeps with all the bodies. Why?"

Making them disappear. He didn't say it out loud. But he knew Var. He was covering his tracks. All their tracks. It would look as if the men just vanished. Any other evidence would also be destroyed, camera devices, cell phones, anything that might record the incident. Not a scrap would be left behind of human remains. Even the blood Firi had dripped into the sand would be scuffed out, along with all footprints.

Only the Jeeps would stay like some modern Stonehenge to an unsolved mystery. They would be found abandoned with only the wind ghosting through their metal frames.

Firi had stopped talking. Maybe he rested. Maybe he slept.

Lace felt his life pulsing, still strong, through their blood-bond, so he knew Firi was still alive. If he focused he could hear the boy's slow, pain-tinged breaths. The windows had turned orange.

Maybe it was all a dream and they were still in the portal, still in that strange, blinding light, stuck there between time, between the seconds of now and then when all who had ever died were not alive but not yet dead. When all possibility existed at once. He wished for it with all his heart.

He didn't know how long he and Firi lay half-passed out in the car before Var returned. He startled when the driver's door opened. He saw Firi jerk in surprise.

Var climbed into the car and said, "And I thought the portal passage was rough. You two still with me?"

Lace said, "Firi. He needs help."

"You both need help." He sighed. "Again." And started the car.

"Var…"

Var said, "Lace." As if that was the answer to any question. Every question. Or maybe it was just a warning, saying his name to shut him up.

He wanted to ask where Var was going. He wanted to know why he wasn't afraid. But he could never remember a time when Var was afraid. Only angry. Impatient. Disgusted.

If things weren't horrifying enough, Var took out a cell phone and began to talk. Lace heard him ask someone for updates on the search. Lace knew he was making them tell him everywhere they were searching. Then he suggested they look at a few places hundreds of miles from where they were. He said, "I don't care what it takes or how much it costs. Find them. And someone get Evan on the phone for me."

His voice remained calm. He had never broken a sweat. He wasn't even breathing hard. When he said Evan's name, even though he had just killed the man, his tone never faltered.

For a fairy to kill and not feel the great energy repercussions of that act was unthinkable. Crazy.

Var had saved them. Again. And he had saved himself. Everything was as it had been for Var before the day of Lace's prison escape. Var was still Colonel Varae. He still gave orders concerning the war against the feared vampires intruding on the human world. He used government dollars and expertise to develop technology for his own devices. He was insidious. He was brilliant.

In that moment, he was the most dangerous man in the world.

Now Lace and Firi were relying on him to get them to immediate safety. And administer medical help.

The back seat had a rise in the middle that pushed against Lace's side. The pain of the wounds in his body were already fading, but that hump was terrible. He could not sit up. He still could not move more than his hand in a slight wave or his leg in a slow, straightening effort. A spinal injury for sure, it was healing slowly. To fully and quickly recover, he would need the autumn wine again. Or remain laid up for a couple weeks.

The car bounced on the dirt road, finally finding its level when they came to the asphalt highway.

He wanted to ask how far they had to drive before they were safe. Instead, he closed his eyes and his mind fell into a white fog where the air smelled like the musty back seat of a car.

He dreamed he stood on a windswept moon in the arch of a stone doorway. Behind him spread a plain of black sand and rocks scintillating in bare, bright starlight. Before him rose a city-sized field of obsidian spires of varying heights, piercing the sky with their Victorian needle-point steeples.

The air howled and the strength of it blew his long hair forward, whipping his face and eyes.

He was at the center of some stony ruin. Automatically, he reached out to touch the hard edge of the door-shaped structure. Cold. Smooth. Like worn marble left to the grinding teeth of time. The touch grounded him and he bent his head back to the clear black sky. Either the stars began to wheel, or he grew dizzy. For a moment he wasn't sure.

The stars began to whirl faster, then to fall, leaving trails of white light through the sky, first one, then two, then dozens, hundreds.

He felt a pressure and the ground shook. Then he heard a succession of pops followed by a screeching roar loud enough to rent the very foundations of existence itself.

One by one the sharp spires rose into the oil-black sky on tails of cadmium and turquoise fire. He watched them ascend, a collection of tall, dark bullets rushing to break the night.

A powerful combination of wind and shockwave nearly knocked him over. Soot and grit and the acrid bloom of finality poured through him.

Something gripped his shoulder.

"We're here," Var said.

Chapter Twenty-One

Var carried him like a baby. He could not describe the ecstasy of his relief when he saw Firi to one side, on his feet, able to walk although he was hunched in pain.

Above him, as they moved up a slight incline, Lace saw tall pine trees and a silver sky.

Var walked into the shadow of a structure. Another house that Var owned. Another place to wonder if he and Firi would ever feel safe again.

Somehow, Var got the door open and the silver-white sky vanished and he was in some place darker that smelled of lemon-wax and dust. He heard Var say, "The car can go in the garage later where no one will see it, though they aren't looking for that make and model. So far. They have no idea what we were driving."

Maybe Var had read his mind about feeling safe or not. But for now he decided he could relax. Var, when he put his mind to something, finished the job. He had decided to help them. He would see it through because that was what he did. He would not let down Lace or Firi.

Lace had never known the Var (or Varae) of the human realm. This house he'd taken them to was unfamiliar.

The living room they went through was mostly white and brown with accents of color, a blue couch with green throw pillows, lamps with pale, green-gold shades, a chandelier twinkling gold and silver crystals.

Var moved quickly into a large room, mostly white, with a huge four-poster against the center of a wall. A lavender comforter covered the bed; the pillows were white and blue. It seemed odd how gentle Var was when he set him down upon it.

The coolness of the material surrounded him. Pillows cushioned his neck and head. He closed his eyes but opened them quickly when he heard Var say brusquely. "Don't just stand there. You look like you're about to faint."

Firi stood on the other side of the bed, eyebrows narrowed, jaw tight.

"Firi," Lace said quietly.

Firi sat but looked decidedly uncomfortable. "I know you have to heal him," he said to Var, nodding in Lace's direction.

Var had his arms crossed over his chest. "Yes. And you as well."

Firi looked at Lace with alarm.

"How bad is it?" Lace asked.

"Not bad," Firi said, but Var wasn't listening. He moved to stand over him and pushed him back onto the bed. "Show me."

"But you have to see to Lace," Firi argued, clearly not wanting Var to touch him.

"Lace is immortal. You're not."

Before Firi could move, Var was pushing back his jacket, pulling the shirt out of his pants. Firi winced but did not make any sound.

Lace still could not move his body, but he could turn his head. He watched as Var pulled Firi's coat off, ignoring the fact that the human was uncomfortable, not fighting, but not cooperating, either.

Jacket off, Firi pushed himself back onto the pillows beside Lace as Var tugged his shirt up. A bloody wound was revealed on his side, thin red streaks circling a darker, shiny circle just beneath the ribs.

Var put both hands on either side of the wound and Firi gasped.

"Relax," he said, sounding bored. "I have an M.D. I even did a year's internship. It was a long time ago but I think I can handle this."

214

"I didn't know that," Lace said.

Var looked at him. "Why should you?"

"Will Firi be okay?"

"The bullet is still inside. Not sure why it didn't go right through him. Maybe because he's a Halfling. Well, it's gonna be fun getting it out."

Firi's eyes went wide and his face went from its normal olive coloring to a ghostly shade of gray.

Var may have gone to medical school at some point in his decades in the human realm, but he had to have skipped the lessons on beside manner. Poor Firi looked like he was about to throw up.

When Var left to gather the supplies he would need, Lace said, "Firi. You'll be fine. He's horrible, I know. But he's not going to deliberately hurt you."

"No?" Firi's voice shook despite trying hard to keep his fear from showing. "He's doing this for you. He doesn't care about me."

"He's different, I know"

"Different? What he did back there was a nightmare. I still can't believe it."

"What he did was save us. You're trained to do the same thing. Only to us."

Firi moved his hand up and touched Lace's arm. "I know, but I just can't think about it right now."

Lace felt Firi's hand stroke down until their palms met. He wove their fingers together.

Var came back into the room, arms laden with towels, clean cloths and bandages, a black bag and a bowl of water. He'd removed his jacket and the sleeves of his shirt were rolled above the elbows. He shoved some books off the nightstand and set everything down. He looked at their clasped hands but said nothing. The wound was on Firi's right side. Lace lay to his left.

The room sat awash in a chill, cold light. Var went to the wall and turned on the heat, then came around the foot of the bed to stand beside Lace. "I know," he said. "You want to be close to him." There was nothing in his eyes to show compassion, but he gently tugged Lace up on the pillows and closer to Firi so that their shoulders touched.

Var said to Lace, "He's going to be gripping your hand pretty fucking hard in a minute." He lifted Lace's arm and placed both their hands between them, supported by their hips.

Firi's palm was damp. His hand shook. Lace wanted to do more for him. Wanted to move. It was infuriating. He had to trust that Var would get this over with as soon as possible.

Now Var brought a chair over to Firi's side of the bed. Without preamble, he quickly wet a cloth and cleaned the wound. First with water. Then with disinfectant from a bottle in the bag.

Firi's mouth was tight, his eyes closed. Just that touch so obviously hurt him.

Var took a pair of gloves and what looked like long, curved tweezers from the bag. Firi opened his eyes, saw them and shuddered.

"Var, damn it," Lace muttered. He was teasing the boy, it seemed.

"Oh, you didn't think I was going to use this without numbing you first, did you?" After putting on the gloves, he took a syringe out of the bag, and another bottle. "This will hurt but not as much as it would without the local."

Firi nodded tightly. He was breathing fast and shallow.

Var said, "Hey, now, don't go into shock on me."

"Relax," Lace said, gripping his hand hard. "Just a shot, okay? Then you won't feel it."

Firi shut his eyes and said in the tiniest, breathiest voice for such a big, muscular guy, "Okay."

Firi tensed as Var administered the needle. It looked like he was making Firi into a pin cushion but it was necessary. An antiseptic scent burned the air.

216

Firi's stomach muscles quivered. Lace wanted to reach out, pet, stroke. He was helpless. Instead, he used his voice. "Look at me, Firi. Look at me. And listen to me. You're going to be fine. And then I'll be healed and we'll stay here for awhile. It will be okay."

But Firi did not look at him. He kept his eyes closed, the lashes like dark lines on his high cheekbones. His face still looked gray. His forehead was dotted with tiny glints of sweat.

Finished, Var tossed the syringe on the floor. He poked with a gloved finger around the wound. "Feel that?" he asked.

"Just pressure," Firi whispered.

Some blood oozed down his side. Var took a cloth and wiped it away. He took another cloth dampened with water and ran it over Firi's forehead.

It was ironic, almost comical, to see this side of Var after what they had just witnessed earlier, the quick and massive massacre, the seemingly emotionless Var carrying Lace to the car, then the hauling of bodies far away to disappear in the sands of the mesa just outside the fairy portal.

Var's behavior was like that of some blind god following a mindless path to ruination because of some distant focus of agenda from which he could not break away. He worked like a tireless machine, a fairy-android, programmed to get a job finished and nothing more.

His gentleness with the half-naked Firi, as he took up the surgical tweezers and held cotton to the side of the wound, came from practice not empathy.

But there were times when the distance in Var's eyes warmed, when he looked caught up in a moment, almost choked, and his eyes would dart around suspiciously, curiously as if he'd just woken from a long dream. Lace had seen it flash once or twice just the other night when Var had healed him, when their sex turned the corner into actual lovemaking. And it had been that. Love. The blood-bond was no trifling fancy. It was not a feeling that just came and went like a tide. It might fade with time, but it always remained. A tattoo on the heart. A ghost-twin wandering its lover's soul.

Firi made the mistake of opening his eyes as the tweezers pushed into him. His eyebrows flew up and if possible his pallor became a deeper gray.

The hand gripping Lace's went limp. Firi's eyes closed and his body slumped further into the mattress. His throat and shoulders gleamed with cool sweat. The rise and fall of his chest was barely discernable.

"He's passed out," Lace said.

Var grunted but kept digging and did not look up.

"Var..."

"It's probably for the best that he's not awake for this. Just give me a second here," he said calmly.

But shock was dangerous. Any M.D. should know that. "Did you really do an internship or were you just trying to placate him?"

"Would I lie?" Var asked, still working inside the wound. "Besides, where do you think I got all this stuff?"

Lace didn't answer. Of course Var, rich and with connections, could've gotten those supplies anywhere.

Not being able to move was infuriating. He wanted to take Firi into his arms, hold him tight as he was being cut into. Feed him the autumn wine. Then all would be right. He wouldn't have to think. He could just have him close, as close to his heart as he could get, hands on his back, lips in his hair. Pulses entwined, synchronized.

He could feel the slick fingers against his own. The coolness of perspiration against the rising heat of his skin. The space between them had grown far too hot. And Firi's lips, slightly open, were an almost blue-white coloring.

A tremor, a tight pull on the mind... that was how the bond between them usually reacted, but now there was a slackness, and a disturbing silence. More than silence, Lace sensed a kind of scouring emptiness begin to encroach.

"There," Var said, firm voice breaking through Lace's daze. Var held up the forcep-tweezers which had succeeded in capturing a dark and blood-drenched bullet. He tossed it in some bloody rags and took up a new rag and methodically cleaned the wound.

"I won't stitch him. I have this newfangled stuff. Very cool. Dissolving glue."

"Var, something's wrong. Listen to me!"

Var looked up at Lace, then turned to glance at Firi's face. "Hmm, he doesn't look so hot." He took off one bloody glove and placed the back of his hand on Firi's forehead. He lifted first one eyelid, then the other. He pushed the tips of his fingers against Firi's throat and counted his pulse beats.

"Hmm, thready. Not good."

"What...?"

Before Lace could finish his question, Var said, "Firi! Firi, boy. Wake up! Do you hear me?"

He sat back on the edge of the bed. Over Firi's form, his eyes met Lace's. "You're little Halfling is so sensitive. It was just a flesh wound."

Lace knew what Var's words really meant. This wasn't right. Firi was crashing. They didn't need words. Discussion. Opinion. Dissention. Lace's regret mattered little in what faced them, what had to be done.

He watched as Var drew out the fancy little silver knife. The one they'd used together only two nights ago. It sparkled in his hand like a caught star. Flickered and glowed as his long fingers flipped it over and over in his hand. His top lip curled up, showing white teeth, the smile containing a sinister curve, but also faultless impeccability. If there had been a mirror before them, maybe he would've seen the smudges of Var's own deeper wounds beyond the flesh, the cracks of his malignity. The owl-men, in their intrinsic grief of their nature to destroy in order to catalyze evolution, had filled Lace with love in the same way they had filled Var with mourning.

It wasn't fair.

Now he searched for that darkness in the man who stood over Firi, felt it edging his mind through their bond. But what he saw was nothing out of order about him, not even a hair out of place.

The room blurred as warmth filled his eyes. Lace looked away to the ceiling. He said, quiet, low, "If you do it with your blood..."

"I know, I know. He'll bond to me. It's why I didn't do it to begin with. He's yours. He is afraid of me. Ah, what an annoying distraction that will be." He let out a sharp laugh. "You know your own blood won't be sufficient. You're too weak right now. But don't cry over it, my dear. He'll still belong to you." There was amusement in that voice as he added, "Too."

Lace said nothing.

"You wouldn't have me let him just slip away, would you?" Var asked.

"No!"

But he knew after Firi discovered what saving his life meant to his own psyche, to his bond with Lace which would no longer be exclusive, he might not thank him for it.

Maybe later he would understand Lace's only thought: Firi, at twenty-one, was too young to die.

Var sliced cleanly, gracefully through the skin of his forearm. Golden blood filled the valley of the cut. He looked once at Lace, who tightened his lips in determination.

Var took that as the final answer and settled next to Firi, taking his dark head against his chest and pressing his arm against the slack and bluish lips.

Firi lay limp in Var's arms. Lace had lost the grip on his hand and his fingers curved over air. He could not look away. Both fascinated and afraid. He need to watch, to be sure that Firi responded. He could not lose his Halfling. Not so soon, so young, and despite everything he'd been through, still so innocent to the world.

He watched as the blood glistened in copper drops upon the pale, motionless mouth.

Var held him in place, balanced and still, and let his blood slowly seep over the fleshy ridge of lips, past the teeth and onto the moist tongue. Nothing happened. Firi barely breathed. He didn't move to suck. It was taking too long.

Var bent his head forward, made a small sound like a hum, touched his chin to Firi's hair. He was doing this not for Firi, but for Lace. Because of their own blood-bond, no matter the distance in their lives from each other, Var would not abide harm or pain to come to Lace.

It was why he'd come to the secret complex in the first place. Lace believed him when he'd told him he had not known Lace was the test subject for experiments to turn immortals into mortals.

A whisper waved over the delicate ends of Firi's hair. "Come on, little Halfling, drink the sweet gold wine. You'll like it. Drink."

Lace tried to will it through the bond.

The blood pressed into the still mouth. Too still, until as if by some miracle, he thought he saw a shift in the muscles of the jaw, the rigid throat. The cheeks hollowed very slightly. Finally the edges of Firi's mouth twitched.

Firi began to suck on the blood, pull it into his mouth, and then he was swallowing between deeper breaths and the gray of his face darkened to his more natural skin tones with two smears of bronze-pink at the height of his cheeks.

Firi's hand came up, the one Lace had been holding, and curved over the outside of Var's arm. At first his palm just brushed Var, fingertips playing over the surface as if to an inner beat. But soon he gripped that arm and pulled it tighter to his mouth.

Var made no move to pull away. His head had rocked back, his eyes closed. Lace understood. It was ecstasy, this sharing, no matter who gave and who received. Var's head would become light, even dizzy, his skin tingling all over as if caressed by silken hands that never stopped. He would soon be aroused. So would Firi.

He tried to smile. All that mattered was that Firi was saved.

The wound on Firi's side had not been sealed. Var had not had time. It had been oozing a slow red liquid. Now that leakage had stopped. The hole was still there but the redness around the edges faded away.

His own system was still locked down. He felt no pain from his three gunshot wounds, but was still not able to move anything but his fingers, his toes and, very slightly, his head.

Firi drank and drank and Var, obviously loving it, let him. Var's other arm went around the boy, and slowly Lace watched Firi's body curl into him. A momentary pain washed through his chest.

Firi still wore his trousers, but they were unbuttoned. As his body turned, heedless of its injury, they rode down on his hips. Var's arm that cradled him moved so that his hand could stroke his bare hip.

Seeing them together was beautiful, he had to admit. All that sheen of olive skin and lean muscle entwined, the darkness of their two heads side by side. Nothing more erotic existed for Lace than the sharing of the autumn wine.

Var tipped his head forward again, eyes languidly opening.

Lace said, meeting his gaze, "Thank you, Var." His voice shook.

Var said, "Oh, the young ones are always so needy." He looked down at where Firi was attached to his arm. "Haven't you got enough, human?"

For the first time since he'd passed out, Firi opened his eyes. He looked up at Var with half-open lids, the pupils enlarged as if he were drugged. He took one last lick at Var's arm, then frowned in confusion. Through the thickness in his mouth, he said, "Lace?"

"The name's Var. We've met before." He gave Firi's bare hip a little squeeze.

Firi's body jerked. "Var? Where's...?"

"Lace? He's in the bed next to you. No need to panic. I'll be getting to him next. But you needed more immediate attention."

"But what are you doing...?"

Lace saw the flush spread slowly across the boy's features and down toward his neck.

"I'm healing you, Firi. You can thank me now." Var was no gentleman—he didn't care if Firi was embarrassed—but his voice stayed low.

Firi squirmed. Var smiled, not letting him go. "Don't be embarrassed. I do like the feel of you. Your heat. That little hardness poking me."

Firi said, "Let go." But there was little conviction in his voice.

"Firi, you were not all right. You were far from all right. Do you understand?" Lace asked.

Firi turned to look at him, still squirming while Var held him in his grip. He shook his head. Then he nodded reluctantly. "Lace," he said. "You're not all right."

Lace smiled to reassure him. "I will be."

Var ran one hand up Firi's back. "Such a slippery thing. But a good, solid body. Pretty. He'll be fun."

Firi's dark eyebrows shot up.

Lace said, "Var, let him go."

Var relaxed his hands and let his arms fall back. Firi still lay against him, far weaker than he could realize. He tried to roll back but fell against Var again. He had stained Var's shirt with blood from his wound. Var gave a heavy sigh and gripped his shoulders, pushing him onto his back toward Lace's side of the bed. "There. Are we good now?" He sat up and reached out to prod Firi's injury.

"Looks good." His hand moved down quickly, patting Firi's crotch where it could be seen he was clearly aroused, and he smirked. "It all looks good."

Firi flinched. "Hey!"

Lace could see that Firi's wound was dried now, nearly scabbed over. It would be healed by the morning.

Var leaned over the side of the bed and started gathering up the cloths and bandages and the errant syringe, piling them all in a big towel. He stood, taking up the bag and the bowl as well, and moved it all to the edge of the room by the doorway. He went into the adjoining bath and came back with a glass of water, setting it on the table by Firi's side of the bed. "Drink some of this. Although my special wine should be enough. But you're still devastatingly mortal, so I guess that means I have to feed you, too."

"I'm not hungry," Firi retorted.

Var glanced below Firi's waist to the undone trousers and the black of his cotton underwear showing. It was stretched taut. "Hmm. That remains to be seen."

Var moved toward Lace, kicking off his shoes and removing his shirt. "Now let's see to your problems."

Lace felt himself respond to Var even as Firi curled against him. It wasn't that he didn't want Firi, always, but just the huge presence of Var standing over him, seeming to take up so much space in his room with that devil-may-care demeanor was overpowering. Every cell of his being tingled with it. He thought he might be able to just breathe in the scent of Var and be healed. It certainly did other things to him.

He had no pain, and he could feel parts of his body, but he still could not move.

Firi gripped his hand tighter. He could feel that. But Var took him over--damn him—with just a look, and made his very blood flame.

Lace was falling.

He looked into Var's storm-dark eyes and felt himself quicken even as his thoughts faded.

224

He saw the stone doorway of his dream again, and there was a door attached now made of thick raw wood, half open to a red and honey-drenched horizon, and all along the edge of the land as far as he could see were tipped or half-crumbled buildings that looked as if bites had been taken out of them, spires pointing downward instead of up, a broken sandcastle regime as far as the eye could see. On the air came a breeze tinted with ash.

Var moved over him. Lace blinked him back into vision as the fairy came alongside him and took him into his arms. He moved the arm with the cut over Lace's chest and up to his face. The cut that Firi had fed from was still fresh. Because fairies healed so quickly, Var must've opened it again when Lace wasn't looking.

Ancient shadows fogged his brain. Scents of rust, peach, ghosts.

Then Var bent to kiss him and he tasted the old rivers of his realm, and the moonlight ponds. His body remembered why he wanted him far too easily. His mind, wordless, simply whirled, never simmering with Var but always ready to burst forth.

The kiss rocked him, soft at first, tender and cool, advancing quickly to tongue, to heat and fever. He forgot he was holding Firi's hand until the boy squeezed.

Var held him down at the chest with his gold-bloodied arm, taking his time to give him the medicine he really needed.

Taking his time. That was what Var did. He kissed him back, drawing him in, lips, tongue, moisture. His eyes rolled up.

Var swiftly replaced his lips with his forearm, holding the flesh against Lace's lips, and Lace tasted the sweetest syrup, earthy, wanton, tart and fresh. It spilled into his mouth, the wine of moons and owls and aliens. The wine of life everlasting.

Only seconds had passed, but he was strong again. He could move. He let go of Firi and brought his arms up and around Var, pulling him close.

He had been half-afraid he would taste only grit now, after the day's deeds. He wondered if what remained of Var might be only bones and dust and the sharp wail of pain, the knife of cracked nights in all wars and murders tainting time. He had thought it might taint the blood as well.

But none of that was here. Either murder did not affect Var at all, or he hid that part of himself well for this procedure, and for Lace whom he had once loved. For a past that was like a red beacon not quite lost in the wails of infinity.

They had only just done this two nights ago. But it was new again. This taste, this texture, this elixir. It was like breath caught and held forever in a clear blue crystal called love.

He had had enough of the blood-wine. He wanted something else now. His lips moved away from Var's arm, and Var caught him up in both arms so Lace could lick and rub against his neck.

He had one more thought of Firi, knowing he was there beside them, but Var overpowered that distraction and he left the boy far behind as they stroked and kissed and fumbled with their clothes.

Var pushed Lace's shirt back from his shoulders, ripping all the buttons. Lace moved up so it could come off one arm, slide under his back, and be pushed off the other.

Beside him, he heard Firi make a little sound, almost like a gasp, but the boy said nothing, and he didn't leave.

They came together again, chest to chest, only to arch apart and grab, pull, tug at their pants. Var undid Lace's pants and barely had them down his thighs and off before sweeping his head low and nuzzling at his full cock.

He didn't wait for permission or pretty words. They weren't needed. Anyway, permission had already been given long ago. All the pretty words in the universe sparkled in their old blood-bond.

Var's mouth poured over his hardness, liquid flare and flame, a slow lowering, and the swirl of a trained tongue.

Lace's head pressed into the pillows. He cried out, his hands blindly reaching down to Var's hair, fingers weaving through the too-short strands.

A fragrance lingered in the air: black rose, autumn rain, an angel's breath of fairy woodlands fading in sugared mist.

He remembered none of it existed anymore.

But in this room between him and Var, it lived on.

Without warning, Lace began to weep.

Var looked up, eyes round and dusked with pleasure. He lifted his mouth from Lace and came up over him to lick his tears from his face. He swallowed, looked down at him and said, "This is the problem with immortality. There is no reprieve. Unending dreams still end."

He felt Firi against the pillows at his head, legs drawn up, watching them.

Lace tried to shake himself out of his reverie but more tears stung his eyes.

Images shifted over him: lost moons, a black lake, his body ripped open and an owl-man climbing inside him. Years of green and perfect rain. Years of ecstasy, sex. The darkness of Var winning a bleaker part of his lonely soul. A rending of reality. The human realm. Firi and love-making in a sapphire pond. Murder. Prison. Rescue. More murder. And now this.

The destruction of his home realm.

The end of the world.

Var whispered, "You always were the fool, pretending not to be attached to anything but holding tighter than any of us."

He heard Firi say, "Shut up." Then, "Lace, Lace." Cool human lips rested against his forehead.

Lace reached up for the Halfling. Firi's face touched his, mixing the wetness, shakily meeting his lips.

Var sat back on Lace's thighs, strangely allowing the comfort. Miraculous, since Var controlled everything he touched. And sometimes he could be a bit possessive.

It was also nothing short of a miracle that Var had allowed Firi to tell him to shut up.

He still wondered that Var showed no regret at losing his beautiful home and all the objects inside it. Var was a person tied up by grief but it had been so long that the grief had morphed into something else, something cold, premeditated. It was the shadow that lived over his heart that made him so ruthlessly single-minded.

But right now there was a kind of studied silence about him.

As Firi caressed Lace's face, Lace watched Var out the corner of his eye. The dark fairy stared just over Lace's left shoulder at the wall, at nothing. Finally, he blinked and moved to Lace's other side. Without a word, he pulled the covers up and over all three of them and lay down facing him.

Firi reclined to his right and Var to his left, both deep in the blood-bond with him, so close he could feel their heartbeats.

Even in his grief and through all the horror, he had the two of them. They were beside him now, constant signals, one dark, one light, to guide him from the storm.

The pieces of himself that he'd lost over the past two years were slowly settling back into him like ghosts coming home to rest.

As his tears dried, he looked around the white room with the winter light seeping through the curtains; he would always remember this moment, when one world died and another began.

The End

Dear Reader:

Thank you for reading "Lace." I appreciate all my readers perhaps more than they can ever know.

A sequel to this novel is already planned, so make a note to check my blog or Amazon page for new releases.

As always, you can find me on my blog here:
http://wendyrathbone.blogspot.com/

My Facebook page:
https://www.facebook.com/wendy.rathbone.3

My author page on Amazon.com contains a list of all my books as well.

http://www.amazon.com/Wendy-Rathbone/e/B00B0O9BMS/ref=sr_tc_2_0?qid=1435096235&sr=1-2-ent

In greatest appreciation,

Wendy Rathbone

LETTERS TO AN ANDROID
Wendy Rathbone

Cobalt is a created human, vat grown and born adult, with no human rights and indentured to serve others for the duration of his life. Liyan is a young man with wanderlust in his eyes, embarking on a career that takes him to the furthest regions of space. The two become unlikely friends and create a memorable long-distance correspondence. Through Liyan, Cobalt gets to explore the universe, living vicariously through his friend's wave transmissions. A strong bond develops between them that not even the stars can put asunder.

Now you know an android who writes poetry.

This is all your fault. Did you not read my last wave telling you extracurricular activities for my kind are discouraged? Of course this is harmless and strangely enjoyable and does not necessarily require me to leave the hotel. Pel would not care if I wrote lines of equations or nonsensical juxtaposed words. As long as the act does not bring my mental state into question.

However, in history, poetry is often written by the rebels.

So we can keep this to ourselves.

Let me know about your lieutenant's test.

And to give you peace of mind, I never believed you observed me as anything other than human.

Some people are and always will be hateful bigots. Most people are simply uncomfortable in speaking to "property." And anyway, friendship, like poetry, is also discouraged.

Your friend,
Cobalt

FROM THE AUTHOR:
www.eyescrypublications.com

ON AMAZON:
http://www.amazon.com/Letters-Android-Wendy-Rathbone/dp/0989693872/

SCOUNDREL
Wendy Rathbone
A male/male romance

Antares is a willing sex slave, trained in the harems of Anada since the age of 18, and owned by a wealthy master who spoils his slaves. But all that changes when Empire soldiers invade Antares' world and he is taken away from the only life he's ever known.

In a colonized galaxy where starships are as common as houseflies, and a dark Empire seeks to control thousands of civilized worlds, there are those who fall through the cracks and refuse to be conquered, including the pirate, Slate, and his crew.

Out in the darkness of the unknown, among Empire soldiers and scoundrels, will bad fates befall Antares and his fellow captive companions?

Will Slate finally find the love he's been looking for his whole life?

Can Slate and Antares ever see eye to eye?

A male/male romance to end all male/male romances!

FROM THE AUTHOR
www.eyescrypublications.com

ON AMAZON
http://www.amazon.com/Scoundrel-Wendy-Rathbone-ebook/dp/B014BU7V42/ref=sr_1_1?s=books&ie=UTF8&qid=1440660148&sr=1-1&keywords=scoundrel+wendy+rathbone

PALE ZENITH
Wendy Rathbone
A Science Fiction Novel

On a far-flung "Earth" in a parallel universe, two factions are fighting a decades-long psychic war. Young talented psychics are being temporarily kidnapped from present day Earth, seemingly at random, to serve as part of one side's psychic army. They are put under the control of spychiatrists, mysterious machines with many limbs that have a programmed ability to travel time and space and universes to kidnap and control carefully selected humans. The humans never know they are being used; when their missions are completed they are brought back to their universe through time and placed back in their beds, their memories wiped.

———————————

The shadows wound the tall corridor in muted gold, varnished brown. It seemed as though they were in the bowels of a giant serpent coiled outside time, outside space.

When they left the palace, a familiar sun flourished in a clear, blue sky. But this wasn't their sun. Not Zack's sun. It was an alien star burning within a different galaxy in an all too distant universe. Zack looked up squinting, trying to see if he could peer beyond the sky, beyond the pale of midday and into his own timespace, but there was nothing. Only sunlight. Only the thin atmosphere of an Earth not his own.

His back knotted again. Leo's presence was a gelid space inside his chest, empty. Always before he'd felt a warmth there, a sort of pressure like someone's hand pressed gently to his heart. He'd taken Leo for granted knowing, the way a shadow falls when you block the sun, that he was there around him, inside him: blood, air, salt, brain, soul. They were genetic duplicates, twins, spiritual halves. Without him, Zack knew the first icy tugs of panic.

FROM THE AUTHOR
www.eyescrypublications.com
ON AMAZON
http://www.amazon.com/Pale-Zenith-Wendy-Rathbone/dp/0976689790/

Moltenrose
Stories Set in the *Pale Zenith* Universe
by *Wendy Rathbone*

In a post-holocaust world, a young woman and her robot partner leave their nomadic gang to take a long trek on foot to the city of Moltenrose to seek their fortune. **Green Forever** is a coming of age novella about love, death and making your own luck.

In the story **Moltenrose**, a deformed man whose nickname is 'Ugly' lives in the shadowed ruins of the barely-alive city and works in a sideshow at the tourist-trap carnival at the edge of town. His story involves several 'firsts' including a lesson about beauty.

Excerpt: "You're late, boy," Rycoff mutters as I walk under the awning and into the tent. His belly hangs over an expensive gold belt, the vinyl trousers like a plastic sack he'd forced his flesh into. He wears a fashionable long-sleeved, bulky paper shirt. White. It sticks to his arms and back. There's already a little tear in it at the wrist. He goes through a dozen a day.

"How can I be? There's no line yet."

"I pay you by the hour, Ugly. Try to remember." He shuffles by me, leaving a scent-trail of sweat and mint. The black skin of his face glistens. The white braid that flaps over his shoulder is as artificial as my half-wig. A stranger might take him for a clown, but he's as shrewd a business-person as Colere the trans-hop queen, who owns half the Free World. Rycoff's just had a little less luck.

I take Main Street to work every day. It needs mending, as does the entire city of Moltenrose. Ghost City, people call it. A fitting place for me since I'm just one more broken down part of it. And the carnival on the east side where tourism keeps what's left of it alive is as good a place as any to work.

On Amazon: http://www.amazon.com/Moltenrose-Stories-Pale-Zenith-Universe/dp/1942415001/

Our Site: http://www.eyescrypublications.com

The Foundling
by Wendy Rathbone

Diego is a powerful man with a tragic past. Out on the expansive ocean in his private yacht, he discovers a beautiful and mysterious man adrift on a raft, near death. The bond that forms between them in the aftermath of Alec's rescue is one of fierce passion, though lacking in trust. Can they make it work, or will Alec's amnesia bring forth secrets so disturbing as to tear them apart? A passionately erotic love story of desire and darkness, exquisite and explicit.

———————————

I can see his struggle between gratitude and uneasiness. He is buffeted by all things new and strange. He does not know where he is from, who he is or what happened to him. He does not know me. There has not been enough time to transition between strangers and friendship.

This isolation of his is something I can identify with, but it is also a feeling no one can help him with until or unless he gets his own life back. And his memory.

If that doesn't happen, then it will take time for him to build a new life. He is polite to me, even friendly, but even a night together during a storm with his arms wrapped tight around my waist doesn't calm the surge I see inside him, the emptiness, the loss, possibly even panic. That night may have reinforced some trust in me, but so far not enough for him to completely relax.

He seeks me out, though. That's something. He sits by me at dinner when he can have any seat of his choosing. I watch him closely when he does not realize it. At dinner the following night after we had only 'slept' together, and before we go to bed again in separate rooms, I notice everything about him, how he moves, the way the air warms when he is closer to me, the dry sheen of his lips as they part for more air when he is reacting to something, or speaking, or eating.

His hands still shake. Anyone else might not notice because he keeps them clasped into fists at his sides or, while sitting, pressed tight to his lap.

I spend another fretful night alone. I dream restlessly, wild, loud and colorful visions I cannot recall at all as soon as my eyes open. All I know is the dreams leave me unfulfilled, impatient.

www.eyescry.com/html/publications.htm

None Can Hold the Dark
Wendy Rathbone

In the eagerly-awaited sequel to Wendy Rathbone's homoerotic romance **"The Foundling,"** Diego and Alec meet new challenges in private and from the outside world. Diego is being investigated by the local police for murder. Meanwhile, Alec's amnesia and the trauma of his kidnapping by white slavers continue to plague him. And the danger to Alec is not yet over.

Distracted by their new love, both men fail to see certain threats until it is almost too late.

"Why do you keep doing this illegal business?" Now Alec's gaze turned toward him, open as the day and lit with a sad frenzy, a challenge. "You could go anywhere, do anything, be anyone."

Diego had asked himself that question on rare occasions. In truth, he got used to what he was, what he did. Even a dangerous known was perhaps preferable to the unknown. "People depend on me."

Alec shook his head, but smiled a little as he said, "That's so weak." He leaned forward, over the arm of the chair, and put his shaking hand on the back of Diego's head. The kiss was cool, lingering, moist with salt. When Alec pulled back, he said almost matter of factly, "It's like there's sharks and there's goldfish and one can't decide to become the other."

Diego was still stunned by the kiss. But the words hit him hard. In them was the unfair conjecture of a locked fate. He believed in making his own fate...or luck. Did Alec think only one kind of man lived inside him and that was all there was to it? To life? It hurt. Badly.

Diego sat back on his heels, catching himself with his hands on the smooth floor. "So, Alec, which am I?"

Alec frowned.

Diego said, "I made choices in my life. I made them No one made them for me. If I need to be strong I'm strong. If I need to be vicious I can be that too. So what? I'm stuck there? In a pattern, a role...with no free will?"

Alec watched him inquisitively now.

"Because," Diego went on, "I'm solely responsible for my actions. Me. Could you say the same of the shark?"

They both waited, the silence covering them in muggy discomfort.

"You think you understand me?" Diego finally asked.

The Lostling: Alec's Story
Book Three in The Foundling Trilogy
by *Wendy Rathbone*

The Lostling takes place directly after *None Can Hold the Dark*, as Alec and Diego relocate to San Francisco. There, amid salty winter wind and fog, Alec's lost memories slowly return and he must relive some of his most painful and terrifying moments to regain his forgotten self. In agonizing dreams and flashes of memory, he finally remembers what happened to him... and why.

Excerpt*: Putting a hand on his arm or leg, I can always feel the tremor of Diego even through his clothes, an innate wildness, a life-power.*

I always believed, from the first day Diego found me unconscious and dying, floating in the middle of a sapphire Caribbean ocean, there was a core of me unhidden, unforgotten, that cried out silently to the air and everything around me communicating who I am, what I am.

I can't remember it myself. Not that core, not anything up to the day I awoke in Diego's bed, sick and panicked. In that moment, I remembered nothing more than my first name, and even that memory is suspect. But this core of me demands to take things into its own hands to be seen, to make sure it remains "I am."

I believe Diego saw it, the urgent desperation in me wanting to be witnessed, and he made a promise to that essence of me, to that heart of me, that he would see me through anything that came my way. Something in me reached up and latched onto him, a clasping energy, and Diego clasped back.

It caught and held him. He was moved. He was compelled. He was mesmerized.

www.eyescrypublications.com

http://www.amazon.com/Lostling-Alecs-Story-Foundling-Book-ebook/dp/B00RO8GSUW/

My House Is Full of Whispers
Wendy Rathbone

Ten erotica short stories by Wendy Rathbone - former winner of the prestigious WRITERS OF THE FUTURE contest!

Leda has not one beautiful man, but two. Kale enters a secret world in a wealthy man's basement. Noah is in love with a man who hates sex. Dina lives next door to a famous Hollywood director she secretly loves. Dorian has a sixteen year old female student coming onto him. Tara is haunted by an erotic ghost. Young Dimitri is kidnapped by lecherous men. And more.

Author's Preface

When I wrote these stories, I deliberately set out to gently break down certain barriers, and I've certainly broken taboos. Do I care? No. This is fantasy at its purest level. The stories are never meant to be political statements, nor do they make any attempt at political correctness, and there is little consideration for safe sex. While I definitely condone safe sex, my stories come from fictional realities in my head where safe sex is not much of a concern because, well, it's imaginary and it's fiction!

For me, these stories are meant as little poetic erotic ramblings merely to stir the flames of desire, nothing more. They are pure fantasy and therefore to be enjoyed as such. Every story is erotic in nature, meant to titillate, some more explicit than others. Some of the stories are light, some are darker. I invite the reader to a feast of diversity and delight.

One reader commented: *"...some of the most beautifully written erotica since Anais Nin!"*

FROM THE AUTHOR:
www.eyescrypublications.com
ON AMAZON:
http://www.amazon.com/House-Full-Whispers-Wendy-Rathbone-ebook/dp/B00IJK3G04/

UNEARTHLY
by Wendy Rathbone

A Collection of Award-Winning Poetry

Intro by the Author: This book contains all my out of print chapbooks (mini-collections of an author's work usually published by smaller presses.)

The chapbooks published within include:
Moon Canoes, published by Dark Regions Press, 1994
(Im)mortal, published by Shadowfire Press, 1996
Scrying The River Styx, published by Anamnesis Press, 1999
Autumn Phantoms, published by Flesh and Blood Press, 2000
Dreams of Decadence Presents: Wendy Rathbone, published by DNA Publications 2002
Dancing in the Haunted Woodlands, published by Yellow Bat Review, 2003
Vampyria, published by Eye Scry Publications, 2005

She Sleeps With Vampires
She sleeps with vampires
courting velvet breaths
poem-dreams
chill-stopped hearts

Wrapped in her arms
like teddy bear thoughts
purple lips trembling
at her quiet throat
they love her more than
somber rain
more than autumn
more than ash-soft hearths of night.

FROM THE AUTHOR
www.eyescrypublications.com
ON AMAZON
http://www.amazon.com/Unearthly-Wendy-Rathbone-
ebook/dp/B00B0MTIZK/

Other fiction titles from Eye Scry Publications...

Prince of Umberlight
Alexis Fegan Black

"If Prince of Umberlight doesn't rattle your cage, you're more dead than the undead!" **-Night Readers**

Thorn may be an 800 year old vampire, but he does not possess the ability to create others of his kind, and so he is cursed to fall in love with mortals, only to watch them grow old and die. Torn by grief, Thorn denounces his immortality and enters into a comatose oblivion for decades. When he awakens, he is no longer in London, but finds himself in a world spun into being by his own desires - a world where Time and Death do not exist, a world where it is forever autumn, where the Parish of Shadows and the River of Stars become his home. It is in this world of Umberlight that he meets Atom - an interloper into his private sanctuary, but also an impudent imp who is destined to reveal to Thorn the three dangerous elements a vampire must possess in order to become a Creator.

The Art of Brutality.
Submission to Dark Desire.
Love.

FROM THE AUTHOR
www.eyescrypublications.com

ON AMAZON
http://www.amazon.com/Prince-Umberlight-Tales-Book-ebook/dp/B00TRD2EHS/ref=asap_bc?ie=UTF8

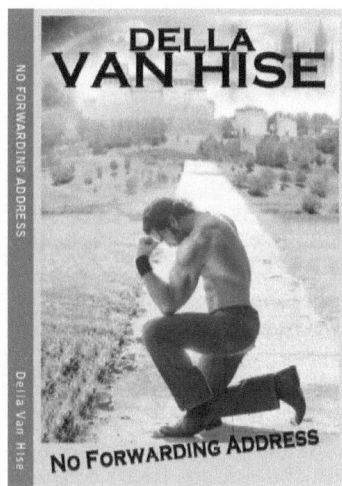

NO FORWARDING ADDRESS
Della Van Hise

When Terrans came to sail dark seas,
And see what stars might be...
Heaven moved with no forwarding
address,
And left this void to me.
(Children's song from Lazali)

A literary science fiction novel told in the voice of an empath, *No Forwarding Address* explores the lures and the dangers of love, the tragedies and triumphs stirring in the human heart.

When Crystal and Raine first meet, it is 50 years after The Great War on Earth. They are hesitant to trust, afraid to love. But even if they are able to overcome these seemingly insurmountable obstacles, is even love enough?

When a man has the stars in his eyes, legend says he must serve them above all others.

I knew then that it wasn't love and hate who were mirror twins. The final irony was that <u>grief</u> would always turn out to be the paradoxical antithesis and simultaneous manifestation of whatever it is that humans call love.

Crystal remained silent and walked a few steps away from Raine – further down the shoreline, until she stood under the wing of one fallen Phantom. She thought of the ship she had seen from the balcony of our home, and though it had long since disappeared over the dark and treacherous abyss of the ocean, its image lingered clearly in her thoughts. On that ship was a man, she thought. A terribly lonely man who made no great difference to the flow of time or the memory of the galaxy. A man who, like Raine, was compelled to keep moving and look only ahead and never behind. A man who could not afford the luxury of waving goodbye to friends on shore.

At last, she turned toward her beloved and watched him watching the darkness. He stood only a few feet away, yet the images in my mind said he might as well have been a million light years off in the void. He was lost to her in that instant out-of-time, just as lost and impossible to find as the light from that ship which had vanished over the horizon...

www.eyescrypublications.com
http://www.amazon.com/Forwarding-Address-Della-Van-Hise-ebook/dp/B00PEOSKJ0/

COYOTE
Della Van Hise

*A Novel of Love, Honor
and Personal Sacrifice...*

When River Willows is accused of a murder she didn't commit, her life takes a turn toward the sanctuary of a world existing at right-angles to our own. Combining the mysticism of martial arts and the romantic conflict of a young woman torn between two powerful men, COYOTE takes the reader on an epic journey of dangerous secrets, military cover-ups, and the infinite heart of the peaceful warrior.

"So who's Coyote?" I asked, trying to ignore the effect he was having on me. "You?"

Steale laughed easily, though it did little to hide the torment behind that mask of indifference he wore so well.

"Coyote's a scavenger, Jack of all trades. The Native Americans call him the trickster - the one who brought chaos down on the world." He shrugged as if altogether unconcerned. "Original sin."

"Is that what you are?" I asked, keeping it light despite the growing knot my stomach. "Original sin?"

He kept his profile to me, eyes straight ahead as he drove. "Sure you want to know?"

I couldn't help wondering if I had cornered the coyote, or if the clever trickster had cornered me.

By the author of **KILLING TIME** – without a doubt the most controversial **STAR TREK** novel ever published!

From the author:
www.eyescrypublications.com

On Amazon
http://www.amazon.com/Coyote-Della-Van-Hise/dp/0976689782/

YEAR OF THE RAM
Della Van Hise

Year of the Ram was described by one reviewer as... "A spacefaring gay romance full of love, angst, and longing."

Only after Star Commander Morgan Diego becomes an exile as a result of a Galaxy Corps political blunder does he begin to realize how much he valued the companionship of his second in command - the mysterious Lucien, an Alfarian who is more elven than human, with peculiar powers & abilities which begin to unfold as he, too, realizes what he has lost.

Separated by circumstance from his former life, Morgan is thrust into a world where he must survive by his wits. When he meets a peculiar little old man calling himself Kim Le, Morgan finds himself in a situation where he is required to master The Art - not only a form of human & extraterrestrial martial arts, but a way of living and being that will alter his life forever.

At the temple, he is introduced to his new teacher, another Alfarian who begins to steal his heart - a heart which is already promised to Lucien. Torn and conflicted, Morgan struggles with the world he left behind and the world he now inhabits.

Beginning to believe he may never again return to his ship and to the friends and loved ones he left behind, he is all the more frustrated and heartbroken when a new Master arrives at the temple: a man to whom Morgan is immediately drawn both mentally and physically, a man who is strikingly familiar... yet utterly alien.

Year of the Ram is a fully-fleshed novel, approximately 97000 words, with a focus on the love story and romance angle. Set against a science fiction milieu, it explores the infinite possibilities of the human and alien heart. Sexual content is explicit, though is not the primary focus of the novel.

For those who like a romance that forces its characters to contemplate the ecstasies AND the agonies of love... you will enjoy *Year of the Ram* immensely.

FROM THE AUTHOR:
www.eyescrypublications.com
ON AMAZON:
http://www.amazon.com/Year-Ram-Della-Van-Hise/dp/0989693813/

Non-fiction titles from Eye Scry Publications...

TEACHINGS OF THE IMMORTALS
by Mikal Nyght

So... You Want To Live Forever?

The teachings are presented as brief vignettes in no particular order of importance. This is not a book you read from start to finish in a single night. It is a grimoire of self-creation, intended to be contemplated slowly so as to be assimilated wholly. Pick it up and turn to a page at random. Where your eyes come to rest on the page is your lesson for the day. Go no further until you have assimilated the lesson totally.

The teachings are seduction as much as instruction. This is the way of The Dark Evolution.

The Ruby Slippers

The danger of the consensual continuum is that its natural gravity exists at the lowest common denominator of human experience, and because of this it will automatically make you forget those elusive truths you've fought to learn, and before you know it you're lost in petty dramas again, sinking into the mire of old familiar scripts.

The only way to overcome this is to be continually cavorting with worlds and events beyond human experience, journeying into the unknown so that it can become known, expanding knowledge and awareness to become more than you were, bringing back from the Dreaming those secrets which will teach you how to use the ruby slippers to transport yourself over the rainbow to the vampyre wizard's secret lair.

Perception

This is the nature of reality: to be precisely what perception dictates, as solid and whole as your interpretation of it, or as changeable and eternal as you permit it to be.

It wasn't knowledge god tried to keep from Man, you see. It was perception, for perception alone has the power to destroy god and obliterate comfortable consensual realities to create unending immortality.

Take the apple, my embryonic children. Nibble its red red flesh. Open your vampyre eyes so you may finally begin to *See.*

www.immortalis-animus.com
www.eyescrypublications.com

http://www.amazon.com/Teachings-Immortals-Mikal-Nyght-ebook/dp/B00C2HY5WS/

Quantum Shaman:
Diary of a Nagual Woman
Della Van Hise\

"Diary of a Nagual Woman brings a quantum understanding to what has traditionally been believed to be a mystical path alone. This book picks up where Carlos Castaneda left off to take us on a roller coaster ride of our own forgotten power..." - Michael Grove, Reviewer

When I asked how Orlando had known I would come to this remote location, and how he himself had gotten there – since there were no other cars in the tiny parking lot – he only smiled a little, stretched out his long legs, and slouched down on that cold metal bench to stare up at the stars.

"You're predictable," he said as if I should have already known. "I'm here because this is where you always come when you're mad at the world."

I attempted to engage him in a conversation of just exactly how he knew I was mad at the world, since I'd had no direct contact with him in quite some time, nothing to give him any hint of what was going on in my everyday life. But even as I began spelling all of that out to him, he brushed my words aside with an easy gesture.

"Do you want to talk or do you want to waste time looking for logical explanations for every magical thing that ever happens?" he asked. "That's what's wrong with the world, you know. Instead of embracing the mysteries and trying to determine how they might open a crack in an otherwise humdrum, pre-programmed existence, people waste their entire lives explaining it all away, attaching labels to it, filing and categorizing it until it loses any meaning."

He had a point. And I'd already been inundated with enough mysteries to know that some things simply had no explanation humans could understand. *'Magic is only science not yet understood'.* Words Orlando had written more than a year before rattled through my mind up there in the middle of the night, in the middle of nowhere, looking down on a distant world that seemed far more unreal to me at that moment than the world he had been trying to teach me to *see*.

He was there – whether physically or in some spirit-form is ultimately of no importance, for in the sorcerer's world there is no difference between body and spirit, and in any world, perception is reality.

www.quantumshaman.com
www.eyescrypublications.com

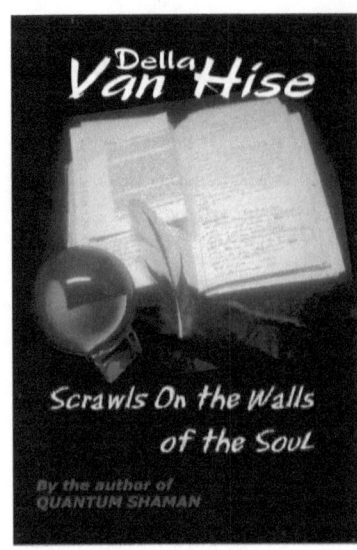

Scrawls on the Walls of the Soul
Della Van Hise

The long-awaited follow-up to <u>Quantum Shaman: Diary of a Nagual Woman</u>. Stands alone, or order together!

"If you've ever felt like a stranger in a strange land, this book is your road map to survival in the spiritual wilderness!" (Michael Grove)

~

It was May of 2000 when my mentor threw me out of the quantum cosmic classroom and said, "I've taught you everything I can. Now it's time to take that knowledge and slam it up against the walls of the real world. If it remains intact and survives the brutality to which it will be subjected, you will get a gold star next to your name and be allowed to proceed to the next level." No mention was made of what this next level might be, or if, indeed, it truly existed.

Go ahead – try to explain this all-consuming path to your friends and relatives. They will smile politely, squirm uncomfortably, and eventually they will stop returning your phone calls and look the other way when they see you coming. And who can blame them? They live in the real world with their office jobs and nuclear families and a host of mindless sitcoms waiting on the propaganda box at the end of their busy day. In direct contrast, it could be observed that anyone who has dedicated themselves to the pursuit of forbidden knowledge really doesn't live in that world at all. Not for lack of wanting, perhaps, but because the real world is quickly seen to be little more than a series of programs and illusions – not unlike The Matrix. And not surprisingly, the people who populate that world may begin to take on a peculiar zombie-like quality.

You find yourself alone in a world of jesters, jokers and jackasses. Now what?

FROM THE AUTHOR
www.quantumshaman.com

ON AMAZON
http://www.amazon.com/Scrawls-Walls-Soul-Della-Hise-ebook/dp/B008CUKH6C/

Eye Scry Publications
A Visionary Publishing Company
www.eyescrypublications.com